RUST SKIES

T.K. Blackwood

Chromatic Aberration

Chromatic Aberration

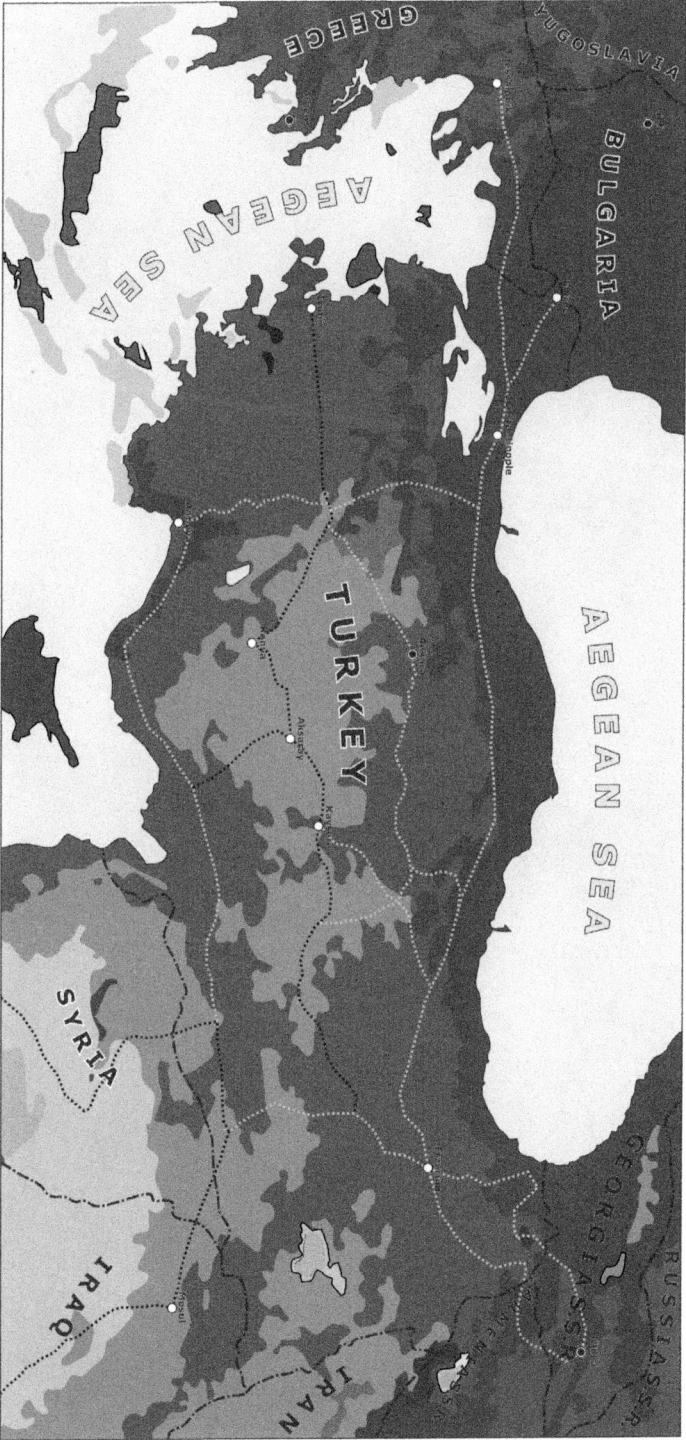

"I found the crown in the gutter. I picked it up and the people put it on my head."

-Napoleon Bonaparte

"Everybody wants to rule the world."

-Tears for Fears

1

October 25, 1992

The sound of gun and cannon fire echoed like thunder through the craggy hills of eastern Turkey. Those hills looked strange to Lieutenant Colonel Kazbek Nabiyev. He felt they looked less like natural formations of rock and earth and more like dollops of dark, lumpy dough dropped at random across the landscape. It was remarkably ugly in comparison to the rolling green countryside of southern Georgia he and the rest of the motor rifle regiment had left behind during their headlong attack into Turkey. They'd traded the green of lush grasses and dark forests for the dull, earthy brown of dusty fields and a tumultuous gray sky. Everything was sparse, barren, desolate. He had to wonder if any of it was worth fighting and dying over.

Nabiyev wiped his face with his hands, fingers brushing across his thick, dark mustache and the beard stubble dotting his chin. It only took one or two missed shaves before he started looking less like a Soviet officer and more like a wild Cossack.

Beside him his commanding officer, Colonel Molchain, swore loudly. Both men were "unbuttoned" with the command vehicle's hatches open to allow the cool air in along with the sounds of nearby battle. They faced west, towards the enemy and toward the distant sound of fighting.

Ordinarily a command vehicle would be on the move, following closely behind its subordinate combat battalions, but in this case it was stalled in place like the rest of the regiment was.

Molchain held a hand pressed to the ear cup of his headset, his brow furrowed in consternation as he listened to the speaker on the other end. Nabiyev took the opportunity to light a cigarette, drawing a smokey breath before exhaling into the rushing wind. It was a small luxury but felt like heaven all the same.

"How many?" Molchain asked before quickly snapping back at the unheard reply. "Then you are to *make* them advance, Comrade! We can't be stopped by every Turkish blocking position between here and Ankara!"

Nabiyev sighed inwardly and took another drag on his cigarette. While Colonel Molchain ranted at his subordinate, Nabiyev listened to the radio traffic of the other battalion commanders as they coordinated their attacks on the Turks. It was the same problem they'd had since their initial explosive crossing of the Soviet-Turkish border in the Caucasus mountains. Death by a thousand cuts.

Soviet doctrine was centered entirely around the mass offensive—and not the crude popular image of waves of peasants throwing themselves forward with bayonets. The Soviet army practiced "deep battle"—the idea that the enemy line should be broken at as many places as possible and then mercilessly exploited. Battle should be brought not just to the enemy front but through the rear areas as well, an operation to drive "deep" into the enemy. A relentless mechanized ballet which was only possible thanks to the staggering industrial might behind the Soviet war machine.

Colonel Molchain swore again, this time directly at the battalion commander he spoke with. "I will not tolerate cowardice *or* insubordination in this unit, Major! Move the enemy whatever it takes! Your men have divisional fire assets at your disposal, use them!"

As if to underscore the Colonel's words, the freight train howl of passing artillery tore the overcast sky above making Nabiyev reflexively duck further down into the BMP. It was pointless. The armored vehicle's thin hide wouldn't protect from shells of that caliber. Besides, these particular rounds were friendly, passing from the gun batteries further to the rear to crash on the Turks holding up the attack. Nabiyev suspected that Molchain's battalions were already making full use of the artillery on offer.

Their offensive had opened well initially, a storm of steel surging across the border and into Turkey with little warning. The Soviets drove the Turks before them, only the terrain and the enemy had both chosen not to cooperate. The Soviet doctrine of the offensive was dependent on penetrating the enemy lines by pinning them in place and smashing through weak spots with overwhelming concentrations of force. So far the Turks had refused to commit to a standup battle, choosing instead to fight a delaying action and trade space for time. It had kept their lines intact for now, but it was surely taking a toll on them.

The Soviet Army steamrolled gloriously across Germany, Sweden, and Norway, yet here in Turkey found itself unable to achieve that critical breakthrough. It had fallen to the men of the 806th Motor Rifle Regiment to tear just such a hole in the enemy line.

Molchain took off his earphones to pin Nabiyev with a fiery gaze. It took force of will for Nabiyev not to flinch away.

As Molchain's executive officer, it was Nabiyev's responsibility to listen to his commander's furious rants and so dutifully lifted his own headset, leaving the combat chatter in his right ear. "Comrade Colonel?"

"That rat-faced bastard Abramov tells me his battalion is bogged down by anti-tank missiles in these damn hills ahead." Molchain swept his arm to the lumpy, dolloped hills around them. The steady drumbeat of distant explosions upped its tempo almost on cue.

The solution to such a problem was textbook: saturate the enemy positions with artillery fire, suppress with rifle and cannon, and sweep their flank with a maneuver element. However, with much of the regiment's artillery assets trailing behind in the rough terrain and the hills preventing rapid, broad maneuver, it was proving easier said than done.

"Comrade Colonel," Nabiyev said, choosing his words carefully, "This terrain suits the defense well. Until we can bring more guns to bear on the enemy, they will likely continue to slow our efforts."

Molchain sneered at Nabiyev. "Are you really so timid, Comrade? Your Turkish cousins have no fear of closing for battle. What is it that you and Abramov are so afraid of?"

Nabiyev's blood surged with anger even as he kept his face placid and unreadable. He hadn't made it this far in the Soviet Army as a Tatar by allowing such barbs to goad him into rashness. While he resented the unending references to the Turks as somehow being more his kin than his native Russia, Nabiyev would never show it.

"I merely suggest that a frontal attack—while likely to succeed —will be needlessly wasteful of men and materiel—" Nabiyev knew better than to lecture his commanding officer and so phrased it as a question, "Don't you think so, Comrade Colonel?"

Molchain snorted. "No doubt, but we don't have the luxury of time." He looked west, "Further along this road is a miserable town called Oltu that sits on a crossroads. Division command expects it to be seized by nightfall in order for us to spring an attack into Erzurum at first light, or perhaps you would like to let General Novikov know the reason for our inability to break through was the want of a few more artillery guns."

This verbal dressing down was needless and reductive. Nabiyev resented being talked down to as if he was some simple-minded junior officer. He found himself gritting his teeth, "Then there may be a third option."

Molchain wasn't interested in discussing it, even less so with Nabiyev. "Take the BTR forward," Molchain said, already moving on from this topic. "Go to Abramov's battalion and get them moving. Whatever it takes, take control yourself if he won't listen."

Nabiyev wanted to protest, to scream, to call his commander unimaginative and bloody-minded. Instead, he saluted. Such protests would be ineffective anyway. "Right away, Comrade

Colonel Molchain."

Since the BMP wasn't moving, it was easy to dismount. Nabiyev felt the hard gravel crunch of loose stones beneath his boots as he stalked stiffly and angrily along the roadside from the command vehicle toward the reconnaissance BTR parked a short distance behind them. The BTR for the HQ detachment was a multi-function vehicle which was physically little different from the angular "battle taxis" that carried the rank and file of the Soviet motor rifle infantry into battle. This particular BTR could serve as an auxiliary command vehicle in the event of a problem with the command BMP; it could also act as a recon vehicle for calling in artillery strikes or—as now—it could be used to ferry staff about.

As Nabiyev neared the BTR, its crew noticed his approach. While only the pale circle of the driver's face could be glimpsed through the square forward viewport, the vehicle's commander and gunner stood out of the rear top hatches that infantry would exit or enter from.

"Comrade Colonel," the vehicle's commander greeted, flicking a cigarette away while the gunner stubbed his own out on the slanted turret exterior.

Nabiyev was in no mood for false pleasantries. He used the hand and foot holds to scale the BTR's flank. He flicked his own cigarette away. "Take me to Abramov's command section."

The commander and gunner traded a look before setting to their task. The BTR started with a coughing roar as the diesel engine caught and a moment later it pulled onto the road, driving southwest along the deserted highway at speed.

The crew didn't speak to each other beyond the occasional command or question, and they certainly didn't speak to Nabiyev. He was considered by many to be a weak element. A Tatar in the army was suspect enough, let alone one serving in combat against other ethnic Turks. Nabiyev never considered his genetic heritage outside of situations where it was used against him. He'd never learned the language and he'd never practiced Islam. Both of those were dangerous prospects, even considering the large ethnic Tatar population of his home of Kasimov. Nabiyev had never been anything but a loyal Soviet. He'd seen a military career as an opportunity for advancement, a stepping stone to bigger and better things. His admittance to Frunze Military Academy had been gruelingly difficult, but he'd made it happen.

The BTR slowed and steered off the road. The vehicle rocked violently despite its large off-road wheels and the men inside pitched about. The padded black leather caps the crew wore protected them from nasty blows against the vehicle interior, but Nabiyev had no such protection and had to rely simply on a firm grip to avoid banging his head. When the rocking subsided, Nabiyev pulled himself to one of the empty gun ports on the flank of the BTR and peered out.

A blackened boxy armored vehicle sat astride the road, forcing them to detour into the uneven shoulder. It looked like an American-made M113, probably killed at range by a Soviet tank shell.

Once clear, the BTR pulled back onto the road and accelerated again. The further they drove, the louder the sounds of battle became. The crash of mortars and chatter of machine gun fire was broken from time to time with the barks of tank and BMP main guns or the shriek of a missile. The hills here scattered and echoed the sounds so that distance and direction became difficult to determine.

"Colonel, Major Abramov's headquarters is ahead."

Nabiyev perked up and looked forward. Smoke dotted the horizon, rising from nearby battles. Here on the side of the road was a burning Soviet scout vehicle which likely marked the place where the Turks first began this particular round of resistance.

The BTR pulled off the road again, rocking and shuddering through a rutted field toward a BTR command vehicle parked in the shade of a copse of narrow spruce trees. As Nabiyev's BTR slowed, he took a deep breath and adjusted his uniform. When the vehicle finally lurched to a halt, he debarked without a word to the crew. The rapid pops of rifle and machine gun fire sounded dangerously close, but Nabiyev didn't hear the telltale whizz and buzz of rounds passing nearby and so forced himself to walk with dignity toward Abramov's headquarters.

The major was close by, a dozen meters from his BTR, crouched behind an embankment with his staff, observing the battle ahead through a pair of binoculars. He looked up at Nabiyev's approach. His eyes were hooded and wary. A visit from regimental headquarters was not a blessing.

"Has Molchain sent you to kill me?" The question was half in jest, delivered with a wry dryness. Abramov was Jewish—at least as much as Nabiyev was a Tatar—as such he knew they were equally detested in their commanding officer's eyes. Placement in Soviet forces here on the periphery of the nation was reserved for those less prestigious than the vaunted forces in Germany, or even keeping watch against the Chinese on the Manchurian border.

Nabiyev's career, like Abramov's, was likely at a plateau. He had once considered himself lucky to get a staff posting in a combat unit, but now he wasn't so sure.

Despite their mutually disadvantaged backgrounds, there was no comradery between them. If anything, it gave them more reason to avoid one another. It would be bad form for "those types" to be seen collaborating. Abramov could speak plainly with Nabiyev simply because Abramov knew Nabiyev wouldn't dare try to report him.

"Not yet," Nabiyev replied coldly, taking a place beside the major and holding out a hand for the binoculars.

Abramov handed them over without hesitation. "I would rather he come here himself so he can look me in the eye before he sends me and my men to our deaths."

Nabiyev pressed the binoculars to his face and swept his gaze over the hills ahead. The Turkish position—at least what was visible—was well-sited. The focal point of resistance was nestled in the divots and creases of a steep hill. From this position they had clear firing lines down the highway and along any reasonable avenue of approach. So long as the Turks held this hill, the 806th Regiment couldn't advance. The hill was subject to a steady barrage of fire from Abramov's mortar section. Shells screamed down and burst on and around the hill like clockwork, one every second or so. It was an impressive display, but not enough to root out well dug-in emplacements. Even the heavy shells Nabiyev heard earlier seemed to have had little effect. He suspected most of the Turkish firepower lay in wait on the reverse slope of the hill, out of sight, ready to smash any brute force attempt to overrun them. Out of necessity they'd established a few forward outposts which now traded fire with the Soviets.

"They've got some kind of anti-tank missile battery up there," Abramov said. "Took out two platoons of my BTRs before we drew back to consolidate and wait for more heavy guns."

"Armor support? Anti-air?" Nabiyev asked, continuing to study the hillside.

"Some of those damn Stingers," Abramov said. The effectiveness of the American-designed anti-air missile system was quickly becoming legendary among the Soviet army. "No armor we've seen, but who knows what's behind the hill. I'm not going to throw a recon platoon away trying to find out and our comrades in the air force must be too busy drinking to be here."

Nabiyev knew the division's air assets were all heavily tasked, primarily with attacking Turkish command and control elements further back to keep larger formations disrupted, but secondarily with fending off NATO's air forces. Unlike Germany, many of the Turkish airfields were well out of range of the Soviet's ballistic missiles.

"Has Molchain sent you to join us on our death ride then?" Abramov asked. "He can be rid of us both in one flick of his wrist."

Nabiyev ignored him, studying the terrain carefully. The surrounding hills were too steep for even off-road vehicles to scale, channeling them perfectly into the valley this hill overlooked. The enemy couldn't be too many in number, but it didn't take much to delay a force like this. If they could get in close, they could sweep the Turks off that hill without much challenge. Whatever lay beyond would then at least fall under their guns, committing the Turks either to a stand-up fight which the Soviets would win, or forcing them to retreat again. The problem would be getting close enough to clear the hill.

"What is that ditch?" Nabiyev asked, gesturing left of the main hill to a furrow in the earth, an eroded track that ran right by the hill.

"A death trap," Abramov said. "If the Turks spot my men in that, they'll slaughter us with machine guns and grenades."

"Do you still have smoke rounds for your mortars?"

Abramov laughed mirthlessly. "Of course, but why not put up signal flares about our plans? They may not be able to see us, but they're not fools, Comrade. If they see us laying down smoke, they will know what we're doing."

Nabiyev shook his head. "No. Not for the ditch. Put the smoke down for what they are expecting us to do. Prepare for a frontal attack, lay a smoke screen, increase bombardment tempo, run your BTRs back and forth in preparation to attack—"

Abramov picked up the thread of Nabiyev's plan. "And we send a company through that ditch to attack on foot."

Nabiyev nodded. "Risky, but better than sending your battalion forward into the teeth of their guns, yes?"

Abramov made no argument to the contrary but held his hand out for his binoculars. "We'll do it your way then."

Nabiyev had no doubt that if this attack failed Abramov would lay the blame on his shoulders, but right now was more concerned with winning the engagement than with covering his own hide. "Just see that it is done."

Scarcely a minute after Abramov radioed the new orders to his companies, the smoke shells began to fall. A mixture of fragmentation and smoke rounds burst across the front of the hill, blanketing it in a thin veil of smoke. Squads of BTRs raced forward to lay down yet more smoke. Turkish return fire—while inaccurate—was fierce. Tracer rounds ricocheted from rocks and armor plate to sail off into the air and Turkish return mortar fire peppered the Soviet positions opposite them.

All attention was focused on the valley, the apparent focal point of the Soviet attack, or so Nabiyev hoped.

The Soviet troopers moving through the ditch were scarcely visible at this range, less so with the haziness to the air from the lingering smoke screen. Minute by minute they drew closer to the Turkish hill, only occasionally glimpsed through binoculars as bobbing, green figures.

Nabiyev and Abramov were far enough back from the fighting that they were in no immediate danger, and yet Nabiyev's heart was racing. He felt both fear and exhilaration in equal parts, and not just for his own safety. No matter how successful this plan would turn out to be, men would die for it—both his and the enemy's. It was a heavy burden to bear, trading lives for meters of ground, but right now Nabiyev was too caught up in the moment to consider the consequences closely.

"There they go," Abramov said.

Three platoons of infantry sprung up from the ditch and advanced in a thin, shaky line, scrambling up the hill as quickly as they could. The junior officers in command held their men in close check, none of them fired a shot until they'd reached the first lip of cover, a scattering of rocky formations jumbled low on the hill's side.

From here, the RPG teams from each platoon opened fire. Their rocket propelled grenades streaked out from launchers to strike Turkish machine gun nests and foxholes. Flat bangs echoed back to Nabiyev, the sound of human life snuffed out.

The Turks responded quickly, shifting fire from the phantom threat of the smoke screen to the infantry assault on their flank. They raked the hillside with rifle and machine gun fire and threw grenades down at the Soviet assaulters.

Nabiyev saw a handful of Abramov's men drop, never to rise again. Another tumbled limply down the hill before his body came to a stop on a smooth boulder, but still the assault pressed on. Bit by bit, the Soviet infantry cleared the hill, silencing fighting positions and neutralizing enemy gunners with bullets and grenades. Like shifting a heavy load with a lever, the whole Turkish line was dependent on this position and the Soviets were unhinging it.

Nabiyev felt it a moment later, that almost imperceptible notion that something had changed, a tipping point had been reached, Turkish fire tapered off or became more sporadic, their responses less coordinated. They were coming undone. Maybe they'd received the command to fall back. "Send the rest of your men forward," he said. "Give them no respite." If they could catch the Turks as they retreated, they could roll them to destruction.

Again, Abramov didn't argue, he relayed the order. The rest of his battalion went forward without hesitation, rising from cover and rushing across the open ground, the infantry leading the way for the BTR personnel carriers. Each BTR laid down heavy covering fire from their turret-mounted machine guns, but the enemy was already breaking.

"Stay on them, Major," Nabiyev said, rising to a knee and brushing caked Turkish mud from his tunic. "Don't give them a chance to break away. I will have Colonel Molchain send the rest of the regiment forward to—" Nabiyev's words caught in his throat at the sight of a pair of F-16 fighter bombers cresting a distant hill to race this way.

It was no secret in the Soviet Army that NATO's ability to triangulate the location of Soviet headquarters through radio intercepts was second to none. They'd come for him.

"Cover!" Nabiyev screamed the word as he threw himself flat on the ground and covered the back of his neck with his hands, interlacing his fingers.

Abramov and his small staff did the same, dropping wherever they were and hoping against hope that the Turks might miss.

The fighters blasted overhead with a deafening roar of jet engines, then nothing. The sounds of battle replaced the roar of the fighters.

Nabiyev lifted his head in surprise, looking back at the withdrawing forms of the aircraft as they continued on northeast. It seemed he wasn't on the menu today. He risked a look at Abramov who looked similarly bewildered, his pale face streaked with dirt.

Both men rose to their feet and vainly brushed their uniforms off.

"I'll be returning to Colonel Molchain with news of your success, Comrade Major," Nabiyev said. He was careful to emphasize *your* success rather than risk Abramov thinking he was trying to undermine him.

"Have him bring the reserves up quickly," Abramov said, looking back at the hill to see his soldiers cresting it before descending down the other side. "The regiment should have a clear path to Oltu now." He saluted Nabiyev, much to the XO's surprise. "Now I have a battle to oversee."

Nabiyev returned the salute and turned back for his BTR idling nearby. The return drive to Molchain's headquarters felt shorter than the trip out, especially with Nabiyev's spirits bolstered by the knowledge that he brought news of a victory. This confident assurance died when Nabiyev saw the smoke rising ahead. The BTR's driver brought their vehicle as close as he dared to the burning BMP, parked just where they'd left Molchain's command vehicle.

Nabiyev opened the top hatch and stood up, staring with disbelief at the pyre. Molchain had been in there. The regiment's commanding officer was dead on the cusp of success. Even from this distance the heat of the flames burned Nabiyev's face, but he couldn't look away.

"Comrade Colonel," the BTR's commander said.

Nabiyev looked at him, feeling numb.

"Yes?"

The BTR commander, a sergeant, looked uncomfortable. "You have orders, Colonel?"

The realization burst like a firework in his mind. With Molchain dead, the 806th was his regiment now. It had all fallen to his shoulders and the weight was crushing. There was no time for that, he had a breakthrough to see to.

"Yes," he snapped. "Get on the radio to the rest of the regiment, inform them that I have taken command, and let them know that Comrade Colonel Abramov has torn a hole in the enemy line. We're advancing."

The sergeant hesitated, but only for a moment before a sharp look from Nabiyev set him in motion. "Yes, Comrade Colonel!"

Nabiyev listened to the distant thunder of Abramov's attack as the sergeant broke the news of the command change to the rest of the regiment. This storm was only just beginning.

***

2

After a tense and agonizingly long journey across the Atlantic, the crew of the *Akula*-Class attack submarine K-461 was at last within sight of their next target. The *Akula* was a technological marvel of the Soviet Union, an attack submarine nearly on par with its more advanced Western counterparts, no small feat for a nation that chronically lagged behind in such developments.

Captain Oleg Yessov was—like the *Akula*—the pinnacle of Soviet achievement, at least in his own estimation. He was already an officer in the premier branch of the Soviet Navy—the submarine forces. Likewise, he commanded a vessel reserved only for the best, but even beyond that he held an achievement no other submariner did, living or not: he'd crippled an American aircraft carrier.

"Slow to one-third speed," Captain Yessov said.

A quick response came from the helmsman, "Slowing to one third."

K-461 was a predator in the open ocean, but in the confines of the Strait of Gibraltar she would be easy prey for submarine hunters. Ordinarily K-461 would at least have the means of defending itself were the boat not also dangerously low on munitions.

Yessov paced to the sonar station. "Contacts?"

"Several, Comrade Captain," the operator said, reviewing his board. "Mostly civilians but there is a pair of military vessels on patrol. They appear to be *Oliver Hazard Perry*-class but the signature is slightly off."

"Probably Spanish make," Yessov said dismissively. He wasn't much concerned about the Spanish surface fleet. They spent most of their time chasing down pirates and smugglers and so had little experience with anti-submarine warfare. It was other attack submarines that he was worried about. His close call with the French attack submarine in the Atlantic still weighed heavily on his mind.

Yessov looked up to see his executive officer—Lieutenant Voloshin—step onto the bridge, navigating carefully around busy command stations to make his way over. Yessov didn't waste time with pleasantries. "How is our inventory?"

"We have ten torpedoes, including four wake-tracking and two more Kalibr missiles," Voloshin said.

Yessov nodded thoughtfully. It was enough for one or two serious fights but not much else. As much as it pained him to let the enemy go unmolested, he was more interested in re-arming to fight a more advantageous battle. A benefit of a submarine's stealthy nature was the ability to decide when and where to engage, ensuring that battles were fought only when the sub held the advantage.

"Have both the Kalibrs loaded," he said, thinking they would make a good last ditch use against the Spanish patrol ships, "and two acoustic torpedoes."

"Yes, Comrade Captain." Voloshin didn't wait before moving on to the weapons control station to relay the orders, leaving Yessov to patrol the bridge anxiously. The Soviet Union was nearly entirely landlocked and had precious little access to the open ocean. Most famously, the expansive naval base in Polyarny was trapped beyond the NATO-controlled GIUK Gap, something Yessov felt prudent to avoid for the time being. It seemed that his foresight was paying off. The Strait of Gibraltar—while a risky passage—was certainly less intensely patrolled than the Gap. He expected to deal with passive sonar buoys listening for his passing but hoped these could be circumvented through a combination of luck, faith in his boat's reduced acoustic signature, and skill.

Minutes crept by as the submarine inched forward, gliding beneath the surface of the sea with its every electronic ear tuned carefully to the activity of the nearby NATO ships. They detected no telltale splashes indicating air-deployed torpedoes or sonobuoys, but it didn't mean there weren't buoys already present. In fact, Yessov was counting on it.

Their luck didn't hold forever.

"Contact one is increasing speed and coming about, Comrade Captain."

The ship was likely inspecting a return on an otherwise silent passive sonobuoy that heard K-461's approach or moving to investigate a sonar anomaly. There was also the possibility of helicopters probing the water with dipping sonar, lowering their powerful microphones into the water via long cables to listen for passing submarine traffic. Engaging with weapons in the confines of the straits was a surefire way to send his boat to the bottom. Even if Yessov was confident he could sink both warships before they could sink him—and he was—they would certainly call in reinforcements. That would mean more ships and even worse, aircraft. Yessov was less confident in his ability to take out those.

"Go to silent running," Yessov said, willing the boat to be quiet.

"Silent running."

The screws stopped and the coolant pumps for K-461's nuclear reactor dampened as much as possible. It was actually the reactor pumps, and not the screws, which made the most noise in times like this. In this way, a diesel electric submarine was actually stealthier than a nuclear sub.

Yessov played his part though, not betraying his anxiety, making a point to study their course on the navigational chart before approaching the sonar station to watch the steadily increasing hits on their hull from a pinging sonar. Each passing moment brought the two vessels closer together. It was time to gamble.

"What's the depth of this channel?" Yessov asked.

"The chart says nine hundred meters, Comrade Captain."

Far below K-461's test depth—the maximum depth the

submarine was allowed to operate in peacetime.

"And our depth?"

"Two hundred meters, Captain."

"Take us down. Set new depth to five hundred meters."

The helmsman didn't immediately reply.

Akula-class ships were only depth tested down to five hundred. Six hundred was the absolute floor of its maximum operating depth. Anything beyond that point was considered in danger of reaching crush depth.

"Yes, Comrade Captain. Setting depth to five hundred meters."

The sinking sensation the crew all felt was akin to riding an elevator down.

"Depth three hundred meters. Three fifty."

"Helm," Yessov said, "One-third speed."

The propeller for K-461 reengaged slowly. The deeper the submarine went, the faster it could spin its screws without cavitating—generating noisy air bubbles.

The hull creaked and popped as the pressure on it increased, putting Yessov's teeth on edge. Every sound made it that much more likely they would be detected.

"Depth four hundred."

"Surface splashes," Sonar said.

"Torpedoes?" Lieutenant Voloshin asked, hissing the question before Yessov could.

"I hear no screws, Comrade Lieutenant. I think it is a sonobuoy."

"Then they still aren't sure we're here," Yessov said.

"Depth is five hundred meters."

K-461 creaked ominously and Yessov's heart skipped a bit. He took scant comfort knowing that if and when the pressure hull failed, it would do so too quickly for him to hear it happening. Now he just had to wonder if the Spanish also heard the sound of his submarine's hull.

"Comrade, shall I flood torpedo tubes?" Voloshin asked.

"No," Yessov returned. "Helm, give me two-thirds speed."

The sonar pings of the surface vessels were now audible

as they thrashed the water around K-461. They came through as high-pitched whines that sounded not of this world. K-461 increased speed, intending to put distance between itself and the searching vessels.

"They are wondering why we're running instead of fighting," Yessov mused. "Maintain course."

Yessov took his eyes from the XO and instead looked at the gauges at the navigation console as the buoyancy tanks took in more water.

"Confidence is high they have detected us, Comrade Captain," the sonar operator said, his voice uneasy.

"Maintain course," Yessov said.

"Captain," Voloshin was at his side, voice lowered, "the tubes —"

"They already have one textbook example of submarine acoustics," Yessov replied. "You would give them another?"

Voloshin hesitated before speaking again. "Captain, this may be our only chance to strike first. If we launch now—"

"Then we will be dead before we have a chance to note the kills in our ship's log," Yessov replied. He deigned to look at his XO again. He hated to explain himself to a subordinate. "It's the Spanish," he said with disdain. "They are amateurs at this. Their commanders will chalk this up as a wild goose chase. Since we did not fire at them, they will begin to doubt we were ever truly here. They will not want to look foolish before their allies, so they won't call for support." It was a guess, but one Yessov was banking on. He knew an untroubled ship was more likely to let them go as a false positive than if they left a burning wake behind them.

Voloshin didn't answer and again Yessov moved away from him, back to the sonar station. "Further contacts?"

"No, Comrade Captain. I think we are losing them."

Every minute carried them into wider, deeper waters and further away from the bewildered Spanish patrol.

Yessov breathed a silent sigh of relief. "Well done." He patted the junior officer proudly.

After another hour, they'd returned to two-thirds speed and Yessov gave the order to come up to periscope depth.

Somewhere in the Alboran Sea between Spain and Algeria, K-461 and its crew got as near to the surface as they dared in wartime, near enough to probe the air above with periscopes. After checking radar and ensuring there were no nearby vessels hunting for them, Yessov tuned into the extremely low frequency radio broadcast that served to feed data to submerged submarines. The data he collected told him the political and military situation of the entire Mediterranean Sea and thus which ports were open and which were not.

The Bosphorus was closed by heavy NATO patrol, cutting off any access to the Black Sea and the Soviet Union itself, but this was no surprise. The Dalmatian coast of Yugoslavia was likewise unsafe, the mouth of the Adriatic being heavily patrolled. Yessov had just slipped one NATO choke point and wasn't eager to try his hand at another.

"What about Syria, Comrade Captain?" Voloshin asked, tapping the small Arab country on the map. "Politically reliable and with good port facilities."

"Distance is a problem," Yessov said. "We are more trapped here than in the Atlantic. I don't wish to get caught by NATO aircraft...." But. Yessov weighed options. Libya was closer. But perhaps less reliable. The Syrians were kept on a shorter leash than Libya and in this case, it might be better to play it safe. "Syria it is."

Voloshin cracked a smile. "As you say, Captain."

"Lieutenant, take the helm for now, if you please. Keep us near the North African coast, within territorial waters. The Algerians and Tunisians won't detect us and the West won't dare violate their sovereignty by conducting patrols there."

Voloshin nodded ascent. "Yes, Captain."

***

3

The VCR whirred to life, tape heads clunking into position as the VHS tape was fed into the slot. Static flickered across the pristine blue of the screen like a storm front on fast forward. A moment later the screen flashed to black and then flickered into motion, coming in on the middle of a scene familiar to President Jerry Bayern: the presidential town hall debate of a week ago.

The television narrated the events as he watched them, recapping the debate, but Bayern hardly listened. Instead, he watched himself as he crossed the open stage to meet his opponent, Harry Nelson, between two podiums where the men shook hands. Their faces were plastic facsimiles of pleasantness. While Bayern held no personal animosity toward Nelson, he also saw him as an obstacle to overcome, a feeling Bayern was sure Nelson shared.

As he watched the tape, Bayern saw Nelson speak briefly to him as they concluded their handshake. The TV cameras didn't pick up what he said, but for a moment Bayern's placid expression faltered. It was imperceptible to anyone but Bayern himself, but he saw it as clear as day. A sentence between political opponents, unheard by any save them. Bayern remembered it clearly.

Remember, we're both on the same side.

Nelson's tone was jovial, almost friendly, but the words seemed more like a warning. Bayern couldn't puzzle their meaning then, and he still struggled with that now.

If Nelson was an obstacle, he was a formidable one. Tall, cool, confident, wearing a neatly trimmed mustache and beneath that a million-dollar smile to rival Bayern's own. If anyone could be said to have a "presidential look," Nelson could. Even now, removed from the debate by time and watching it through a TV screen, Bayern felt intimidated by that confidence. Nelson was a wildcard in many ways. Nelson had long been a fixture in the politics of New York City, ultimately rising to mayor on a platform of social reform and programs to combat poverty. He was charismatic and outspoken. Under ordinary circumstances, Bayern doubted that Nelson had a chance in hell of winning, but with the war going on....

The bottom of the screen proclaimed that what he was watching now were "debate highlights," though they felt far from "highlights" to Bayern.

"After touching on issues as varied as the economy and abortion," the newscaster's voiceover explained, "the debate inevitably turned toward the topic of war and tempers flared."

Bayern, now in the Oval Office, watched one of the audience members of the town hall stand as he was handed a microphone. With the benefit of hindsight, Bayern felt mounting dread in his stomach.

"I'm a veteran, sir. A tour in Vietnam." The man who spoke looked the part, older, hair gone white already. His expression was tired but beneath that exhaustion was anger. "I believe in this country, I've done my part. My boy's serving now, sir." Here the man's emotions broke through his facade of calm and that simmering anger came to the front. "He just caught shrapnel in Germany and he's not alone. This is the third world war this century. The last two nearly burned the planet up and who's to say this one won't be any different? There's no end in sight and people's sons, brothers, and husbands are dying out there." He managed to check himself enough to finish the question. "What exactly are you going to do about this? How many more boys have to get hurt? How many boys have to die?"

Bayern watched his VHS doppelganger stand, taking only a short second to think before responding. Now, a week later, Bayern could hear the nervousness in his own voice. "Firstly, I'm honored that you've taken the time to come and voice your concerns here, sir. When I joined the Navy, I swore an oath to support and defend the Constitution of the United States of America from all her enemies. That's an oath I've continued to uphold since taking office. Fulfilling that oath has required a lot of difficult choices. Sometimes the right answers aren't always clear."

Bayern of the present thought about how this all started in Yugoslavia, an ill-conceived military intervention, followed up with an even worse decision to strike back for a perceived first strike by the Soviets. He'd spent many sleepless nights trying to imagine how he might have made different choices, steered things differently.

His VHS self continued unperturbed. "I wish to God I could change how things have turned out. I wish I could guarantee your son's health and safety—everyone's health and safety—but part of this role is making those tough decisions, putting men's lives on the line—men like your son. All I can say is that I've never sent anyone where I was not willing to go myself. "

It was as diplomatic a response as Bayern could think of at the time, but now he could see just how hollow it was.

Before the microphone could be retrieved from the man Bayern spoke to, he snapped off an angry response, one that broke sharply with the otherwise cordial tone of the debate. "But you're not out there now, are you?" the man demanded, expression flaring into fury. "Boys are burning alive in our ships and tanks. Planes falling out of the sky. I see it on TV every day! Our boys are getting slaughtered and you're just sitting here chatting away."

The crowd murmured and tittered as a more strenuous effort was made by the organizers to collect the rogue microphone. The cameras tightened on Bayern's face as he responded, his voice sounding weak. "War is never easy," he said. "I only know that it's necessary."

"If you had any guts at all it would be *you* fighting this damn war," the man added a moment before the microphone was wrenched from his hand.

The crowd booed at that outburst, at least some of them did, but it was half-hearted. The boos were met a moment later with weak applause as the heart and soul of the audience went to war with itself over that caustic statement.

Bayern didn't let it show at the time, but the remark struck home. Even now he felt the hollow ache of guilt eating at him.

"Mr. Nelson," the moderator said, order restored. "Your thoughts? What would you do to end this war?"

Nelson stood with fluid smoothness. "I could not agree more with Mr. Bayern." He shook his head sadly. "War is a nasty business, but I'm afraid it's unavoidable. We can't simply wish it away as much as we might want to." As he spoke, he paced slowly, each stride measured and precise. "How would I end this war? Simple. I plan to win it."

The crowd erupted into applause fueled by barely restrained patriotism.

Now Nelson turned his attention directly to Bayern. "Mr. Bayern, what you've got to understand is that things have changed now. 1992 isn't 1982. The Cold War is over. World war is here."

VHS Bayern kept his expression as neutral as he could as Nelson dressed him down.

"When it came to the War in Panama, or in Somalia, or even Yugoslavia, we were playing a game. Let's be honest with ourselves, that's what it was. It was a game. This was a game in which men and women's lives were on the line, but it *was* a game, one we could have chosen to stop playing whenever we wanted. This war isn't that. Forget the Great Crusade, this is a struggle for survival. It's not about whether communism or capitalism thrives, it's about who is left standing when the dust settles and—I'm sorry—but there is no price too great to pay for us to come out on top."

The audio of the debate cut out, replaced by the calm commentary of the newscaster. "As casualties continue to mount from the fighting in Europe, polls have shown President Bayern's popularity flagging with American voters, reaching the lowest point since his taking office."

The graph which replaced the debate video did nothing to boost Bayern's mood.

"The latest news from Europe comes a week after a titanic naval clash in the Norwegian Sea. The Department of Defense reports that the Soviet Northern Fleet has been 'neutralized and rendered operationally ineffective.'"

Bayern watched video footage of burning warships at sea, Soviet sailors being taken prisoner from life rafts, and a battle-damaged aircraft carrier cruising into port at Aberdeen, pocked with craters and splinter holes.

"Despite the heavy death toll and loss of many warships including the battleship *Iowa*, the war shows no sign of slowing down. Now we go live to Greece where we have Associated Press war correspondent Jean Carson reporting from Thessaloniki. Hello Jean, what is the situation like on the ground?"

The video image froze before fuzzing back to static as the tape reached its end. A moment later the VCR stopped whirring and clunked to a halt. **STOP** displayed on the screen.

Returned to the present, Bayern tried to shake off the lingering dread he felt from the drubbing he'd received in the debate. It was a necessary but painful part of preparing for the upcoming joint session address and his presidential campaign at large.

"That's the news coverage you're getting," Bayern's campaign manager said weekly. "We were expecting Nelson to play up his domestic experience and downplay the war."

"Which left us looking soft when he went all-in," Bayern replied with a sigh. "I know. I was there."

"We've got to put out some ads to push back," Walt Harrison, Bayern's chief of staff, said. "Emphasize naval career, emphasize the wins we've had so far. By God, we sank their whole northern fleet. That's got to count for something!"

The campaign manager was unsold. "People get enough of that on the daily news. We should play to our other strengths instead. Business, domestic policies—"

"Come on now. Who's gonna buy that with the Red's screamin over the border?" Bill Dewitt said. Dewitt—who Bayern still couldn't quite bring himself to call "Hoss"—was Bayern's Vice President, recently appointed since Bayern himself had vacated the role on President Simpson's death. Dewitt—a potential political rival before—had become a powerful ally since assuming the vice presidency. As Bayern managed the day to day of the job, Dewitt had been on the campaign trail for him, drumming up support in battleground states.

"That's exactly why I don't think we should harp on it," the manager argued. "Every day all they see on the news is war. We need to remind them that we still have a country to run. Emphasizing the war is a losing game. The latest poll numbers have slumped since the Russian breakthrough in Turkey. After Ezurum fell your approval rating—"

"Don't bother reading me the latest polls," Bayern replied. "I've already seen them. They're worse than when this was recorded. What about Nelson? What is he running?"

The other men exchanged glances.

"A lot of attack ads mostly," Bayern's campaign manager said dismissively.

Bayern knew it was naive to act like his own party wasn't running equally slanderous ads. "About the war?"

More awkward glances.

"Come on," Bayern said, "I know what people say."

Harrison spoke up since the campaign manager seemed reluctant to do so. "There are quite a few attack ads calling the war a mistake. Saying that belligerent foreign policy caused it, saying that we weren't willing to live and let live with the Soviets."

If only the public had known just how hard Bayern had worked to preserve the peace. Sometimes they acted like all the Soviet Union wanted was to hold hands and hug puppies. He knew that it took two to tango and that he'd played his part in the escalation—hindsight made that clear—but it was foolhardy to suggest this was a war that didn't need to be fought. The

Soviets would never give up, not until NATO was on its knees.

"So he's positioning himself as a 'war winner' while framing me as a 'war starter,'" Bayern said. "I'm just not sure that running some rah-rah jingoist ads are going to get us what we want."

"If the electoral count goes the way the polls are suggesting, then we're going to need Florida and either Virginia or Ohio to hit the magic number," the campaign manager said. "It'll take some serious maneuvering. Virginia is a maybe, but Ohio is looking grim for us."

"We can't pretend like the war isn't happening. If Nelson is pushing himself as a war leader, then we can't give him an inch," Harrison suggested.

"Then we don't," Bayern said. "I've got an address to give to a joint session of Congress in a week. We'll find a way to leverage that. Nelson's going to rake me over the coals over every mistake I've made and, if I'm not willing to cop to that, then I'm going to look like some kind of idiot." Bayern sighed and rubbed the bridge of his nose. "Run the ads, okay? Run them but I want to pivot to something less blood and guts. Rick and I got brought in to streamline this country and get everyone back to work after Slater stalled the economy. Let's remind people of that."

No matter how much the others in the room might have wanted to, there was simply no arguing with the president when his mind was made up.

"Hoss," Bayern addressed Dewitt, still feeling foolish using his preferred nickname, "I know you've been on the trail a lot, but can you tackle Ohio for me?"

"Say no more," Dewitt said. "It'd be my pleasure."

Bayern couldn't pull himself away from the Oval Office for more campaigning, not with the war in full swing. Though the truth was that the day-to-day operation of the war rarely involved him directly. He was a figurehead more than anything else, a symbol. It was up to his generals to do the actual fighting.

A subtle look from Harrison and a tap on his watch reminded Bayern of his schedule.

"I'm late for a meeting with the Security Council," Bayern said, rising from his desk as an aide wheeled the TV out of the room. "Gentleman, thank you. Bill, call me from the trail if you need anything."

"Will do," Dewitt said.

Eventually the others filed out leaving Bayern alone with Harrison.

"What's next?" the president asked.

Harrison didn't need to consult the schedule, he knew it by heart. "Barry wanted a minute of your time before the meeting."

"Is he ready?" Bayern asked, answered with a nod from Harrison. "Then bring him in."

Barry Gillis had been secretary of defense under Simpson, a role he carried over in Bayern's cabinet.

"Mr. President," Gillis said on entering.

Balding and with thick glasses, Bayern had always thought Gillis looked more like a substitute history teacher than a secretary of defense and the ever-present smell of cigarettes that followed him did nothing to dispel that image. Gillis carried a dark leather briefcase as he entered.

"What's up, Barry?" Bayern asked. "Something for me?"

"A proposal from the Joint Chiefs that's going to need executive sign off," Gillis said. "You'll get more details at the security brief."

"About Turkey?" Bayern guessed.

"Something like that," Gillis produced a manilla folder from his briefcase and laid it down on Bayern's desk before opening it up to a pre-typed sheet waiting for a signature. An executive action. "The front in Turkey has cracked. The Russians are really pushing hard from every direction. Landings on the Black Sea Coast, Romanians pushing on Istanbul, and Soviet tank formations coming from the Caucasus Mountains."

"We expected the Turks to hold longer on their own," Bayern bemoaned. "They're one of our big traditional militaries."

"Yes, sir," Gillis agreed. "They probably would have too except for the Russians chopping their heads like we chop theirs. Decapitation strikes on Turkish HQ units, mostly long-range cruise missile strikes from the Black Sea Fleet, but also some aircraft coming from Iraq."

"Iraq?" Bayern blurted. "You're kidding."

"I wish I were. We've tracked a couple sorties back to an air force base outside Mosul in Northern Iraq. Soviet aircraft based on Iraqi airfields."

"I know last brief we talked about the Iraqi and Syrian army units stacked on the Turkish border, but basing Soviet aircraft is a hell of a neutrality violation."

"That's not mentioning the satellite recon we have of sub pens on the coast hosting Soviet boats. So far, all the intel is that it's 'when' not 'if' they join in against Turkey. We were delaying that as long as we could but...." Gillis shrugged.

"But now they're shooting at us," Bayern supplied.

Gillis gave a nod of assent. "Worthy of shooting back."

Bayern looked down at the executive proposal before him. "They want to nail the Iraqis?"

Gillis nodded. "It's a proportional response on Iraq and Syria. We've got recon photos on Soviet submarines in hidden pens on the coast. The proposal is for a retaliatory strike to be executed by the *San Juan Hill* carrier group in the Eastern Med. Enough to shake them or drop them out."

Bayern read over the proposal. "Well if the alternative is to let them keep pounding us, we might as well act." Bayern scrawled his signature on the blank line, closed the folder, and slid it back to Gillis. "Just make it clean. No civilian deaths."

"I'm assured there's little risk," Gillis said, tucking the signed paper back in his briefcase. "Iraq is involved in this war whether we strike or not; hopefully this will remind them why it's in their best interest to stay out."

"Let's hope so," Bayern said, remembering the last time Gillis suggested a retaliatory airstrike to stop escalation.

"There's something else," Gillis said, adjusting his glasses anxiously. "Something I wanted to talk with you about away from the security council."

Bayern sat on the edge of his desk and gestured for Gillis to take a seat nearby.

"It's the draft," Gillis said, easing himself onto a couch.

The words were a curse, conjuring images of anti-war protests and domestic turmoil. Bayern remembered the Vietnam draft vividly and all the animosity and fear surrounding it. He swore under his breath before realizing he's said anything.

"We've got to pass it, sir," Gillis pressed. "And we've got to do it before it's too late."

Bayern forced himself to listen without reservation.

"No one wants to bring it up," Gillis said, "but it's got to be done. If we wait too long, our professional army is going to get ground away to nothing and we'll have to start from scratch. The plain facts are that our volunteer enlistments just aren't keeping pace with losses and manpower requirements. Even reserves and national guard aren't going to be enough. Right now we're riding high on a wave of patriotic enlistments, but it won't last long, not if people keep seeing dead bodies on the news."

"That's political suicide," Harrison interjected, drawing both men's attention. Harrison flustered for a moment. "Forgive me for speaking out of turn, sir, but if we push this in now it's going to be the last nail in your presidency's coffin. No amount of TV spots can turn that around. Election is in ten days. Wait two weeks and either you can pass it safely or let it be Nelson's problem."

Gillis shook his head. "Respectfully, it can't wait that long. Every day we wait is another day we're going to be without proper replacements. We don't just need boots on the ground, we need specialists. That takes time to find and to train. In all honesty, we should have done this a month ago."

Bayern knew that. Deep down he knew they should have gone all in from day one, but he'd bought the hype that this would be a short war, an armored Armageddon at the Fulda Gap and then on to Moscow.

Bayern swore again. "When do you need a decision by?"

"Soon as possible, sir. Congress will have to authorize it, but if you put it forward, I think it stands a better chance of getting traction."

Bayern nodded. With his impending address to Congress he would have the perfect chance if he chose to take it. Even as he thought it, he thought about the man whose son had been maimed in Germany, all the other men and boys butchered across Europe. Signing a draft would continue that slaughter onto a fresh class of boys.

"I'll get you an answer before then," Bayern said.

Gillis nodded, looking somewhat relieved. It was no longer his choice to make after all.

With Turkey bending and Iraq and Syria aligning to the Soviet Union, it seemed like the war was threatening to turn against NATO. They'd only just checked the Soviets in Scandinavia, the last thing they needed was yet another crumbling front to shore up.

"At least Germany is quiet," Bayern said.

**

4

The German night was quiet enough that the crickets—normally suppressed by the thump and bang of gunfire—felt bold enough to chirp, oblivious to the danger all around them. Simple insect minds remained blissfully unaware of their own mortality, but Warrant Officer Michael Heathcliff didn't have that luxury. He crouched at the end of a grassy field all too aware that each breath could be his last. His platoon's last CO, a captain named Werthers, had nearly demonstrated this point a few days ago. Werthers had ultimately survived the Soviet mortar shell that landed on him, but he would go through the rest of his life without any hearing in his right ear and without his right leg.

This was far from the first time Heathcliff had put himself in danger—his baptism by fire happened weeks ago in a place miles from here—but familiarity with danger didn't lessen its hold on him. He was all too aware of the numbers at play, each time he went into combat the chances of him coming out alive and intact shrank.

Heathcliff sat with the rest of his platoon, nearly thirty men in all, crouched in a rutted road on the edge of a grassy field in the middle of the German countryside. Though it was dark, there was enough moonlight to see what they were doing. In this case, they were preparing themselves for a raid.

Heathcliff turned his face side to side, examining all angles in the mirror to ensure he'd properly applied smudgy camo paint to reduce the shine from his pale skin. His mustache, once carefully trimmed to stay within regulations, now blended in with the weeks of stubble on his chin.

The rest of the men were Canadians like him, members of the

reserve who'd flown into the country as a part of REFORGER to blunt the Soviet attack. That part of the plan had worked, slowing and then stopping the enemy. So far, however, they had been unable to throw them back and an uneasy stalemate was forming.

Satisfied with his makeup job, Heathcliff tucked the small mirror back in his kit, slung his rifle, and walked among his men, looking over their preparations with a keen eye. "Riggs, stow that canteen. Make sure it's full, no sloshing."

"Yes, sir."

Heathcliff patted another soldier on the helmet. "Stomach feeling better, Mandeville?"

"A bit, sir," the private gave an awkward grin.

These men were Heathcliffs's responsibility. Their lives fell to him to preserve, against the enemy, and against stupidity—their own and their officers'. Heathcliff had come over here with most of these men and every time one of them was sent home in pieces, he regarded it as a personal failure on his part. That was a family who'd lost a son, a husband, a father, a brother. Every time it happened he swore to himself that it would be the last and every time he swore it, he knew he was a liar.

The faces of the men who looked up at him were drawn, pale, haggard. Their sallow skin seemed to glow in the moonlight where they hadn't been covered with camo paint. Facial hair was untrimmed, uniforms were scuffed, torn, muddy. Everyone was tired in a way that sleep couldn't touch. It was as if some deeper essence of their beings was being pulled taut and could never relax again.

Heathcliff took life here one day at a time, but this particular raid held deeper significance to him and to his men: it was going to be the last one they undertook before rotating off the line to a rear area. It was all but certain they were simply going to be re-deployed elsewhere, but Heathcliff would welcome any break he could get no matter how small.

Near the end of the platoon he came to Lieutenant Driscoll, his new commanding officer, the man replacing the hapless Werthers. Heathcliff frowned to himself. It wasn't that Heathcliff didn't like Driscoll, he just didn't trust him.

"Sir," Heathcliff said, voice soft and low. "We're all just about ready, I think."

"Nice work," Driscoll said, looking over the platoon. Driscoll was young, a few years younger than Heathcliff. He'd been transferred in just after Werthers had been flown back to Canada. Driscoll was quiet, earnest, and level-headed, by all accounts a good officer. His only sin was inexperience, but that was a sin Heathcliff wasn't prepared to forgive. "We'll get under way once the recon team reports back that the path is clear."

Heathcliff nodded and tried not to sound like he'd rehearsed his next line too much. "I'll be going in with First Section," he said, a statement, not a suggestion, not a request. "If things go south I want to make sure we've got good command and control at the spear tip."

Driscoll seemed momentarily taken aback so Heathcliff pressed on before he could object.

"Probably better if you make sure the other sections don't fall behind too much, don't you think, sir?" Heathcliff forced himself to keep his face blank and to keep his eyes on the lieutenant's.

"If you think that's best, Heathcliff. I was planning on leading First Section in."

Heathcliff feigned apathy. "If that's what you want to do, sir. I'd be worried about getting cut off from you though."

"No," Driscoll shook his head. "No, I guess you're right. I'll stay with the main body. You'll be alright on your own then?"

Heathcliff didn't bother to point out that he was still on his own as far as he was concerned. "Fine, sir."

Driscoll nodded, "I figured you would be. Sergeant Dupont's section is carrying the Carl G," he indicated the anti-tank weapon. "We'll be relying on that to knock out the Gainfuls."

Heathcliff mentally translated the NATO reporting name to resolve an image of the self-propelled anti-air missile launcher in his mind. The target of Heathcliffs's platoon was a squad of Soviet AA vehicles standing watch over the highway interchange at Biemsen-Ahmsen. Currently the half-demolished crossroads was worthless, but inevitably the front would loosen up and when it did, NATO would need such arterial roads to feed its advance.

At least that was the thinking.

Movement at the edge of the clearing caught Driscoll and Heathcliffs's eye. The men of the platoon tensed up, weapons ready until they saw the side-to-side sweep of a small flashlight. It made two passes before it snapped off. The signal of returning friendly forces.

"The scouts," Driscoll said. "I'll debrief them assuming they say all is clear. You get with Sergeant Dupont and make sure his team is ready to move. We'll head out in five."

Heathcliff nodded in reply and picked his way back to Dupont. The sergeant and First Section were posted on the far end of the rutted farm road the platoon waited beside. Heathcliff found Dupont adjusting a bulky pair of night vision goggles on his face, the long, narrow lenses giving him a strange, bug-eyed look.

"Sergeant," Heathcliff said.

"*Bonsoir,*" Dupont said. "What news from our lieutenant?" He asked the question in French though Heathcliff understood perfectly.

"He says we are to be ready to move." Heathcliff had been told he spoke French like a maniac wielded a hatchet, but it was passable enough to be understood.

"There are glories to be won of course," Dupont said, lifting the goggles to give Heathcliff a wry grin before continuing in English. "You are with us then?"

"To the bitter end," Heathcliff said. "Once the Germans give Driscoll the all clear."

"No doubt." Dupont turned to one of his section leaders and switched to English. "Lydecker, you have the Carl G, yes?"

The young soldier patted the anti-tank weapon's tube muzzle. "Yes, Sergeant."

"Don't let her get away from you."

Heathcliff raised his voice enough to be heard by the platoon.

"Alright guys, one last show before we rotate off. Let's do this right. Quick and quiet, no one shoots anything unless it's about to shoot you. Clear?"

There were a dozen replies. "Clear, sir."

"Stick to your training and stick to the plan. The Germans found a clear path to the launchers, we just need to follow them in. Me and Sergeant Dupont will clear the way in. Stay together, don't wander off."

Driscoll finished talking with the German recon team and watched Heathcliff finish his address.

"Once we set those guns off, Second and Third Section will lay down cover fire and First Section will pull out." They'd gone over this plan a half dozen times with the section leaders, but Heathcliff wanted to impress the broad strokes of the operation on every man. He wasn't going to lose anyone in this operation because of a mistake. "We good?"

The men responded affirmative. They were nervous, but too proud to let it show.

Heathcliff looked at the lieutenant. "Sir?"

"We're good, Warrant Officer."

It was enough for Heathcliff. He snugged his own night vision goggles into place and so viewed the world through emerald-fuzzed tunnel vision. He wouldn't be able to shoot worth a damn wearing these bulky things, but at least he could move swifter in the dark.

The platoon set off by sections. Dupont and First Section led the way with Heathcliff in their midst. Darkness cloaked their movements, but Heathcliff knew it was scant little protection, his own goggles peeling its layers away easily enough. While the Soviets were more hard pressed for night vision gear, they weren't completely without it. At least if they were using infrared spotlights, he would be able to see the invisible beam with these goggles.

They didn't come across a single soul as they traveled. The battlefield they crossed was empty, without any sign of friend or foe. The front was far from a solid line. In actuality it was a permeable barrier. While huge numbers of men faced one another in the dark, they simply didn't have the numbers to occupy every square meter of ground, nor did they need to. In a modern war, weapons could reach out to the horizon and beyond. Widespread motorization meant entire divisions could shift in a heartbeat, lashing out to close or exploit gaps. Such unprecedented mobility and firepower had ironically resulted in utter stalemate.

Gunfire chattered in the dark, close enough to make Heathcliff and the others tense and drop to cover, but too far away to send them scurrying back. Someone not far away was having a bad day, maybe the worst of their life, but right now it wasn't them.

Certain the coast was clear, Heathcliff set the men moving again with a handwave.

Everyone kept their weapons at the ready, heads swiveling for threats as they walked along the deserted back road. Given the open nature of the front, a small attack on foot was a safer method of conducting a raid than all but the most high-tech aircraft. They could travel undetected and strike without warning, provided their target was within walking distance.

Before long, the illusion of sterility the empty fields posed to them began to melt away. This war wasn't a chess game played across the fields of Europe, it was a bloody and merciless struggle. Werl was a testament to that.

Sited just outside the suburbs of Bad Salzuflen, the town of Werl was hardly anything, a crossroads centered on a gas station, a gathering of houses.

The smell of decay and ash preceded the sight of the town in the dark.

It had once been a charming village in a country dotted with them, but now it was a disordered charnel house, a collection of empty homes. Some were destroyed, gutted by fires, others had caved in on themselves, victims of shellfire. Burned out cars lined the road like a grim ceremonial guard. The air was full of the smell of burnt wood, melted plastic, and the fetid stink of rotting bodies trapped in collapsed homes and half-buried in cellars. If anything still lived here, it didn't dare poke its head out.

Heathcliff resisted the urge to cover his face and instead focused on breathing in through his mouth and out through his nose. As awful as it was, he wasn't here to eulogize these unfortunate souls, he had a deadly task of his own.

Dupont's section emerged on the other side of the town and halted on the edge of a fallow field. The sergeant looked at Heathcliff. "Mines. I think."

Heathcliff nodded. "This is definitely the field the Germans said got sowed." He looked over his shoulder and pointed at a rifleman. "Abernathy, stay here and make sure Driscoll doesn't let anyone wander in there. Have them stick to the road."

"Yes, sir."

Heathcliff nodded to Dupont. "Lead on, Sergeant." He didn't like sticking to the roads, which was obviously what the Soviets wanted. They were more visible and easily bottle necked, but without proper minesweeping gear it was the only option they had. The Germans had checked this way and found it clear though. Even the Soviet Army didn't have enough tank divisions to drop one on every road, but Heathcliff hated dancing to their tune all the same.

The sound of rushing water made itself known over the chirp of insects. Maps called it the Werre River, but it was hardly a creek. Narrow, shallow, and slow, it was no obstacle to men on foot, which was good since the bridge was out. One side or the other had blown the bridge at some point with some carefully deployed explosive charges, dropping the paved road sections into the river. A dozen meters downstream was a section of shallows, only knee deep, a perfect crossing place.

Dupont eyed the ford. "Bevin, cross and check."

A narrow, two-story pub sat on the opposite end of the creek. Its windows were dark and empty, the parking lot deserted.

"I'll go," Heathcliff said.

Dupont gave him a quizzical look.

"I'll signal clear," Heathcliff said, giving Dupont a look, daring him to object.

The sergeant said nothing and Heathcliff set off, carefully picking his way through the tangled undergrowth that lined the river, keeping his eyes on the silent pub. He crouched at the water's edge, listening to the soft gurgle of the stream and scanning the opposite bank for movement. Nothing.

He tightened his grip on his rifle and gave one last visual sweep of the far bank before stepping in the creek. The water was cold as ice and filled his boot in an instant. Heathcliff didn't react and followed through, one step at a time across the shallow water, weapon at the ready. An eternity later he reached land again and brushed through the leafy foliage until finding shelter in the dark.

Heathcliff took a knee and scanned his surroundings before starting to signal the all clear to Dupont. He was just beginning to lift his hand when he saw the flash in the dark, a tiny circle of red light in the undergrowth nearby. The warrant officer froze, eyes fixed on this sudden threat.

The light flared and died only to return a moment later. The cherry of a cigarette. As his mind processed the scene, he resolved the smooth dome of a helmet and slouched form a soldier in a small foxhole on the bank nearby. A sentry, a Soviet sentry less than ten meters away. Through some miracle, Heathcliff hadn't been spotted. It was likely that this soldier was here as a sort of tripwire. This man's death would warn the rest of his comrades of an impending attack.

Heathcliff gently laid his rifle down on the ground, careful to keep the mechanism and muzzle clear of dirt. Slowly he removed his night vision goggles and waited to let his eyes acclimate to the darkness. His gaze didn't leave the sentry as he drew his bayonet from its sheath. This guard had to die before Dupont and the others could cross, and it had to be quiet. He circled through the vegetation slowly, moving arrhythmically so as not to make too human a sound. The muscles of Heathcliff's neck were as tight as piano strings. His breath came quicker than it should have and his hands trembled.

The sentry looked side to side, scanning the river, and occasionally taking a drag on a cigarette that Heathcliff was now close enough to smell. It was a nervous habit, a bad habit. A deadly one.

Heathcliff dropped into the foxhole behind the sentry and struck. He clapped a hand over the sentry's mouth and chin, pulling his face up to the sky.

The man let out a startled, muffled cry a moment before the silver blade of Heathcliffs's bayonet traced a fatal line across his throat. He felt the gentle pull of sinew and flesh as he slit the Russian's windpipe, cutting him from ear to ear. Hot blood spilled from his neck across his tunic, his severed jugular spurted red. The Soviet fought back, or tried to, grabbing at Heathcliff even as his life waned from him. He was dying, but not fast enough.

Heathcliff thrust his knife into the man's side. The blade chipped on his rib cage. Drawing back, Heathcliff plunged it in again, searching for his heart. He stabbed him a third time, and then a fourth, each stroke whispered through the Soviet's tunic and his vulnerable flesh, sliding between his ribs. The Russian's struggles became weaker and then stopped altogether. Heathcliff let him drop into the foxhole, a blood-soaked heap.

Heathcliff stood, panting, and stared down at his handiwork for a moment, trying to catch his breath. The dead man's lifeblood was sticky on his hands and he felt a sudden rush of nausea. Only the thought of the mission kept him focused. With a man dead, they had limited time to complete the mission before someone missed him.

A moment after Heathcliff gave the all clear signal, Dupont and his men waded quickly across the river. Dupont saw either the blood on Heathcliffs's hands or the look on his face. "Are you well?" Dupont asked.

"Took out a sentry," Heathcliff said, picking up his rifle and pulling his night vision goggles back on. "We need to move quick or they're going to wise up that we're here."

Dupont nodded. "We will be quick then."

Under Dupont's direction, the section advanced in the dark, moving across open fields at a trot, following local landmarks to their target. Most of the men navigated simply by moonlight, but Dupont and Heathcliff both had the benefit of night vision. Upon reaching a low hill, Dupont directed them to skirt the base, not wanting anyone silhouetted against the night sky. The cold ache in his feet and the wet squishing of his boots hardly registered in his mind.

Rounding the hill, Heathcliff and the others reached a weed-choked fence on the edge of a pasture and fanned out. Riflemen took positions to either side, sighting weapons through gaps in the vegetation, Dupont settling in beside the warrant officer, each of them peering out into the dark with their night vision goggles.

"There," Heathcliff said, his voice just above a whisper.

Three tracked anti-air missile launchers sat arrayed in a wide, triangular formation in the field, each partially concealed by camo netting. From the air they might have appeared to be clumps of trees, but from the ground they were unmistakable. The range was short, just under two hundred meters, well within the Carl Gustaf's effective range.

"Where's the rest of the platoon?"

Both men looked back the way they came and saw nothing. Driscoll and the others must be running late, delayed by some unforeseen obstacle, maybe lost in the dark, or simply moving slower than Dupont's men had.

Heathcliff scanned the Soviet AA battery again. He didn't see any movement around the tracks, even their launcher assemblies were still, their missile racks angled skyward. All the same, he knew these launchers weren't defenseless. There would be security troops nearby somewhere, maybe closer than he expected, hidden by the tall grass and hedgerows. The sentry he'd killed would likely belong to the soldiers in charge of protecting this launch site, and he would be missed sooner rather than later.

"What do you want to do?" Dupont asked.

It would be safer to wait until Driscoll and the rest of the platoon arrived, but it might be too late by then.

"We're gonna have to go for it," Heathcliff said reluctantly.

Dupont lifted the night vision goggles from his face, he looked worried. "That will put us in a lot of danger, yes?" he asked the question in French, keen apparently that his men not understand his doubts.

"*Oui*," Heathcliff said. "We will have to be quick. Get Lydecker up here."

Dupont made no further argument. "Corporal!" he whispered, gesturing for the soldier.

Lydecker half-crawled over to them, the Carl G launcher slung on his back rocking side to side.

"Are you a good shot, Lydecker?" Heathcliff asked.

"Good enough, sir."

Good enough would have to be good enough. "Get in position to take out those launchers. Three shots, three kills, understand? Quick as you can. Start shooting as soon as you're ready. We'll provide cover for you."

Lydecker craned his neck to look over the distant launchers again, sizing them up. "Sir." The corporal and his assistant moved down the hedgerow, doubled over at the waist to keep low, looking for a good vantage point.

"Get word to everyone," Heathcliff told Dupont. "Once Lydecker starts firing, all hell is gonna break loose and we need to keep any security troops suppressed.

"*Oui*," Dupont vanished, moving down the line and readying his men.

Heathcliff himself settled into position, shouldering his rifle and ensuring it was primed and ready. The field ahead was silent, dark, empty save for the launchers, each one was separated from the others just enough that a single bomb or missile couldn't kill them all. Heathcliff would rather have a tank platoon come in and do this work. He had to remind himself that a tank platoon wouldn't be able to get this close undetected.

The sounds of the crickets continued unabated until the bang of the Carl Gustaf cut the night. The first missile launcher flashed with an impact of the round. Since the Gustav was a recoilless rifle, it left no missile trail, it was more like a small, shoulder-mounted cannon than any anti-tank missile.

The exploding shell flashed in the dark, momentarily lighting the area around the launcher before the missiles on the launch rack sympathetically detonated, incinerating the camo net draped over top in a blazing fireball. The flash whited out Heathcliffs's night vision goggles and he swore, pulling them off his face and blinking away after images.

A long burst of machine gun fire stitched through the night, tracer rounds cutting the dark, probing for the enemy. The tracer rounds were hued green, Soviet-made, in contrast to the red-colored return fire of the Canadians.

Pandemonium ruled the night as the Soviet security troops flew into a frenzy, firing in all directions trying to determine the source of the threat.

Heathcliff couldn't allow them the chance to realize just how outnumbered he and his men were, and that meant fighting with all the ferocity he could muster. The origin points of the machine gun spray made for a perfect targeting point. He returned fire in bursts, mindfully bringing his rifle down and re-sighting it every time it stopped jumping in his hands, forcing himself to remain disciplined and not burn off an entire magazine at nothing.

Return fire hissed, whizzed, and cracked by, making Heathcliff duck down lower. If there was any chance he could have escaped by fleeing, he would have. Every fiber of his body was tense, afraid, the primal core of his brain alive with fear, like a trapped wild animal. Only the faint, rational thought that the only way to get out of this alive was to keep fighting kept him in place.

Lydecker made his second shot just before Heathcliff finished emptying his magazine. The round flew true, striking the rear of the launcher vehicle. Burning diesel fuel spewed from the stricken tank, lighting the pasture on fire and silhouetting the shapes of human figures dashing for cover.

Heathcliff scythed them down like wheat with a burst of gunfire. When his rifle ran dry he yanked the magazine and quickly replaced it, snapping the charging handle back. His hands trembled, white knuckling the grips on his rifle. Heathcliff swore out loud and returned to firing on the enemy, his fear kept at bay only by his training.

One launcher to go.

Up and down the hedgerow the Canadians fired off staggered bursts, focusing on enemy machine guns as they found them. The longer the gun battle drew on, the more fire became focused on their position. Confusion was giving way to order, reason burning away the panic in the enemy's minds.

They couldn't stay here much longer. Soon enough the Soviets would fully come to their senses and begin maneuvering aggressively, sending out squads to pin, flank, and destroy the outnumbered Canadians.

Heathcliff looked at Lydecker who knelt at the far end of the line, Gustaf shouldered as his assistant worked to slide a fresh round home. The private got as far as unloading the spent round when he jerked and fell away from Lydecker, writhing on the ground.

Without thinking, Heathcliff rose to his feet and raced to the wounded man, moving behind riflemen firing from cover. He recognized the wounded man at once, even in the dark. "Riggs!"

The private shook his head, hand clamped to his ribs, face contorted in pain.

Lydecker looked from Riggs to Heathcliff, eyes wide with fear.

"Eyes on that launcher!" Heathcliff snapped, stepping over Riggs to pick up the next round for the Carl Gustaf.

"Sir!" Dupont reached Heathcliff, yelling to be heard over the fire fight.

"Get Riggs out of here!" Heathcliff said, working the mechanism to lock the Carl Gustaf's breech. "Get the section back!"

"Sir, you cannot stay!"

Heathcliff spared him a look. "We finish this or they send someone else to do it! Go!"

Sergeant Dupont didn't have time to argue. "Section fall back! Fall back! Riggs, hang on."

The infantry broke the engagement, falling back from the hedge line and moving for the relative safety of the rear.

Heathcliff grabbed Lydecker's sleeve. "One more then we go!" he had to yell the words into Lydecker's ear over the cacophony of gunfire.

The soldier nodded and then pressed his eye to the sight on the side of the weapon, angling it toward the last Soviet launcher. Heathcliff remained with him, steadying him with a free hand. His training with the Carl Gustaf was only half remembered but he had enough presence of mind to check the backblast area of the weapon to ensure no friendly soldiers would be caught in the blast. "Backblast area clear!"

Lydecker took an extra second to center the last launcher in his sights.

Enemy fire ramped up without the covering fire to suppress them. Rounds snapped through the branches overhead, dropping leaves on two remaining men.

Heathcliffs's heart rattled the cage of his chest as if it were trying to surge its way to freedom.

The Carl Gustaf boomed, blowing out Heathcliffs's hearing worse than it already was. This shot followed the others, striking the last launcher vehicle on its flank and setting off the missiles it carried. The blast shook the night and spread yet more fire to the grass around it.

"Let's go!" Heathcliff shouted, the last words Corporal Lydecker would ever hear.

A Soviet rifle round punched through his forehead, snapping his head back and toppling him to the ground lifeless, dead before he finished falling.

Heathcliff recoiled away, gaping at the dead soldier as he sprawled back against him. "Ly—" Heathcliff didn't finish. The man was dead. More Soviet rifle fire tore through the foliage around him. Lydecker was dead, but others were still counting on him.

Heathcliff crawled away, moving as fast as he could without lifting his head high enough to get it taken off. Worming his way through the grass, he was keenly aware of gunfire snapping by just overhead. Finally, he crested a low hill and started down the other side, now sheltered from the enemy. Rising to his feet he jogged down and found the others regrouping further back.

"Where—" Dupont began.

"He didn't make it," Heathcliff said bitterly.

Dupont swore. There was nothing more to say.

The section retraced its steps, moving as fast as they could back the way they'd come, only this time with the staccato chatter of enemy gunfire echoing in the night behind them only now firing at phantoms.

They didn't stop until they'd crossed back over the creek. Driscoll and the rest of the platoon were there, deployed for combat.

"We heard the shots," Driscoll explained on meeting Heathcliff. "What happened?"

Heathcliffs's mind was still racing, the sight of Lydecker's dead eyes staring into the dark sky burned into his mind. "We took out a Soviet sentry on the crossing," He said. "So when we found the guns, I gave the order to engage before we were found out. Private Riggs was wounded, Corporal Lydekcer was killed, sir."

Driscoll's mouth tightened. "I see."

"I gave the order, sir," Heathcliff said. "I knew we wouldn't get another chance at this."

Driscoll nodded, "For what it's worth, I think it was the right call."

Heathcliff could only nod. He felt numb.

"Let's get the platoon back before the Russians pay us back."

"Yes, sir," Heathcliff said. He knew they'd be rotating back now. Things would be quieter—safer behind the lines. Not that it would matter anymore for Lydekcer.

T. K.BLACKWOOD

***

5

Yessov ascended the ladderway and emerged from the cramped confines of his submarine and onto the small navigation bridge atop K-461's conning tower.

The moonlight was filtered to a strange brown glow by the enormous camouflage tarp that hung across the vessel, transforming the submarine into an apparent rock when viewed from the air. Advanced thermal scans would reveal the submarine's presence and indicate Syria's violation of their own supposed neutrality, but Yessov was betting the West had no such optics to spare on humble Syria. It was a risk that had to be taken.

A single sailor stood on sentry duty here, smoking a cigarette and holding the sling of a Kalashnikov rifle draped over his shoulder. On seeing the captain, he turned his head and spat the cigarette off the side of the boat. Smoking while on sentry duty was expressly forbidden, as was smoking while submerged. Nicotine was a nasty habit for a submariner, but Yessov was in no mood to dress down this young seaman.

"Get below," Yessov snapped. "Gather a detail to remove this." Yessov gestured to the overhead camo netting.

"Y-yes, Comrade Captain!" in his haste to flee, the sailor didn't salute and instead scampered down the ladder.

As a submarine flying a Soviet flag in time of war, K-461 legally had no business being moored in Syrian territorial waters, but they'd been docked here for two days taking on weapons and supplies. By international law the Syrians were required to imprison the trespassing sailors and impound their submarine until the war's conclusion or forfeit their neutrality.

In practice, the Syrian government was happy to assist the Soviet Union and her allies in this global struggle so long as their assistance remained undiscovered. Whatever the feelings of the general population, Syria was in effect an Iraqi client state and went where Iraq led, and Iraq pointed firmly toward the Soviet sphere.

The shallow waters of the coastal sub pen were a deep black, a glossy contrast to the *Akula's* matte finish. The waves flashed white when they caught the light of the moon as they lapped the curved sides of the sub. This pen—once a small, sheltered harbor for fishing boats—was deserted by all but a skeleton force of Syrian naval personnel to assist with the rearming of the two vessels held here. Blank-faced tenement housing lined the water, their windows cold and dark—the homes of fishermen and their families in happier times. Yessov imagined they'd been relocated at some point in the recent past to preserve the secrecy of this operation.

He looked from the buildings to his neighboring vessel in the sub pen. The other submarine was also Soviet, a *Sierra*-Class. To an untrained observer, the *Sierra* looked nearly identical to the *Akula*. A black, teardrop-shaped hull topped with a gracefully swept conning tower and a tail also mounted a teardrop-shaped towed sonar array. The *Sierra* was second only to the *Akula* in terms of technology. This particular submarine had arrived the day after Yessov's boat and began its own arduous re-arming process, a process still unfinished.

Yessov inwardly wondered just how many submarines the Soviets had left in the Mediterranean. With the relentless pace of combat operations and the lack of easy reinforcement here, it couldn't be many. Somehow, being an endangered species did not bother Yessov. It only made him more determined than ever to fight on.

He puffed his chest with pride at the thought, inhaling the cool salt air through his nose. There was nothing especially aromatic about it if you were used to living close to the coast as he was. It was special only in that it would likely be one of his last breaths of fresh air for the foreseeable future. A submarine and its captain had no business on the surface, their work lay under the waves.

Yessov watched as the forward deck hatches were sealed. The black rubber acoustic-dampening panels which covered the submarine's metal hide were looking worse for wear. Some had come loose over time and sea growth has started to spot the bare hull. It was an unavoidable symptom of a long combat deployment with little time for maintenance. Yessov hated to see it here in the open air. It felt naked and exposed. In peace time a submarine in dock was a beautiful thing, but in war it was better left unseen. It would feel good to get underway again.

As Yessov savored the fresh, salty air and the muffled crash of nearby waves, a team of sailors returned to hastily begin unfastening and rolling up the camouflage netting. He took one more wistful look at the moon and then descended into the guts of the boat.

Unburdened by any sort of claustrophobia, Yessov navigated the tangled interior of the boat with no apprehension, ultimately making his way to the bridge. K-461's bridge was not much to look at, built entirely around function rather than form. Dull, beige paneling lined the walls, broken only by display panels and gauges. To the uninformed it might look more like a power plant control center than a weapon of war.

A junior officer announced his arrival and the crew snapped to attention.

Yessov saluted them and they relaxed, returning to their duties. From the ranks of junior officers, Lieutenant Voloshin stepped forward, his tired, shadowed eyes scanning a clipboard which held a heavily marked readiness report. "Comrade Captain, we've finished loading the last of the torpedoes and missiles."

Yessov nodded, pleased. He picked his cup of tea up from the tray where he'd left it before going on deck and sipped thoughtfully. Despite his safe arrival here, Yessov had not yet been able to properly relay his situation to high command. He'd sent a coded dispatch by courier to the Soviet embassy in Tripoli, but he expected no swift response.

"Beyond this," Voloshin continued, "all stations report ready to cast off."

"Very good, Lieutenant," Yessov said, "take us out."

K-461, now unburdened by his camo net, cruised from the safe harbor with a thrum of screws, re-armed and ready for action again. Combat, Yessov thought, was where he belonged and that was precisely where he intended to put his boat.

As they sailed out, Yessov toured through the bridge with Voloshin trailing closely behind. He stopped from time to time to look over the shoulder of sailors at their posts, monitoring computers and making adjustments for the submarine's multitude of systems. It wasn't long before they'd gone far enough out.

"All stations report ready to dive," Voloshin said.

"Depth?" Yessov asked.

"The ocean floor is twenty meters down here and getting deeper," Navigation returned quickly.

"Take us down to periscope depth as soon as practicable." Yessov gave the order to his helmsman conversationally.

"Yes, Comrade Captain!"

Outside of K-461's double hull, the ocean waves swallowed the submarine, leaving only a single, narrow radar mast held aloft above the water, trailing feathery white wake.

"Any orders from high command on the ELF?" Yessov asked.

Since they'd arrived here, he'd had his crew monitoring the extreme-low frequency transmissions that were regularly sent out by Soviet naval command in the hopes of getting some actionable orders.

"No, Comrade Captain. Nothing beyond our standing orders to interdict NATO shipping in the region and attack targets of opportunity."

Yessov clicked his tongue. "A shame. The Mediterranean Squadron all but destroyed. Ourselves trapped in this little lake."

After their efforts to interdict the North Atlantic had met

with mixed success, the submariners of the Soviet Navy had been forced to make the dangerous journey to friendly ports to re-arm. Conventional wisdom had been that the conflict would already be decided by this point, so little thought had been given to the re-supply of the Soviet submarine fleet. It was an oversight they were all paying for now.

Friendly Soviet naval forces in the Mediterranean had been virtually annihilated. Certainly no major surface combatants remained, and precious few attack submarines. Those that were left were either lucky or clever, or more likely both. With the Bosphorus firmly closed by the Turks, they had no way to make it into the Black Sea and return home. To try to slip that cordon would be akin to suicide.

He was the Hero of the Adriatic. He was the slayer of *Gettysburg*, the vaunted Soviet champion, and now he was stuck far away from the true war: the Norwegian Sea, the North Atlantic. It was in that theater that the future of the war would be decided. He who controlled the sea lanes controlled the fate of NATO. All he could hope to do now was to draw in as many NATO assets as possible and wait for Soviet land forces to reach the Bosphorus and clear it.

"I do not see our situation quite so negatively," Voloshin said, choosing each word with care.

"Is that so?" Yessov asked, peaking an eyebrow.

"In fact, Comrade Captain, I believe we are quite fortunate."

"Fortunate?" Yessov looked back at his XO with a mixture of disdain and disbelief.

"Fortunate to be alive at all," Voloshin explained. "Given the fate of our comrades in this region."

Yessov and his crew had narrowly made it through Gibraltar, not discounting the close calls they'd had with NATO ships in the Atlantic. It had been a close-run affair in many ways. Of course, acknowledging that was a form of cowardice. Yessov scowled at Voloshin. "We can be thankful for our luck once we have won this war, Comrade. I feel no gratitude so long as the enemy remains standing."

He might have seen something like exasperation flicker on Voloshin's face, but his XO recovered himself before Yessov could be certain. "Of course, Comrade Captain."

"News will come soon," Yessov said, choosing to ignore this half-display of insubordination. "North. Our comrades in the Red Banner Northern Fleet will sally forth and deal a deathblow to NATO soon enough. A climactic engagement to put Jutland to shame. Soon. If we are truly lucky, we will find a way to return in time to see it won."

Voloshin stared back, face blank.

"Comrade Captain," a seaman at a radar monitoring station spoke up.

Yessov tore his eyes from the stoic Voloshin. "Report."

"We read heavy concentration of NATO targeting and acquisition radars dead ahead, one hundred kilometers out."

"Already?" Yessov forgot his irritation with his XO and strode to the tactical plot in the center of his bridge, his eyes sweeping the chart as a junior officer marked approximate bearing and distance or radar transmitters.

"Near Cyprus," Yessov said to himself.

"A NATO task force?"

"Likely," Yessov said. The sheer number of radar transmitters was daunting, representative of a large battle group, a difficult target to crack, certainly if they were expecting him. For all his bluster, Yessov wasn't keen to engage such a formidable assemblage of ships, certainly not alone. "We'll divert south," he said. "Skirt the Lebanese coast." Yessov felt Voloshin's cool gaze on him, along with a sudden need to explain himself. "Our mission is to keep NATO engaged. I'd say they're already well engaged here."

Voloshin made no comment and the submarine banked silently through the water, turning south to avoid this potential snare.

As they accelerated and descended into the ocean depths, Yessov felt his mind relax, his fear fading away. As it did so he was left wondering: just what was the enemy doing gathered here in such strength?

**

USS *Wisconsin* was a relic of another age. One of the last big-gun battleships in service, an *Iowa*-class behemoth which had first plied the waves during the Second World War, and now again sailed under a flag of war during the third. While once *Wisconsin* would have been king of the seas, now she sailed in the proverbial shadow of the new master of the waves, the *Antietam*-class aircraft carrier *San Juan Hill*. These two massive warships formed the core of a carrier battle group holding station one hundred kilometers off the Syrian coast.

Around these two capital ships was a series of concentric protective rings of defensive firepower, collectively forming a nigh-impenetrable defensive barrier. At the center was a *Ticonderoga*-class cruiser armed with the advanced Aegis Combat System. Further out were destroyers and frigates, and beyond them patrolling aircraft. These forces were primarily on anti-submarine patrols. While it was unlikely a Soviet attack sub would make a run at *Wisconsin* or *San Juan Hill*, it wasn't impossible. *Gettysburg* had been torpedoed while thought to be safe during the Yugoslav War. While the ship had been saved, it was currently dry docked in Italy undergoing extensive repairs. None of the men of this carrier group had an interest in winding up like *Gettysburg* or worse.

The night sea was quiet and calm, giving no indication of the deadly intent aboard these warships. They were here to carry out a punitive attack against Syria and Iraq for violating the terms of their neutrality. They would pay in blood for the NATO lives they'd allowed to be taken on their watch.

The first salvo of the strike was fired by *Wisconsin*, though not by her aged sixteen-inch main guns. Rather it was the battery of tomahawk missiles on her flanks that fired. Each missile rocketed from its cell in sequence, lighting the sea with fiery rocket boosters as the cruise missiles accelerated to speed and leveled off, screaming east toward Syria. These particular weapons weren't targeted at Syria itself, but instead were aimed beyond her borders at the Iraqi air base outside Mosul. With their low flight ceiling and high speed, there would be little warning for the base crew. They were targeted via GPS arrays, aiming for hangars, aircraft maintenance bays, fuel silos, and ammunition bunkers.

For Syria the fleet exercised its other primary killing arm, the aircraft of *San Juan Hill*.

The men who piloted the F-18 Hornet squadron which rocketed off the deck were veterans, no strangers to this type of mission. Their ship had arrived in the Adriatic too late to save *Gettysburg*, but just in time to later on clear out the remnants of the Soviet Mediterranean squadron which attempted to interdict them. They'd since conducted innumerable strikes against the Soviet and Warsaw Pact military forces threatening Greece and Turkey.

Now their target was the ostensibly secret Syrian naval facilities on that country's coast. Armed with a mixture of anti-radar and anti-ship missiles, as well as laser-guided glide bombs, they were escorted in by a handful of F-14 Tomcats and—perhaps more importantly—a pair of EA-6B Prowlers. The Prowler was—unlike the sleek Hornet and Tomcat—a bulbous, stocky, and awkward-looking craft. Its unassuming appearance masked the potent electronic warfare equipment stuffed within. So long as a Prowler was in the air, enemy electronics would be unreliable and ineffective, including anti-air missiles and radar.

Masked from Syrian ground-based radar stations until they were close enough that even the Prowler's electronic counter measures couldn't hide them, the Hornet squadron dove and attacked. Anti-radar missiles were unleashed, targeting the radar arrays and air defense batteries that dotted the landscape around their primary target.

Fireballs lit the night as these emplacements were neutralized one by one.

Finally, with the Syrians left defenseless, the remaining

Hornets struck, unleashing missiles and bombs to systematically destroy port facilities, storage, repair, and control bunkers. The prize of a lone *Sierra*-class submarine was particularly invigorating for the airmen of the squadron. The submarine had no chance to flee, caught at anchor in the midst of being re-armed—red handed.

As the remains of the *Sierra* burned and sunk, the squadron broke off and returned for the carrier, confident in the blow they'd dealt to the enemy. Early intel had suggested there was an *Akula*-class in port as well, but there was no sign of it here after their raid. Maybe it had been a case of misidentification, or maybe they'd just missed it.

**

6

Compared to the chaos and intensity of the battlefront, the military base at Laikovo felt almost lifeless. Lieutenant General Pyotr Strelnikov had spent most of his military career at facilities like this one, though had never been to Laikovo specifically. Laikovo was part of a ring of military bases which surrounded Moscow, each one responsible for the defense of the city to one degree or another. In peacetime it would have been considered a desirable posting, certainly better than being stationed in the frigid and remote Far East.

Instead of feeling honored, Strelnikov felt like the particle board desk he sat behind was a prison. He'd taken this role some days back after the debacle in Germany. He'd stuck his neck out too far and this time it was his head which rolled. It was a step above being shot for incompetence but spelled an end to his career just as surely.

Your division is no longer considered combat effective. It will be rotated to the rear for replenishment. General Turgenev's smirking arrogance bled into Strelnikov's recollection. In violation of his orders, Strelnikov had attacked, blunting an American operation which otherwise might have savaged the whole front. He'd been rewarded with exile, and by Defense Minister Tarasov himself no less.

Strelnikov felt aimless and disillusioned. How could they have any hope of winning the war with fools in charge? Germany had devolved to a stalemate, the Soviet offensive in Scandinavia was being rolled back bloodily, and operations in Greece and Turkey were likewise not panning out. The victory which Strelnikov had dedicated himself to was further away than ever, wrenched from his grasp by incompetents infesting every level of this rotten command structure. Politicians expanded the war and mismanaged the home front. The Stavka was a viper's nest of fools and sycophants and the whole Red Army was sagging and groaning beneath the multitude of failings piling on its shoulders. He shuddered to imagine the inevitable outcome.

A polite rap on his office door lifted Strelnikov's head from the letter he was penning. "Yes?"

His chief of staff, Colonel Mishkin opened the door a crack. "My apologies for the interruption, Comrade General."

"An interruption implies that I was being productive," Strelnikov said. He looked down at the half-completed letter. It was a perfunctory notice to his parents that he'd been recalled from the front to Russia. He didn't expect anything by way of reply.

"You'd asked to be informed on the arrival of the fresh transfers," Mishkin said.

"Yes," Strelnikov said. "They are here?"

"Arriving now, Comrade General."

Mishkin was one of Strelnikov's "old guards," men who had served alongside him since their early days in Yugoslavia. He was by far the best chief of staff Strelnikov had ever worked with and it made it all the more tragic that he, like his general, was now wasted on a garrison posting.

"Thank you, Comrade."

Mishkin retreated, closing the door behind him.

Strelnikov tucked the letter into a drawer, rose from his desk, and left his office. Mishkin waited outside to escort him to meet the new arrivals, their footfalls echoed loudly off the linoleum tiles as he followed wall-mounted placards through the empty halls of the administrative building. It felt strange to be so dressed. He'd become used to wearing the simple uniform of an infantryman. Now in full regalia he looked fit for the May Day Parade, perhaps fitting with October Revolution Day approaching. From his peaked cap to the well-starched creases of his trousers, he cut an imposing figure: tall, gaunt, and stern.

When Strelnikov saw himself in the mirror, he couldn't help but note that he was looking more and more like the "old men" who'd run the army in his youth. His chest was even starting to become heavy with medals and ribbons.

A pair of waiting sentries pulled open the double doors leading outside and Strelnikov strode past them. Both were older than he would have expected, easily into their thirties, likely reservists called to replace the younger men sent off to fight. Strelnikov himself was a sort of replacement. He only had to look at the unfamiliar rank pinned to the shoulder boards of his uniform. He'd become a Lieutenant General after his old commanding officer, Lieutenant General Gurov had been killed in a NATO airstrike, along with his entire staff. He'd climbed ranks with unheard of rapidity, but now expected he was at a plateau. After his initial success in Zagreb during the Yugoslav War, now Strelnikov found himself a pariah, unable to replicate that stunning victory. He'd been blunted at Metz, fought to a standstill outside Worms, and now had been recalled to Moscow in shame. He'd failed to live up to his initial promise and so here he would stay. Not bad for the son of collective farmers, he had to admit, but still beneath what he thought he was capable of.

The late October air had bite to it, the first hints of the brutal cold which would descend in the coming months. He took a moment to pull on the heavy greatcoat offered to him by Mishkin, quickly buttoning it against the wind.

Right away Strelnikov was struck with the strangeness of the situation. From the steps of the administration building entrance, he could see the distant assembly grounds filling with vehicles. What had once been an overgrown cement expanse was rapidly becoming a parking lot for row on row of military vehicles.

"What exactly is arriving?" Strelnikov asked.

"I'm afraid I can't say for certain, Comrade General," Mishkin said, frowning. "We were provided no information about their numbers or composition." Mishkin prided himself on his sharp administrative skills and it was clear this lack of organization bothered him as much as it bothered Strelnikov. "I know that we have a group of fresh inductees and returning replacements."

Fresh meat and returning wounded lumped together into the "stew" of the army.

Strelnikov saw easily a regiment's worth of equipment already arrived with more queued up along the road. Strangely, he noted that what seemed to be arriving was new equipment, not old generation gear.

When Strelnikov had assumed command of this base, he'd arrived along with the battle-hardened shreds of his once proud 121st Motor Rifles, the "Zagreb Guards." That honor, issued in the heady days that followed the victory in Yugoslavia almost seemed farcical now. The division had only just restored its strength after Yugoslavia when they'd been thrown back into the fray in Germany. That experience was a hell all its own.

As bitter as he was about his posting here, Strelnikov was a man of duty and set about at once training these fresh conscripts. While he'd been provided manpower—an induction group of fresh-faced teenagers—they'd had precious little equipment to go around. Strelnikov's trainees had been forced to make do with weapons and vehicles had been deemed too old to be sent to the front, mostly castoff tanks and APCs from the 1960s.

It had been clear before that Strelnikov was meant to be thrown away, forgotten, but now with the arrival of modern weapons, he had his doubts. He'd expected to welcome another batch of inductees and get them doled out to training units. This was something else entirely.

"Fetch me a UAZ," Strelnikov said.

Mishkin saluted sharply, apparently happy to have a task laid before him. "Yes, Comrade General!"

Strelnikov spared one more look at the vast assemblage in the depot yard. It made him long for a combat command again, a dream that now somehow felt less impossible than it had the day before.

Mere minutes later his adjutant returned with a 4x4 truck and rolled to a stop. Strelnikov boarded the vehicle. "Let us see what's been brought to us."

They set off at speed through the base weaving around parked vehicles and drawing steadily closer to the growing assemblage. Strelnikov eyed the nearest vehicles once they reached them. They were BMP-3s, the latest infantry fighting vehicles produced by the Soviet Union. Strelnikov had never had the privilege of commanding these newest units in battle, but had heard rumor that the firepower they wielded was legendary by virtue of the 100-millimeter gun joined with a 30-millimeter autocannon and their armor more capable of surviving hits. Accompanying the BMPs were main battle tanks that he recognized as a new variant of the T-72.

At the edge of the depot, they came into sight of a command company overseeing the delivery of this equipment and slowed to meet them.

Strelnikov climbed from the UAZ and started walking toward the command vehicle where he found a paunchy major watching the delivery.

"Comrade Major," Strelnikov said as the two of them traded salutes. "What have you brought me?"

"Replacements," the major said, apparently uninterested in this conversation.

"What are these tanks?" Strelnikov asked.

"The new T-72BUs, Comrade General," the major said, "fresh from the factory floor at Uralvagonzavod." He gave Strelnikov a humorless smirk. "You can still smell the paint on them. They share sixty percent commonality with old T-72 parts which makes maintenance easy. Fast, hard hitting, with new composite armor. I'm quite certain you'll find them sufficient for your purposes."

So, the rumored next generation tanks had finally been approved for use. It wasn't impossible that the upper echelons of command hoped to use Strelnikov's old command as some kind of proving ground for them.

As much as Strelnikov was awed by the sight of fresh

weaponry, he couldn't help but remark on the insanity of deploying them *here*. "And they are for my division?"

"Yes, Comrade General. Your division has been given the honor of marching in the October Revolution Day parade. I imagine these will make a nice showing." he gestured to the factory-fresh tanks.

Strelnikov furrowed his brow, unable to stop himself. "Do you think instead they might be more useful killing fascists on the front lines?"

The major flushed red but didn't back down. "It is not my place to question orders from the Defense Minister!"

Tarasov signed off on this? Strelnikov was surprised to hear that based on what he knew of the old man. To waste new gear on a parade was borderline criminal. Unless these new weapons weren't as effective as Strelnikov imagined?

Without warning, Strelnikov felt a strange feeling creep over him, almost a sense of deja vu. He was not a spiritual man. Strelnikov was a materialist, an atheist. But he couldn't shake the feeling now that he was becoming a part of something larger.

It was almost beyond belief that the Soviet high command would earmark an entire division—nearly ten thousand men— for rear area garrison duty in such a dire time. Let alone a division equipped with the latest gear and staffed with battle-hardened troops.

"Unless you have any further objections, *Comrade*, then I would like to finish this equipment transfer."

Strelnikov nodded absently and watched the vehicles as they parked in phalanxes of armor, tires, and treads. There was no practical strategic reason for holding an experienced frontline division in garrison around Moscow and why the secrecy of these movements? Why had they not received advanced notice of these reinforcements? The only reason Strelnikov could fathom to keep such a volume of elite troops on standby was if trouble was expected. He turned his head east, toward the unseen city. Trouble in Moscow. Political trouble.

The thought turned his stomach. What exactly were the men in the Kremlin up to?

***

The restaurant was nearly empty when Soviet foreign minister Andrei Gradenko stepped inside. Gradenko would gladly take the gloom of the deserted establishment over the cold nip of the air outside. Moscow's warm spell had ended suddenly, with temperatures dipping down to hover just above freezing. The weather would only get worse of course, but it was an unwelcome change all the same.

An unsmiling attendant took Gradenko's coat without a word, hanging it beside the others on a nearby coat rack. With the Soviet Union still in the early stages of transitioning to a more nimble market economy, a privately-owned cooperative restaurant like this was a rarity, a luxury largely confined to cosmopolitan urban centers like Moscow and Leningrad, and even then, limited only to the elite. In peacetime demand for such amenities far exceeded supply and reservations were nearly impossible to come across—unless of course you were one of the most powerful men in the Soviet Union.

After collecting his information, the server took Gradenko to a waiting table where his host sat waiting.

"Comrade! Sit!" General Anton Tarasov said, beckoning Gradenko over. Despite his age and poor health, Tarasov was just as imposing as ever. In his youth he'd been a bear of a man, but hard years in the Red Army had worn his back and knees, and solid muscle had given way to a gut. All the same, there was no mistaking that Tarasov was dangerous even given his physical shortcomings. As head of the Soviet military, Tarasov was not a man to trifle with. At one point, he had been a part of the troika controlling the Soviet government alongside Gradenko before being politically outmaneuvered and ousted by General Secretary Karamazov.

Gradenko sat opposite Tarasov as a waitress poured a glass

of water for him. He couldn't help but notice that the staff appeared to only be women. Presumably the men who worked here had been called up to their military postings in the reserves or had been requisitioned by the state for more vital work.

"It's good you could make it on such short notice," Tarasov said. "Reservations are nearly impossible here, especially now. Their pelmeni is excellent. I recommend it."

Gradenko was too tense to feel hungry. He carried the weight of the world on his shoulders and felt as stooped as Tarasov looked. He waited for the waitress to leave before speaking.

"The American attack on Mosul air base has given the Iraqis cold feet."

Tarasov eyed him levelly. "No time for pleasantries, Comrade?"

"I have too much on my mind," Gradenko said sourly.

"Your son?" Tarasov's voice was low, the mirth gone from his voice.

Gradenko nodded, but that was only part of it. As the top minister of the Soviet Union's foreign policy and diplomacy, the responsibility for the conflagration the world had fallen into lay in large part with him. The knowledge that the men meant to be working in this restaurant could now be dying on the fields of Europe by his word was a bitter pill.

His son being taken as a bargaining chip by the KGB was a more personal tragedy, one he did his best to keep separate from his other duties.

"The bastard," Tarasov growled.

"The bastard" was Alexei Karamazov, formerly Chairman of the KGB, currently General Secretary of the Soviet Union. Karamazov was without a question the most powerful man in the nation and undoubtedly the primary architect of the Third World War. He was also the man responsible for imprisoning Gradenko's son in the bowels of the KGB's headquarters here in the city.

"Cold feet?" Tarasov prompted.

"The Iraqi government has added additional terms to their cooperation," Gradenko said. "And Syrian participation is conditional on Iraqi participation."

Tarasov sighed, shoulders sagging. For a moment he looked his age. "And what are the Iraqi terms?" Tarasov asked.

"Iraq will enter the war so long as we back their territorial claims on Kuwait," Gradenko said. "They insist on full diplomatic recognition of their so-called 'nineteenth province.'"

Tarasov snorted and shook his head. "Hardly a surprise. They've been eyeing it for years. No one to say 'no' to them now, I suppose. This explains why they've mobilized so many divisions to the south."

"Perhaps we let the bastards hang," Gradenko said. Personally he was furious over the expansion of the war, not to mention the fury he felt over their client state dictating policy to them. The Soviet Union truly had fallen on dire times. "See how much longer their economy staggers along without our assistance."

"It would be different if we did not need them," Tarasov said. "Let them make demands now. We will collect our repayment in due time."

Gradenko couldn't care less what fate befell the decadent monarchy of Kuwait. In truth he saw them as no better than Iraq, though he hated to be led by the nose.

"If the military signs off on this proposal, then so will the foreign ministry," Gradenko said.

Tarasov waved dismissively. "You have our cooperation. We will coordinate it all through our military advisors. It's time to see if all our military aid paid off."

The Iraqis were second rate clients at best, behind even the likes of the Polish who were infamously contentious. All the same, snatching Iraq away from the Western Bloc in the wake of the Iran-Iraq war had been a diplomatic coup. This bloc switch had come right after Persia fell to Iranian revolutionaries. Now the Americans were left only with Pakistan which was safely sandwiched between lukewarm India and hostile Iran.

In the turmoil after the Republican Guard coup following the Iran-Iraq conflict the Soviets had found a ready and willing partner in the Middle East to replace the wayward Egyptians.

While the Iraqis were fair weather socialists at best, they were relatively large and stable enough, something of a success story as far as the Soviet Union's Arab client states went.

"We paid damn near enough for them," Gradenko said. Extensive economic aid to Iraq following the war and the coup had come at a steep cost for the Soviet Union. Rebuilding that shattered nation hadn't been easy, but it would hopefully pay dividends now.

"I can make arrangements to coordinate our attack with theirs," Tarasov said. "With Erzurum in our hands now, we're in position to launch attacks south to link up with the Arab states. The operation should be simple."

Discussion of politics and war was curtailed by the return of the waitstaff. Gradenko and Tarasov ordered in turn. After the food arrived they continued, now onto the United States.

"The latest poll figures from America show Nelson rising," Gradenko said.

"Nelson? He is Bayern's opponent, yes?" Tarasov asked before shoveling food into his mouth.

"Yes," Gradenko confirmed. "It is rare for a sitting president to lose," he said. "It has never happened in wartime, but the news media and public lay a substantial amount of blame for the war at Bayern's feet."

"Rightfully," Tarasov said before he'd finished chewing. He swallowed and wiped his mouth. "We had gotten exactly what we wanted before that little son of a whore popped off and bombed our naval bases."

Gradenko couldn't argue with Tarasov, though he felt that they also bore some of the blame. It was all academic now though. "It means that a higher chance of Nelson winning come November. If he wins then we might be able to negotiate an end to this mess." Even as Gradenko said it he doubted it. Whatever hopes he had of Nelson suing for peace died when he watched the American televised debate. Nelson, if anything, seemed even more hawkish than Bayern. Though it was possible it was an act, one of America's many political charades, he couldn't count on it.

Tarasov raised an eyebrow, possibly seeing through Gradenko's lie. "Is that so? Are you sure Nelson will be more amenable?"

"Nothing is sure in politics," Gradenko said, "but Nelson represents a change in leadership. Perhaps they will have less stake in continuing the war than Bayern's administration."

"Then we will hope for the best," Tarasov said, "though I will not relent militarily before then."

"I did not assume you would," Gradenko said. Tarasov was many things, belligerent among them. Gradenko finished his drink and stood. "If you'll excuse me then, I'll cable our reply to Baghdad right away."

Tarasov frowned, "You've only just arrived, Comrade. Surely you can take a moment."

Gradenko eyed his mostly untouched plate warily. "My appetite eludes me." Tarasov caught Gradenko's sleeve as he turned to leave, startling him.

"Things are in motion, Comrade Gradenko." Tarasov's face was deadly serious, his eyes fixed on Gradenko's. "Things will not remain static forever. Change is coming." He glanced around to ensure they were far enough away that no one else would overhear their conversation. "I have now a division of loyal men gathered just under the bastard's nose. We only wait for the right time."

Gradenko wanted to take comfort in that, knowing that Tarasov was working out a plan to dethrone the tyrant Karamazov, but he also knew the cost of political change in history. Russian history was full of such horrific tolls. He didn't respond to Tarasov directly, he couldn't bring himself to. "Farewell."

Gradenko's trip across the city back to the foreign ministry was contemplative. He relished the relative warmth of his car as his driver navigated from one security checkpoint to the next. All traffic in the city was heavily curtailed, KGB security troops manned street corners and chokepoints replaced the army reservists who'd previously handled this role. Through a combination of military call ups, double work shifts, and people leaving the city center for the perceived safety and quiet of the countryside, there were few men beside the KGB troops out on the streets. Most of the men Gradenko did see were work gangs commuting to different job sites around the city. Hungarians, Poles, Romanians, Czechs, and Germans filling roles as guest workers. They were easy to spot from their demeanors and the way the KGB rigorously checked their work papers at each checkpoint.

The Stalin-era high rise that served as the focal point of the foreign ministry was as busy as ever. Cement barricades and razor wire surrounded the building, patrolled by yet more KGB men. In a tight plaza across from the building, an anti-air missile battery sat waiting and ready, weapons pointed skyward, yet another reminder of the constant threat the city was under.

Gradenko stepped from his car as his driver circled around to park in a nearby garage. He sighed into the cold air, dreading that he would most likely be spending the rest of the night coordinating diplomatic messages to their Arab allies. It was going to be a long day. Gradenko's melancholy broke in favor of surprise when he saw a familiar figure emerging from the foreign ministry building and walking briskly but calmly along the sidewalk toward him.

"Comrade Chairman Dragomirov, hello," Gradenko said.

Dragomirov blinked behind the round frames of his glasses, his face blank. "Hello Comrade Minister. How fortuitous running into you here. I was just overseeing the delivery of some foreign intelligence reports to your office."

Right away Gradenko knew it was no coincidence running into Dragomirov. Delivering reports was far below his station, and the timing was too perfect, especially for someone like Dragomirov.

"Keeping busy with Karamazov out of town?"

Dragomirov shrugged. "General Secretary Karamazov has little day-to-day role in the committee for state security. He leaves these matters to me."

"With good reason I'm sure," Gradenko said.

"Certainly." Dragomirov smiled in a way that made Gradenko uncomfortable. How such a spidery man ever earned Karamazov's trust was beyond Gradenko. Dragomirov was ostensibly Karamazov's most trusted right-hand man, his hand-selected successor to rule the KGB. That made it all the stranger that Dragomirov had done nothing but drop hints that he was in league with Gradenko's plans to depose the erstwhile leader.

Of all the conspirators in the unfolding coup, Dragomirov was perhaps the most enigmatic. He had volunteered his services without requesting anything in return. Gradenko knew that Tarasov was a patriot of the old school. He believed in the Motherland and believed in the promise of Soviet supremacy. Gradenko himself favored a middle path between conquest and subjugation. East and West, he believed, could peacefully cohabitate if only they could stop the fighting. Dragomirov's ultimate motivations, however, remained a mystery. Gradenko could only assume the soft-spoken KGB chairman was after simple power, one of the oldest and most potent motivators of men.

"I'm lucky to encounter you this way so I can tell you directly," Dragomirov continued. "I have received word that your son Vladimir will be released in five days."

The words hit Gradenko like a freight train. He was left speechless, his mind reeling. Released? From KGB custody?

Dragomirov pressed on regardless. "There is to be a final hearing, purely a formality, and then he will be free."

"Free," Gradenko repeated.

"Yes." Dragomirov clapped a hand on Gradenko's arm. "Good news I am sure."

"Yes. Yes, very."

"I'm glad I was able to secure this for you, Comrade. Truthfully, Vladimir's arrest never sat well with me. I am afraid that's not the sort of thing I want my organization to deal with. We have too many enemies externally to start conjuring them domestically, don't you think?"

Gradenko nodded slowly, haltingly as he collected his thoughts. "Yes. I think so."

"Then I believe it is time for a change, Comrade. There are men who would love to see such a thing." Dragomirov patted Gradenko's arm again and gave him a tight smile. "Until we meet again, Andrei." Dragomirov walked on toward a waiting car, leaving Gradenko's mind swirling with joy over his son's release and the exhilarating terror of the unmistakable truth. A coup was on the horizon.

***

7

The last thing Nabiyev expected on reaching Erzurum was snowfall. It wasn't much, just a light dusting, nothing compared to the subarctic fury his native country was capable of. Still, it was a surprising change after the endless brown hills and green mountains of Georgia. The city itself was out of sight to the south. Erzurum Airport was identifiable to their west from the columns of rising black smoke, the result of Soviet missile strikes. Now with the city under their control, flights of helicopters cruised periodically toward the waiting runways and hangars, either clearing out lingering resistance or consolidating their foothold here.

Centrally located in Turkey's eastern reaches, Erzurum was an ideal staging ground, one which the Soviets were putting to work already. Other motor rifle divisions were hard at work driving back the Turkish defenders. They pried and blasted them from the craggy hills around the city with lethal force, shoving them westward, clearing out this vital chokepoint.

The trip from the Georgian border here to Erzurum had been a grueling one, even excluding the combat. Though the tires and tracks of their vehicles did the hardest work during the drive, it had been little easier on the men packed into those stifling metal coffins. It was no secret that the vehicles of the Soviet army were built to be economical, and economical construction didn't make allowances for creature comforts. In the heat, crews were lucky to have a single, unshielded fan to combat the beating heat of the sun which seeped through the steel hides of their tanks and APCs like water through a cloth. Unseasonable warmth in the border regions had mercifully broken to be replaced by this cold snap. Where before sunlight had baked the men inside the BTRs, now snow and cold breezes made their cramped interiors feel almost hospitable.

Nabiyev, by virtue of rank, had access to a roof hatch of his command BTR and could enjoy fresh air whenever he chose. He did so as the BTR crossed the snowy freeway toward the division's assembly point. Frigid gales snapped by, blowing bursts of snow across the APC and his face, stinging his cheeks. Nabiyev adjusted the dust goggles protecting his eyes and frowned deeper.

With the command BMP destroyed back in Turkey, they'd been issued a rust-spotted replacement with dry-rotted tires from some forgotten Caucasian depot. For now, it was holding together but when it inevitably broke down Nabiyev and his meager staff would have to transfer command to the spare recon BTR which lacked all of the advanced communication gear onboard this one.

Men were exhausted and machines were pushed to their limits. Whatever slight satisfaction he'd felt with their rapid drive south had been replaced with apprehension as they reoriented and prepared for the unknown.

"Comrade Colonel!"

Nabiyev ducked back inside the hull of the APC.

"If the map is correct," one of his aides said, "we are approaching the meeting point for divisional command."

If the map was right—and there was no guarantee of that—then it was almost time for Nabiyev to learn exactly why they were orienting away from the fighting that truly mattered. He was told nothing of operational goals or the larger strategic picture, but he could pick up on what was unsaid. His division was re-orienting, turning from west to south. There was nothing of strategic value that way—nothing he knew of anyway. Nothing but Iraq and Syria. He had an inkling of what that could mean, but also knew that his opinion didn't matter. He was here to see orders executed, not ponder the wisdom behind them. Nabiyev only nodded and counted the minutes as they neared the meeting point, an open stretch of empty snowy field on the edge of the highway.

The farmland around Erzurum was far from deserted. As they topped hills, Nabiyev could see vehicles in all directions, the division arraying itself according to a hastily drawn up plan. Black, slushy tracks through the snow left a tangled pattern of movement as vehicles assembled.

"Park us nearby," Nabiyev told the driver.

The vehicle slowed to a shuddering halt and Nabiyev debarked as his staff lit cigarettes and took swigs from canteens, congregating on the side of the BTR sheltered from the wind.

Nabiyev was afforded no such luxury as he made straight for the division HQ ahead, tightening his jacket and tugging his dust goggles to hang around his neck.

Each moment more men and vehicles arrived from the road, guided by snow-dusted junior officers into proper parking spots. The drab tans and greens of the rifle division stood in stark contrast to the wintery terrain around them. Some enterprising vehicle crews set to work remediating this, wrapping their tanks in white sheets they had appropriated from nearby houses in an effort to blend in better with the snow. One crew hung a leather-cased cassette player from one of their tank's explosive-reactive armor panels where it churned out tinny, washed out rock music as they worked.

Ahead, familiar faces. "Comrade Colonel," Major Abramov saluted. Beside him, one of Nabiyev's other battalion commanders, Baranov, only tipped his head slightly before uncapping a canteen and taking a swig of something that likely wasn't water from the way it made him grimace.

"Comrades," Nabiyev said with a nod of his own. "Have we all arrived in one piece?"

"Major Alexandrovitch is lost somewhere north," Abramov said.

"The bastard could not navigate himself out of Red Square," Baranov replied, breath reeking of alcohol.

Nabiyev scowled at him. "Pour that out, Major."

"For what reason?" Baranov returned, frowning.

"Because this is a war," Nabiyev said. "I won't go into it with a drunk helming one of my battalions."

"One of *Colonel Molchain's* battalions," Baranov said defiantly. "Blood rank doesn't mean anything. Tomorrow you too will be dead and then it will be my regiment. Or Abramov's."

Abramov said nothing, only watched as Nabiyev's face darkened with anger.

"If my life is measured in hours then yours is in minutes. Empty it."

With exaggerated slowness, Baranov uncapped the canteen and poured its clear contents onto the ground, eating a hole in the snow crust.

Nabiyev wasn't sure what he would have done if Baranov refused again. The bastard was right, he had a rank but no respect and little more authority. Molchain was insufferable but the men feared him enough to obey. It was within Nabiyev's power to order his insubordinate major shot, but where would such a purge end? And who would carry it out? If he killed everyone reluctant to take his orders, he would decimate his own regiment.

"What is it that we're doing here?" Baranov interjected. "The moment we unhinge the Turks and send them running they stop us and turn us south."

"That is what I aim to learn here," Nabiyev replied, glancing toward General Novikov's headquarters tent. "But I can guess."

"We will be linking up with the Iraqi army," Abramov suggested.

Nabiyev nodded. It was his guess as well.

"What use do we have for internecine, tribal nonsense?" Baranov exclaimed. "Iraq?" He shook his head in disgust. "More trouble than they are worth. Backwards people with a backwards military." He kicked a furrow in the snow with a boot.

"They are one of the largest armies in the world," Nabiyev said.

"The fifth," Abramov added.

"Well equipped and well trained," Nabiyev continued,

ignoring Abramov's interjection.

"Equipped with what we have deigned to give them," Baranov retorted. "I leave it to your superior judgment if you think that means they are *well* equipped. As for their training—" He looked back around the division. "I would sooner trust the dregs they give us than whatever the Iraqis have dredged up and shoved into uniform."

"Whatever the job, we will do it," Nabiyev said, looking each of his subordinates in the eye. "If we do it well then we may earn ourselves a rotation home or at least somewhere more comfortable. More civilized."

Baranov and Abramov didn't look enthused by the prospect. Besides, Nabiyev himself couldn't imagine any army deployment was truly comfortable now. They'd heard little news from the meat grinder that was the German plains and the flood of exuberant news from Scandinavia seemed to have dried up, followed by a painful silence.

"See to your battalions," Nabiyev said. "When I learn the details of our deployment, you will be the first to know." In response he got two weak salutes. Better.

Nabiyev watched the majors leave before he at last set off for General Novikov's command tent and the news of their work to come.

Nabiyev brushed the snow off his sleeves as he stepped into the command tent. The relative warmth of the tent caused his face, which had been numbed by the relentless wind, to tingle with sensation. He loosened his coat and returned the salute of a nearby junior officer before joining the command staff who were already assembled further in.

As Nabiyev looked around the tent at the divisional and regimental officers gathered here, he couldn't help but feel a nervous tension in his gut. He knew that they were taking a significant risk by gathering like this with the ever-present threat of a NATO airstrike hanging over their heads. He'd heard of entire divisions being decapitated by a single well-timed airstrike in Germany. They were fortunate the Turks weren't as well armed as the western NATO nations. The chances of such an attack slipping through the Soviet air defense network were remote, but not impossible. Colonel Molchain's absence here was evidence enough of that.

Nabiyev had only just enough time to take a seat facing the standing map of Turkey before General Novikov arrived. His expression was stoney. He always looked as though he'd just been given bad news. Maybe in this case he had.

"Comrades," Novikov began, clearing his throat and looking over the assembled army officers. "I have just received confirmation from the Stavka that Iraq and Syria are to join in our push into Turkey."

Nabiyev had suspected it but was surprised all the same. The last thing he'd expected was to discover allies out here in remote Anatolia. How useful the Iraqis would prove to be remained to be seen.

Novikov continued unfettered. "The Arab Front will consist of a motor rifle corps of the Iraqi Army as well as an elite Republican Guard division, the 1st Hammurabi Tank Division. The Syrians have provided a single rifle division as well. With the support of our Arab allies, we will turn the entire Turkish line and start driving them west. To that end our division is tasked with a southward strike—" he thwacked a wooden pointer against the standing map, sending shockwave ripples through the paper and rocking the folding stand it sat on. "—linking forces with the Iraqi tank division which will begin driving north tomorrow morning at dawn, pincering the Turks here and trapping them in a pocket to be eliminated by follow-on Iraqi army forces. Then we can turn west for Ankara and Izmir, crushing the Turks against the Aegean Sea."

For the first time Nabiyev saw Novikov show an emotion besides irritation, an almost child-like glee at the prospect of destroying his enemies. Nabiyev tried to take as much comfort from that sadistic smile as he could but found there wasn't much to be gained.

T. K.BLACKWOOD

***

8

Bayern's heart was in his throat as he stood in the hall just outside the House of Representatives. He was nervous, extremely so. He'd faced trials beyond what most presidents ever had to contend with and he wasn't sure he'd handled them all as well as he could have, but what stood before him here was something he was sure he could do right. He only had to see it through.

"Mr. Speaker," a voice inside Congress boomed. "The President of the United States!"

Bayern stepped in and fixed a smile on his face as he was met with a roar of applause, his party cheering for him. He shook hands and traded remarks with the party leadership who lined the crowded aisle, all too aware of the television cameras tracking his every move and of the unsmiling faces of the political opposition around him.

He hardly listened to what he said as he said it, a kind word there, a jibe there. He couldn't help but wonder if his party would applaud him after they'd heard what he had to say here. He'd wrestled with the decision for days, spoke at length about it with Harrison, his cabinet, and his wife. But now he had to commit, there was no going back. What happened here would be historic, for all the good and ill that entailed.

Gradually he worked his way down the aisle and to the podium where the unsmiling Speaker of the House stood beside a friendly face, Vice President Dewitt, acting in his capacity as the president of the Senate.

Bayern greeted the speaker and Dewitt, shaking hands with each of them before coming to stand at the podium, looking over the sea of faces—politicians, reporters, VIPs, and dignitaries. Among the crowd, looking down on him from the upper gallery, he could only just make out the oval of his wife's face and the small forms of his children close at her side.

Bayern gave a little wave and felt some of his fear subside when they waved back.

He hardly listened as the Speaker of the House introduced him to Congress, eliciting another round of applause.

At last, and all too soon, it died down and fell to silence.

"Mr. Speaker," Bayern said, "Mr. President, thank you." He looked out over Congress and took a steadying breath. "When I first accepted President Simpson's invitation to serve as his running mate I never anticipated where that course would eventually lead me. I have heard it said that the best leaders are those who don't seek to lead, and as someone who sought just that, I have come to suspect that's true."

Bayern's unexpectedly self-deprecating words stilled the chamber even further, settling over the audience. They set what Bayern thought was an appropriately melancholic tone for this somber address. He glanced up at his wife for support before continuing.

"I had hoped that my career would ultimately take me to exactly where I am standing right now—" Bayern tapped the surface of the podium with a pointed finger—"the highest office of this great nation, but had I known the terrible price paid to make that dream a reality I would have never pursued it to begin with." He paused before continuing. "At the dawn of the decade, we stood at what some argue was the peak of our nation's power. The economy was on the rebound and international peace was the rule of the day. Across the ocean—across the Iron Curtain —we saw, for the first time in decades, a sliver of hope. As democracy finally comes to the people of China, there were many who saw the same future for the Soviet Union: an end to communism and an end to tyranny. An end to the Cold War. Maybe an end to history. Barring that," Bayern continued, "we had hoped at least for continued coexistence. We had, after all, survived for forty years with our Eastern neighbors, each on our side of the Iron Curtain."

Bayern allowed himself a frown. "It's clear to me now that this war was always inevitable. Not a question of 'if' but one of 'when.' We had deluded ourselves for decades into thinking that we could live alongside oppression, militarism, and despotism. We had come to believe the lie that the world could continue on—to steal a turn of phrase— half free and half slave. Maybe," Bayern said, "if things had played out differently, maybe if things had developed to our favor, then I would be bringing you a very different report. One of triumph, one of freedom, one of peace and prosperity."

Bayern shook his head. "I'm sorry. But all I bring is bitter news. News that our struggle isn't over. We have survived, and will continue to survive, only through blood, sweat, tears, and sacrifice." Bayern paused here for a moment. "In 1864, our nation was in the middle of the greatest threat it had ever been subjected to. America had been torn by three long years of war, misery, and death. In the midst of that bleakness, President Lincoln wrote a letter to Mrs. Bixby, a widow who had lost three of her sons to that war." Bayern effortlessly called the words from memory, lines he'd once memorized for history class in high school and never since forgotten.

"He said to her: 'I pray that our Heavenly Father may assuage the anguish of your bereavement and leave you only the cherished memory of the loved and lost.'" Bayern swallowed. "'And the solemn pride that must be yours to have laid so costly a sacrifice upon the altar of freedom.'"

He looked across the silent House. "We have always lived with the blessings of freedom while seldom considering its altar. In scarcely a week our nation will practice one of its greatest traditions and we will exercise our right to vote, ushering in a new leader for our nation."

Some members of the audience murmured at Bayern's apparently overlooking his own candidacy, but he continued on, unphased.

"What we have forgotten—or perhaps what we have ignored —is that freedom often requires sacrifice. This was not a right which was handed down to us from heaven, it was one we took for ourselves with the blood of patriots and tyrants." Bayern steeled his nerves. "And so, I come to you as President, as a sailor, and as an American to ask that you acknowledge this horrible truth. If we are to secure the blessings of liberty to ourselves and our posterity, then we must fight for them."

Bayern turned, looking back over his shoulder to the wary Speaker of the House and the solemn Dewitt. "To that end, Mr. Speaker, I formally ask that you submit an amendment to the Military Selective Service Act with all due haste, authorizing me to induct personnel into the armed forces of the United States."

As the gravity of this request became clear, chaos erupted on the House floor. Shouts, weak applause, and boos competed in equal measure as emotions clashed.

Bayern stood alone with his thoughts, silent as the Speaker of the House banged his gavel and called for order. Order came in due time. Bayern almost wished it hadn't.

"Such a change is beyond the powers of my office alone," Bayern said, "though I accept responsibility for proposing this measure. Should such a bill cross my desk I can only promise to sign and enact it as soon as possible."

Silence lapsed. Bayern hated to break it, but he forged on, mind set.

"During my last debate with Mayor Nelson," he said, voice soft, candid. "We shook hands and he said something to me which I didn't understand at the time, but I do now. He said: 'Remember, we're both on the same side.'" Bayern studied the silent men and women of Congress before he continued. "When President Simpson asked me to become his running mate, I saw this House as two halves—divided—perhaps as many of you do. Right and left, red and blue. My side of the aisle and that of the opposition." Bayern shook his head. "Today, I see only one body: Americans. Whatever your party affiliation, whoever you vote for in November, we all hold that in common. Like the cost of freedom, I think this is something so universal that it's often overlooked. But we're all on the same side. We all believe in the tenets of the Constitution and the future of this great nation. I cannot promise you there will be no suffering. If anything, I can only promise you the opposite. All I can say is that the struggle is a worthy one, the cause hallowed enough to undertake. I would not ask you to sacrifice your children on the altar of freedom if I did not think it was necessary."

Bayern swallowed. Now came the real bombshell.

"And," he continued, "were I not willing to meet the call of that sacrifice myself. To that end, I am formally withdrawing my candidacy in the presidential election in hopes of reactivating my naval commission."

Again, the House erupted in confusion before the Speaker reined it in.

"I give my full support and confidence to Vice President Bill Dewitt—" Bayern turned back to Dewitt and smiled slightly. "'Hoss' to his friends."

Dewitt's bewilderment gave way to a confident grin. He nodded at Bayern, part thanks, part admiration.

"I hope that my final act as president will be signing the draft into law," Bayern said. "After that, it is my intention to fight." The words were full of iron, passion. When he spoke again, he was more resigned. "I'm more comfortable with that."

With that, the collected representatives rose to their feet and applauded. It was a reaction Bayern was unprepared for and found himself staring dumbfounded out as they—Republican and Democrat—clapped. The applause went on and on before Bayern held his hands up, bidding for silence.

"I'm beyond honored to have had the chance to serve this great nation," Bayern said. "And I hope to continue to do so in another capacity. Should my desire to be reinstated to my old rank be honored, I would be likewise honored to join the ranks of the brave men and women around the world who fight on in the face of overwhelming odds. And America is not alone in the struggle against tyranny! Our allies soldier on, side by side with us. From the United Kingdom and Norway to Turkey and Greece."

***

9

The breeze coming up from the Thermaic Gulf, south of Thessaloniki, tussled Jean Carson's short hair playfully. She stood expectantly on a waterfront rooftop, earpiece in her ear, microphone in hand, staring into the dead, black glass eye of the video camera.

Half-visible behind the harsh light of the camera's lighting rig was her cameraman, Pete Owen. His faded, navy blue ball cap was turned backwards allowing him to press his eye into the viewfinder. Behind him, Jean stared out over the darkened bay south of the city whose mouth opened on the wider gulf beyond. The bay was full of freighters and cargo ships unloading the tools of war. Many others were civilian passenger craft, evacuating, hopefully, for safer locales.

Jean waited as long as her limited patience would let her while she watched Pete fiddle with the focus and zoom. "How are we looking?"

"Good, just trying to get the best framing."

Jean scowled slightly. "Good enough for Pete is perfect for me."

"Har har har. Almost got it."

"Roses."

Jean tucked the microphone under her arm and tried in vain to smooth her hair out into a semblance of style. Whenever she felt she had it tamed, the wind would pick up and ruffle it again. She sighed and gave up. It was strange, she reflected, thinking back to the dim beginnings of all this death and strife. It all started with her, Pete, and Dario—poor Dario—discovering that trainyard in Belgrade overrun with Soviet soldiers the way a stray dog is overrun with lice. After they broke the story of the Soviet intervention, their lives had become a whirlwind of activity. She remembered the feeling of relief she and Pete shared when it seemed that the cat had—in fact—been put back in the bag. All that changed when President Simpson had been killed.

From there they'd been expelled from the newly restored borders of Yugoslavia in short order—now unified again in name if not in spirit.

"Okay," Pete said. "Got the network signal." He listened intently to his earpiece. "Patching you in."

A second later Jean heard the chatter of the network anchors back home, safe and sound in the United States. Though she worked for the Associated Press, she often acted as a special war correspondent to news networks in the US. This was one of those times.

At first Jean had been bitter about missing the fighting in Europe as the war shifted north. She'd pulled all the strings she could to get redeployed—first trying for Germany and then Sweden—but with the chaos of war, transport across Europe, especially over hotly contested territory, became nearly impossible. Now though the action seemed to be shifting south again, toward Greece and Turkey, and where there was action, you could expect to find Jean Carson.

"Here we go," Pete said, making a final adjustment to his camera before checking the network uplink equipment was working as expected.

Jean took a steadying breath and froze her expression as she listened to the anchor introduce her.

"Joining us now, live from northern Greece is Jean Carson. Jean is a field correspondent with experience in war zones from East Africa to the Balkans and beyond. In fact, it was her reporting which initially broke the story of Soviet forces in Serbia."

As the anchor listed her qualifications, images of places and people flashed through Jean's mind. Deserts, steppes, jungles, cities. People divided by geography, language, and ethnicity but united in suffering under the bootheel of war.

The anchor's voice came through, small and thin in her ear. "Jean, hello and good evening. What's the situation like there on the ground?"

Jean gave the camera a tight smile and spoke into her microphone. "Good evening, or should I say good morning, Scott. It's just past two in the morning here in Greece. I think you can see the night sky of Thessaloniki here lit up with fire, and you can hear the sounds of the aftermath of another enemy bombing raid on the city. I'm standing on the roof of the Meridian Hotel in what was once a peaceful resort district which has now—like so much of Europe—been scarred by war. All night long myself and my cameraman, Pete Owens, have been watching Bulgarian missile attacks on the ships and port facilities here. You can see—if we pan the camera—"

Pete did so, slowly to take in the crowded nighttime harbor.

"Some vessels are burning at anchor," Jean continued. "I haven't been able to confirm if those ships are military or civilian, but it doesn't seem to make much difference to the Bulgarians."

The camera finished scanning the harbor and came back to her face.

"They've since focused this missile attack on the Thessaloniki international airport north of us. Greek missile defenses have been working around the clock to protect the city, but they don't get them all. You can see—I think—the glow of fires from the airport. I don't know if the footage has made it to you yet, but we sent along video of the explosions last night."

"Yes," the anchor answered over her earpiece. "We've been playing it alongside other missile attack footage tonight. Harrowing stuff."

Jean nodded. She tried not to dwell on the fact that *her* missile attack footage made up just *some* of the missile attacks going on across the continent. "Harrowing is the word," she said. "Certainly, for the people being targeted. The bombardment stopped just over two hours ago now, but I'm sure if the Bulgarians had the stocks for it then this bombardment would go on night and day. I can't comment on the efficacy of the attack as far as the military is concerned, but I can say that the result on the civilian population here has been horrific. With the fighting further north, we've seen a flood of refugees flock into the city filling hotels, streets, and hospitals."

"What's the mood there, Jean?" the anchor asked. "How are people holding up under all this pressure?"

"One thing I have been continually amazed by," Jean replied, "is the human capacity to endure suffering. They're continuing on, Scott. Like Londoners during the Blitz, they are going about their days like always, trying to hold a sense of normalcy. Air raid sirens cut the day and night, but between them life goes on."

"Life goes on," Scott repeated. "From your position have there been any changes in the front lines?"

Jean resisted a scowl. "We're far enough from the frontlines that I can't comment too much on the situation there," she said. "However, I can tell you that the city defenders have shown no signs of a willingness to withdraw, nor can they. If Thessaloniki falls then the Soviet-Bulgarian army will cut Greece from Turkey not to mention gain control of vital port facilities. I don't see any sign of the Greeks giving up here."

"And," Scott continued in her earpiece, "what about news of Iraq and Syria joining the war? Has this had any impact where you are?"

It might as well have been on the opposite side of the world. Even if the average Greek could be persuaded to care about the plight of the Turks, it wasn't high on their priority list with a Russo-Bulgarian army breathing down their necks. "I haven't heard anything specifically about it to be completely honest with you, Scott. I think the Greek people have their hands full here. You can be sure that no one is happy to hear that the war has expanded, but ultimately they are determined to fight on. In short, I don't think anything has changed, Scott."

"Jean, thank you. Stay safe out there."

Jean forced a smile. "Thank you, Scott."

A moment later the chatter from the network died in her

earpiece.

Pete capped the camera. "We're out."

Jean lowered her microphone and finally allowed anger into her expression. She looked around at the fires on the horizon. "That's a commonality of war, isn't it?"

"Suffering?" Pete asked as he packed the camera.

Jean nodded. "War is something most people see on maps and photographs. Wars happen in fields and ruins. People forget that those ruins used to be someone's living room."

"War isn't just for soldiers," Pete agreed.

Jean unplugged the mic and started winding the cord. "You know, I'm kind of sick of our celebrity status."

"Celebrity?" Pete finished packing his camera and tripod.

Jean rolled her eyes. "Oh come on, Pete. If I have to hear about Belgrade one more time I'll puke. I swear."

"Jeez, Jean. You can't just pretend like it didn't happen."

Sometimes Jean wished it *didn't* happen. After all, wasn't this all really their fault? If she and Pete hadn't broken that story, if they hadn't provided undeniable proof of Soviet intentions, then Simpson wouldn't have deployed troops in Croatia and if he hadn't done that—

"Hey," Pete said, voice soft, reading her expression. "You can't think that we caused any of this."

"I never said that."

"We report the news, Jean, we don't make it."

Jean didn't answer directly. "Tired?"

Pete shook his head although Jean could see it was a lie.

"Then let's get packed. I'm sick of sitting around this place waiting for something to happen. I can feel myself growing roots."

"You have a plan?"

"That Greek army convoy that showed up last night, let's follow them to wherever they're going."

Pete frowned slightly. "Did Tony get us embedded?"

Tony, their Stateside producer, had been working to get Jean and Pete officially embedded with a Greek military unit but Jean had resisted that idea. She didn't like the idea of the military telling her what she could and couldn't report while hanging the carrot of insider access in front of her face. They'd always acted unilaterally and this time was no different.

"No," she said. "But we'll make it work."

Pete smiled wryly. "We always do."

"We always do," she agreed.

***

10

Lieutenant Colonel Nabiyev cut the starry night with a bulky night vision headset. Though the monocular goggles reduced the world to a grainy, depthless, green morass, they provided more visibility than the naked eye, at least until dawn. As the division drove south overnight, they left the snowfall around Erzurum behind in favor of the arid scrubland of central Turkey.

It was impossible, Nabiyev thought idly, to keep the tanks and vehicles of his regiment in appropriate camouflage on this trip. Their olive-green paint had worked well enough in the woodland around Georgia and the Turkish border region. Then it stood out starkly against the snow. Now those crews who'd draped sheets on their tanks and APCs found themselves stripping them away to match the dry brushland around them.

Right now, it was too dark to worry about camo patterns though. He peered down from the hilltop his command vehicle was parked on, looking along the darkened highway and a snaking column of armored vehicles toward the faint glow of the town of Bingöl. The open plains around the city were striped with massive expanses of farmland, ringed on all sides by craggy hills and dotted with scrub, brush, and other drought-tolerant plants.

This terrain made a perfect avenue for the Soviets to advance, their APCs and battle tanks throwing enormous dust clouds into the chilly night air. The same was true for the Iraqi formations already attacking Bingöl from the south. The town was caught in a pincer, like hot iron between a Soviet anvil and Iraqi hammer.

With one headphone on, Nabiyev listened to the radio chatter of his regiment's constituent battalions as they cruised forward, mostly concealed from the Turks by the hills north of the town as an Iraqi attack crashed onto Bingöl ahead of them. He ducked briefly into the BTR to adjust the radio frequency to the Republican Guard channel. In an instant his headphones were filled with Arabic. He understood none of the language and only little more about the men themselves, but he could recognize fear, elation, anger, confusion, and determination. The Republican Guard were the elite soldiers of the Iraqi regime, though "elite" was a relative term. Nabiyev had never worked directly with any of the Soviet Union's Arabic client nations, but he understood that they seemed to all share the same basic problems: siloed knowledge, tribalism, religious schisms, elitism, and a general lack of motivation. When coupled with sycophantic leadership, poor equipment, and nonexistent training, it was a miracle the Iraqi army functioned at all.

But function it did, and with deadly effect.

Helicopter gunships chopped by overhead, splotched brown-tan camouflage met the red, white, and black colors of Iraq. The gunships shot a flurry of unguided rockets into the town followed shortly by a spray of autocannon fire.

Dawn was just breaking to the east, providing enough light that Nabiyev pulled off his goggles and squinted in the twilight. Shells shrieked as they flew overhead before falling on Bingöl. Cubic, beige homes and shops were obliterated by artillery fire. Clouds of dirt blossomed into the air as other shells struck earth and exploded.

In the wake of this ferocious, indiscriminate attack, the Iraqis advanced.

"There they go," Abramov said over the headphones.

Nabiyev watched older model tanks fire on outlying structures as they closed in, demolishing yet more buildings while Republican Guard infantry fanned out with sprays of automatic fire, surging into the town.

The helicopter gunships circled wide around the town drawing sporadic fire from the ground. Tracers cut parabolic arcs through the night sky as they felt for helicopters. Ignoring this, the Iraqi gunships descended toward a hill east of the town and blanketed it with more rocket and autocannon fire before settling down to unload assault troops to sweep and clear the hilltop.

"Lieutenant Colonel," Major Alexandrovitch said over the radio. "Targets sighted in the open. Battle tanks. M-60s."

"M-60s? You're certain?" Nabiyev asked.

"As I can be," Alexandrovitch replied without hesitation.

Assuming the report was correct, they were likely to be Turkish forces withdrawing before they became trapped in the town.

"You are clear to engage," Nabiyev replied. "Have your gunners ensure beyond any doubt they are not Iraqi tanks." The last thing they needed was a friendly fire incident to start their cooperation together.

"Acknowledged."

The bark of main guns was met with exploding fuel and ammunition. Sabot rounds whistled invisibly through the dark to strike and destroy targets in the open. Fireballs climbed skyward, lighting the valley floor and momentarily silhouetting Alexandrovitch's battalion driving forward as they skirted the edge of Bingöl, looping the town as the Iraqis plunged into deadly urban fighting.

"Wasteful," Nabiyev said to himself. He toggled his radio on. "Alexandrovitch, veer east. Our objective is the D300 highway. Cut enemy access to it, ensure the Turks cannot slip into the city. Steer clear of that maelstrom. Report any resistance."

"No resistance at all, Comrade," Alexandrovitch said a minute later, voice masked by the hiss and crackle of the radio. "We're crossing the highway now."

Nabiyev felt a small sense of satisfaction. They'd crossed the border and secured their first objective without difficulty. He turned his attention back to the Iraqi forces subduing the town. At this distance it was impossible to be certain of how skillful the attack was but, skillful or not, it was succeeding.

Perhaps weight of steel and fire would be enough to win

here. It seemed to have worked in Yugoslavia. Nabiyev tried not to worry about tomorrow, not while he had to worry about today. He could not win this war without first winning this battle. Before he devoted any more attention to his men, General Novikov's voice broke over his headset.

"806th Regiment, advance west. Follow in behind the Iraqis."

Nabiyev saw a battalion of Iraqi T-72s forming up east of Bingöl and moving onto the D300 highway. They passed by Alexandrovitch's men at speed and formed into columns, a spearhead racing west.

"Acknowledged," Nabiyev said before toggling to his battalion leaders. "The time is here, comrades. We go forward. Follow the Iraqis."

The Soviets, unleashed, raced on, following the Iraqi armored advance and driving, together, toward the Aegean coast.

***

11

The White House Situation Room was deceptively plain—wood-paneled with a single square conference table and a drop ceiling. The far wall was taken up with a bank of televisions all linked together to display one large image, an addition from the renovation done during President Slater's administration.

Here the National Security Council was gathered. By now, these meetings were commonplace for President Bayern and all involved. Bayern had practically slept in this room during the two-day battle in the Norwegian Sea, living and breathing for each update, each loss tallied on a dry erase board.

Bayern sat next to Secretary of Defense Gillis as General Orville and a handful of intelligence experts walked through briefings on the war fronts.

"Good news first," Orville said. "The Soviets in Scandinavia are reeling." The Marine smiled grimly. "Between Swedish and Norwegian resistance, overstretching their own forces, and a relentless air campaign conducted by the carriers just off the coast, we've worn them to the bone. After the Norwegian Sea battle, we've secured a sea corridor to Norway and broken the Soviet Navy's back. Counterattacks are underway now; we're providing all the aid we can but at this rate we'll liberate Stockholm within the month."

Bayern forced himself to savor this. It was not a war-winning move, but liberating Scandinavia was another paving stone on the Soviet Union's grave.

Orville pressed on. "In the Middle East we plastered the Iraqi air force on the ground in Mosul. Follow-on attacks by stealth aircraft operating out of Greece have savaged them pretty well, but they're not out of it yet."

Bayern nodded appreciatively. "So, what's the bad news?"

Orville's tight smile grew grimmer still. "Where do you want to start?"

"The Mediterranean."

"Greeks are holding the line so far but taking a beating, primarily north of Thessaloniki. They'd been arrayed mostly in the east of Thrace," Orville explained, "anticipating a Bulgarian attack from the north. This line has been broken by two primary factors. The first is a lack of meaningful cooperation between the Greeks and Turks in the region."

"We shouldn't have expected any different," Secretary Gillis said dismissively, sitting back in his chair. "NATO members or not, they're far from allies."

Greece and Turkey were the only members of the alliance to have ever nearly gone to war with one another. They made undeniably poor bedfellows.

"Secondly," Orville continued, "Bulgarian forces outflanked the Greeks in the west, crossing into southern Yugoslavia and back into Greece through the city of Gevgelija."

Another half-surprise. Whatever neutrality Yugoslavia had aspired to across the majority of the Cold War had vanished after the failed NATO intervention there. They were a Soviet client state now, an ally in all but name, although the country had so far remained out of the war.

"Are we recommending action against the Yugoslavians?" Bayern asked.

"Not at this time, sir," Orville said. "You've already been briefed on our next stage planning; this neutrality violation only aids our future plans. Their turn is coming."

Bayern nodded.

"Otherwise, the situation is grim," Orville continued. "The Turks are facing Soviet forces in the east and Soviet-backed Romanians in the East. Greece is likewise struggling to hold on against the Bulgarians."

Ordinarily, third-tier Warsaw Pact allies like Bulgaria and

Romania would be no challenge for NATO, but with the bulk of that alliance's forces already engaged, it fell to Greece and Turkey to defend themselves.

"What about Turkey?" Bayern said. He'd already seen urgent pleas from the ambassador of that nation, yet more lost souls in a maelstrom of death and violence.

"Turkey is facing attack from every angle," General Orville said. "In the European bit they're holding their own against the Bulgarians and Romanians for now. The Soviets have a naval infantry brigade in the Black Sea that they could land pretty much anywhere along the coast but haven't yet. It's tying up a lot of Turkish troops watching the coast right now. However, the main threat to Turkey is coming from the east, from the Caucasus mountains. The Soviets are pitting about ten rifle divisions against an equal number of Turkish troops. The Soviets were making slow and bloody progress until the Arabs got involved."

"What's the damage there?" The question came, not from Bayern but from Vice President Dewitt.

"The Iraqis seem to be far more concerned with Kuwait than Turkey, the bulk of their army is occupied with gobbling it up. As far as Turkey goes, it looks like the Arabs have sent a reinforced army corps all told. Mostly Iraqis, a token force of Syrians. The troops themselves aren't good, but the real problem is positioning." The general leaned forward, steepling his fingers. "They've basically outflanked the whole Turkish line and are rolling them up."

"We're talking battle hardened troops, that right? The Iraqis I mean." Dewitt continued. With Bayern stepping back from politics, he was content to let his vice president take the lead. After all, if they managed to beat Nelson, then it would be Dewitt sitting in that spot come January.

"That's our assessment," Orville said. "Iraq is one of the only nations to have fought a peer-to-peer ground war in the last decade. The lessons of the war against Iran are likely fresh in their minds, and the Soviets have spent the last few years pumping them up with new gear."

"The big counterattack we've got planned," Dewitt asked. "What's it called again?"

Orville didn't miss a beat. "Operation Patriot Resolve."

"That's a little on the nose, isn't it?" Bayern said.

Secretary Gillis sniffed. "We pick the names ourselves now. Otherwise, the computer might spit out 'Blue Spoon' again."

"Or maybe we'd get another 'Overlord,'" Bayern replied.

"And you think Patriot Resolve is too on the nose?" Gillis said.

"Can't we pull troops from Patriot Resolve to bolster the Turks?" Dewitt asked. "Jerry, we agree on that, right?"

Bayern nodded. "Absolutely. If it's doable." He looked to the Joint Chiefs. "What do we have on scene?"

This time Admiral Gideon, the Chief of Naval Operations, answered. "*San Juan Hill* is operating off the Israeli coast. We've got airspace access over Israel and Jordan, straight shot into Iraq and Syria."

"It's going to be months before Patriot Resolve can be put into action," Orville added. "Those units, especially rapid-reaction forces like airborne and marines, are fully tasked with those preparations."

"So, what can we get?" Bayern asked. "There's got to be something."

Orville looked at Gillis.

"We can't spare much more than we already have," the secretary of defense said. "We can't be everywhere."

"But we're not alone," Bayern said. "What about our allies?"

"Third corps?" Gillis asked Orville.

The General mulled it over. "We can maybe tap the Anglo-Canadian force we had earmarked as follow on for Patriot Resolve. I'm sure the French have something on hand."

"How fast can we get them on scene?" Bayern asked.

"How fast?" Orville looked to Gideon.

"Maybe a couple days if the Europeans cooperate," Gideon said.

"They'll have to," Bayern said. "I'll talk to the State Department and we'll figure this out."

"If we get what we want, I think we can pull both Canadian mechanized brigades, maybe a British armored division too. It all depends on what our allies can put up."

"Make sure we pass off any gear that might be useful," Bayern said. "Anything that could help."

"Will do."

After the meeting concluded minutes later, Bayern caught up with Admiral Gideon as he was leaving the Situation Room, folders tucked under his arm. "Admiral, do you have a moment, sir?"

"Christ," Gideon said under his breath, giving Bayern a sharp look before glancing around. "Don't you 'sir' me. I know what this is about. You think I don't watch the news?"

"Then you know exactly what I'm asking."

"And you know exactly why it's a problem." Gideon turned to leave before Bayern spoke again.

"Any word from Admiral Alderman? Last I heard was just that *Anzio* got hit."

"Fine," Gideon said, smothering any emotion he felt concerning his friend. "That son of a bitch is going to get a ship class named for him for sure. But we lost a lot of good people."

Bayern pressed on, undeterred. "I need to be out there, sir. That's where I belong."

"We'll talk later," Gideon returned. "You're way outside of the norm, Jerry. You're my goddamn boss but you don't have the right to put me in this position."

"I know." Bayern made no excuses.

Gideon sighed. "Later," he said. "Ask me after the fourth."

"Yes, sir."

"And no 'sir' shit. Christ."

***

12

The strangest thing about the whole ordeal so far to Brigadier John Gates was the fact that there had been no climactic tank battle.

Conventional military wisdom held that any shooting war with the Soviet Union would culminate in a mass breakthrough by one side or the other followed by a massive exploitation by armored forces. The Soviets had tried outside of Metz and been swatted down hard by the French and Americans. NATO had tried the same at Worms and gotten stalled.

He wondered if this was how his predecessors in the British army felt during the First World War when the Germans didn't break after the Marne. Were they as lost as he was now when no glorious cavalry breakthrough spelled an end to the fighting?

Gates stood on an ancient cobble street, looking up at the cathedral of Saint Patrokli—Patroclus—the center of the town of Soest, West Germany. The street was devoid of any non-military presence and even now only played host to a line of trucks and soldiers waiting apathetically for their turn to move on.

It was difficult to fathom the scale of human history at times. This church, or at least the oldest incarnation of it, had existed for about a thousand years. It had seen the rise and fall of kingdoms and empires as well as centuries of war, and now it was acting as a silent observer to another. Gates had to wonder how many more wars this church might see yet and he wasn't sure if he hoped it managed to see another one or not.

"General, sir!" The officer who approached stopped, snapped his heels smartly together, and saluted. It was textbook perfect. "Colonel Benson to see you in the headquarters, sir." He was new, a fresh face from back home, like so many others in the brigade after Paderborn. Gates wasn't sure if he was a reservist recalled to active duty or a freshly minted officer. Either way, the lieutenant was symptomatic of a wider problem the brigade and consequently the whole British Army of the Rhine faced.

"Very good, thank you, Lieutenant," Gates said, returning the salute albeit more stiffly. His little walk for some fresh air hadn't taken him far from the marketplace that now served as the assembly point for Gates headquarters company and so he started back on foot.

Gates had always been critical of the Army of the Rhine and its lack of preparedness. They always needed more gear, better gear, more soldiers, better soldiers. That made it all the stranger when he found himself mourning the loss of that force. For all its flaws, the Army of the Rhine had been a well-polished, well-honed machine, an organization of professionals with their mind about their business. It had been led by men like Colonel Dunworth, the late commander of the King's Royal Hussars. It felt like years ago, though it had only been weeks.

And now those well-trained men were largely gone, dead and maimed across the fields, woods, and hills of northern Germany, bled away to buy time with their lives. The gambit had worked, ultimately the Soviet onslaught had been stopped cold. For Gates that place had been Paderborn and the cost had been immense. The 4th Armored Brigade simply wasn't the same after Paderborn, not after the way death had swept their ranks clean.

The death of Colonel Dunworth had been hard for Gates to take. He was hardly the only man under his command to die, but he'd known Dunworth personally; the man had a wife and children. As part of his "rest" duties, Gates had penned a letter to Dunworth's wife, explaining that her husband wouldn't be coming home.

The streets of Soest were packed with military equipment, trucks, tanks, APCs, and all associated support vehicles. Gates's brigade was meant to be resting up after their brutal grind on the front. This was meant to be time for the brigade to gather strength, assimilate their reserves and bring them up to speed; however, Gates knew that there were wounds that even time couldn't heal. The fact of the matter was that the old 4th Brigade was dead, never to return again. What had come out after Paderborn and what now filled the streets of Soest was a new unit for better or worse.

Gates checked both ways before quickly crossing a narrow street and entering the marketplace. Where once stalls of produce had stood, now sat only military vehicles: APCs and anti-aircraft guns, Gates's command units.

Outside one of the slab-faced APCs was Colonel Benson.

Gates put aside his despondent melancholy and approached.

"General," Benson saluted. "You wanted to see me, sir?" Of Gates's battalion commanders, Benson was the only original one left. Dunworth had long been Gates's shining star. Imaginative, agreeable, bold, brave, he'd been destined for great things, and perhaps in a way he'd achieved them. Before the war Gates had considered Benson merely adequate. It was an assessment he'd been forced to revise, now that Benson was his most trusted subordinate.

"What's the status of your battalion, Colonel?" Gates asked, not bothering with pleasantries.

"We're short of everything, sir," Benson said. "Especially ammunition."

The news came as a shock to Gates. "We just received resupply yesterday, didn't we?'

Benson bowed his head, "Yes, sir, only it wasn't a complete replenishment. Just whatever was on hand, I suppose."

Gates sighed loudly. "How are we meant to win this bloody war without bullets and missiles?" The question wasn't directed at Benson, and the colonel didn't provide an answer. The intensity of combat they'd seen was unmatched in modern times and stocks of all weapons were low. Tank rounds, bullets, mortars, artillery shells, missiles of all types: anti-tank and anti-air. "The Russians could blow right through us," Gates said.

"They would have to go through the Belgians first, General."

Gates didn't put much stock in the Belgian troops that had replaced them on the line and ignored that comment. "Our only saving grace, Colonel, is that the Russians are just as bad off as we are."

"Sir?"

"You've read their doctrine. The Red Army makes no allowance for the defense. It's a non-option for them. If they're not attacking, then they're losing."

"Yes, sir."

"Well, they aren't attacking, are they, Colonel?"

"No, sir."

"No," Gates agreed. "They only trained for one thing: attack. Endless attack. They drove themselves to exhaustion. They're vulnerable, you see."

"With respect, General, I believe there is still fight in them."

"No doubt," Gates said. "But they lack cohesion. For every one of ours, we took ten of theirs. They're certainly hurting. The only reason we're not forming up and driving for Moscow is because we're stretched so thin as it is." Gates turned east, squinting up at the lightening sky. "The Soviets have deep pockets, Colonel, but they aren't bottomless. They must be starting to weaken. Surely they are."

"We can only hope, sir."

"Hope and fight like hell," Gates added.

"Yes, sir."

A moment of silence lapsed between them as Gates pondered the future of the war. It took only a moment for him to return to the business at hand. "Colonel, I called you here because I wanted you to be the first to know. Our brigade is coming out of reserve and going south."

"South, sir? Italy?"

Gates grimaced to himself. "Not exactly. Marseille. We'll redeploy by ship."

Benson's face contorted in confusion. "Ship? To where? Greece?"

"Have you heard about Iraq?" Gates asked.

"They've gone after the Turks, is that right?"

Gates had to think of operational security, even with Benson. "I can say this much: we've been issued desert pattern gear and told to repaint our vehicles."

"God," Benson said. The colonel took a moment for this to sink in. "When, sir?"

"We start moving later today. I understand that there's not a moment to waste."

"Are they going to give us adequate ammunition?" Benson asked.

"I only have the assurances of my superiors. I'm told the necessary gear will be waiting for us in Marseille."

"Odds of that?"

Gates's frown deepened. For all his boldness with maneuver, he wasn't inclined to take a guess. "I'm not a betting man."

"God," Benson repeated.

"I'm sure the Turks are in even worse shape than we are," Gates continued. "After fighting the Soviet Red Army to a standstill, I'm less worried about a Third World rabble."

"A bullet's a bullet," Benson returned. "Arab or otherwise."

"It matters more who's shooting it. More than that, it matters what he's fighting for and who's leading him. The Turks have been knocked down and I imagine they're eager to reverse that. Shouldn't be a problem for us."

"Hopefully, sir."

Gates appreciated Benson's cautious pessimism much less than Dunworth's bravado, but he reminded himself Benson had reason to be cautious after what the brigade had just gone through.

"How ready are your men?"

"Ready enough," Benson said. "We haven't had enough time to break in the new lads."

"I don't expect we ever will," Gates said. "War will have to be a teacher."

"Again," Benson said.

"Always, Colonel," Gates reminded him.

Benson smiled wryly. "Always, sir. There's that and the matter of ammunition. Can't very well fight without it."

"I'll put in another word with command," Gates said. "If we're expected to go on the offensive, then they bloody well better get us the proper weapons and ammo."

"Yes, sir."

Gates clapped a hand on Benson's shoulder. "Get your battalion in line and ready to move. We've got an appointment to keep."

***

13

"Target one maintaining speed and heading, Comrade Captain."

"Sonar activity remains heavy," Lieutenant Voloshin said, adding to the sonar operator's report.

The NATO reporting name for Yessov's submarine, *Akula*, meant shark. Yessov felt frustratingly far away from being a shark at this moment.

Double rows of air-dropped sonobuoys paralleled the course of the NATO convoy as it steamed eastward across the Mediterranean. These lines of buoys occasionally left tantalizing gaps, gaps Yessov knew were heavily patrolled by sonar-dipping helicopters. Traps. He was too wise and too paranoid to fall for that old trick. The ships of the convoy traveled slowly, slow enough not to drown out their sonar with their own engines.

In all, a frustratingly well-protected target.

It didn't help that there was still no news of the anticipated naval battle in the Norwegian Sea. Yessov wasn't expecting an air-dropped copy of *Pravda* with a photo cover and in-depth articles, but he would have expected at least a triumphant announcement via ELF, something to bolster the spirits of him and his crew. Anything. Anything but silence.

Silence rarely indicated success.

"Comrade Captain?" Voloshin prodded.

"Set heading triple zero," Yessov said, disgusted. "Take us north at half speed. When we are beyond maximum sonar range take us to two thirds." Another retreat.

"Yes, Comrade Captain!"

Yessov paced as they sailed north, away from the heavily

guarded convoy, hopeful he may locate easier pickings. What good were all the torpedoes in the world with no targets to use them on?

He was alone with his thoughts for so long that Voloshin's appearance at his side hours later startled him. "Strange for you to return to the Ionian Sea, Captain?"

"Strange?" Yessov asked.

Voloshin nodded. "So close to the site of your victory over the American carrier."

Seven hundred kilometers northwest of their current position, Yessov had struck a carrier. A miracle, some might say. Weaker minds, he thought. The only miracles were the actions of men. "Hardly," Yessov said. "Simply an accident of fate."

"An accident," Voloshin smiled slightly to himself. "Isn't that all anything really is?"

Yessov didn't approve of his XO's inane philosophizing and opened his mouth to say so.

"Fresh contacts on sonar!"

Yessov turned from his planned scolding, forgotten. "How many?"

"Four signals traveling northwest 300 at fifteen knots."

Yessov watched as they were marked on the tactical plot with a grease pen, a line of ships sailing toward Italy. "Set our course to match theirs, shadow them." One small upside to their disadvantageous position here in the Mediterranean was the lack of friendly targets to worry about. As they shadowed their prey, more information about the vessels trickled in over minutes.

"We've identified one escort, *Charles F. Adams*-Class."

"*Charles F. Adams*," Yessov repeated the foreign name.

"Probably Greek," Voloshin said.

"The others are civilian freighters," Sonar added.

"A milk run to Taranto," Yessov said. He grinned savagely. "For us, breakfast. All hands to combat stations."

K-461 readied for battle as it cut silently through the crushing ocean depths. The lone escort was easy pickings. With no onboard helicopter and aging sonar equipment, it wasn't aware it was in danger until just before the first torpedo pair struck it amidships.

"We have a hit, Captain."

It would be catastrophic. Two torpedoes below the waterline was a death sentence. Back broken, the destroyer would slough bonelessly into the ocean waves.

With their only protection dead, the freighters ran but there was no running from the wake-following torpedo spread Yessov unleashed. He watched breathlessly as one by one the herd of helpless livestock were immobilized with torpedo hits. He chased these successes with another spread of torpedoes to ensure that these freighters were destined for the bottom, finishing them off. Satisfied that his butcher's work was done, Yessov gave the order to dive deep and flee south, back the way they'd come.

The bridge crew's spirits were leavened, as they usually were, by the slaughter.

"Four fewer ships for the fascists," Voloshin said, beaming.

Yessov took no pleasure in it. He felt not an ounce of sympathy for the men he'd dropped into the ocean, but he knew the victory was hollow. What difference would the loss of an obsolete destroyer and a handful of transports make? "Mark the estimated tonnage in the ship's log."

Yessov was left alone with his thoughts as they cruised away from the battle site before being interrupted by a subordinate.

"Comrade Captain, we have something on the ELF," the radio operator called. "Coded message from command."

The communications officer on K-461's bridge handed Captain Yessov the slip of paper before returning to monitor his equipment.

ALL AVAILABLE NAVAL ASSETS RETASKED. PROCEED TO POINT FYODOR AND ASSUME INTERDICTION OF ALL TRAFFIC.

Yessov crumpled the scrap into his pocket.

"Good news or bad news?" Voloshin asked.

"Nothing about the Norwegian Sea," Yessov said bitterly. "Find me Point Fyodor on our navigational charts, Lieutenant."

"Yes, Comrade Captain."

Yessov paced from the communications station back to the center of the submarine's bridge as he awaited Voloshin's return. It wasn't long in coming.

"The latest changes indicate Point Fyodor is just north of Crete," Voloshin said, "the mouth of the Aegean. A dangerous task," Voloshin mused.

"But rewarding," Yessov said, mind racing with possibilities. A specific interdiction order meant that high command was eager to prevent NATO movements and re-supply. The heavily guarded convoy they'd abandoned was likely part of that very movement. The Aegean was the gateway to the Turkish Straits, which were in turn the gateway to the Black Sea. Maybe the Soviet Union and her allies were heightening military operations there.

"If the Romanians are successful, then perhaps we can clear the Bosphorus and go home," Yessov mused aloud. "Not to Libya or Syria but *home*."

The prospect was just as appealing to Voloshin as it was Yessov and both men were momentarily united by a desire to once again stand on Soviet soil.

Yessov was already dreaming of his next target, a juicer one than the handful of cargo ships they'd just torpedoed. He was dreaming of catching another fully laden NATO convoy in his sights. "Set a new course. East. Take us into the Aegean. When our quarry arrives, we will already be waiting for them."

***

14

Jean, Pete, and Hristos, their Greek interpreter, walked down the line of idling tanks. The late afternoon air was thick and hazy, full of the throaty rumble of engines and acrid stink of diesel exhaust, which Jean was starting to think of as the hot, fetid breath of the war machine. Each tank was a fearsome thing on its own, bulky and imposing with armored slab sides. The crew and soldiers perched on and around these tanks watched with idle curiosity as Jean and the others made their way down the line, Pete filming some B-roll footage as they walked.

Jean doubted it would see any airtime—if there was one thing this war had in abundance it was dramatic footage—but she consoled herself by imagining it may someday be of value to historians or show up in a documentary when this war was behind them. It was a strange thought, the knowledge that someday—inevitably—this war would end. It hardly seemed possible even as it crossed her mind. People must have felt this way about the Second World War, or any war. It seemed almost ludicrous to imagine it, but someday this war would become just another piece of the collective zeitgeist. History. There would be movies about it, and not just tasteful documentaries, but gaudy action films, video games, comic books—Jean reminded herself that she wasn't a documentarian, she was a reporter.

"Hristos, can you ask if anyone is willing to be interviewed?" She prodded her interpreter.

The older man nodded, his short, gray, ponytail bobbing. Turning to the nearest tank crew, he repeated the question in Greek without avail.

The tank column blocked nearly the entire street, which was

hemmed in on both sides by multi-story, balconied apartment buildings. This town, Kilkis, was remarkably untouched by the war given its close proximity to the Bulgarian border and what population remained watched the soldiers in their midst, curiously peering down from balconies and out of windows and doorways.

One of the soldiers, sitting atop a tank, called back to Hristos and gestured further down the column.

"What did he say?" Jean asked before Hristos had a chance to relay it.

"That there are already reporters," he said, "at the head of the column."

As much as Jean hated to pick through another team's leftovers, she knew it might be her best bet to get a story here. That said, Jean was nothing if not persistent. "Ask if he wants to be interviewed. Tell him we'll make him famous." She smiled at the soldier.

The soldier laughed and climbed from the tank, apparently willing to oblige them. Pete framed out the ad hoc interview against the soldier's tank. What followed was the painstaking process of prying the story out. It was made more difficult by two main constraints, the first being the language barrier, the other being time. Anyone who'd done this job long enough could tell you that people were layered. They were guarded and private, or starstruck and babbling. To get the most out of an interview, you had to find the best way to cut through the natural defenses and artifices of a person's character and get to the truth—the story within.

They did not have hours to dig through the layers with this man. To Jean it felt like performing surgery wearing iron gauntlets while under a strict time limit, but she made it work. Gradually the story came out.

"We will win," the soldier—a captain, whose name was Kalatzis—said with easy confidence. Greek was Greek to Jean, but his tone and attitude carried as clear as lightning. It wasn't a boast, it was a statement of fact. Kalatzis looked tired, worn thin, half-awake, but he also looked certain.

"How can you be sure?" Jean asked. "You seem certain."

"We are certain," Kalatzis responded through Hristos. "The Bulgarians are a slave army. They fight from fear. We are free and we fight to stay free. We have rifles and tanks and bombs, but we would fight them with sticks and stones if that was all we had. We will fight them as we fought the Nazis and we will win."

Jean only wished he spoke English. It would make a great soundbite.

Hristos and Kalatzis talked back and forth a moment before Hristos returned to English. "He says there are prisoners if we wish to speak with them to see for ourselves."

Jean's interest was piqued. "Prisoners?"

"Bulgarians."

A scoop. "Definitely."

The Bulgarians were a block away, sitting together, hands on their heads under the careful watch of a handful of armed Greeks. The Warsaw Pact soldiers looked pitiful. Their uniforms were tattered and dirty, their faces streaked with grime. Many were wounded with bandages wrapped around heads, arms, hands, and legs. A few lay on stretchers, tended to by their comrades. The war was likely over for them, and none of them looked too sorry about it.

Pete took all this in with a sweep of his camera, capturing the scene on videotape.

"Hristos, you speak Bulgarian?" Jean asked.

He shook his head.

"Can you ask if they speak Greek?"

Hristos tried, though none of the POWs responded.

Jean, stymied, refused to give up. She tried a Hail Mary. "Anyone here speak English?"

"I speak," an accented voice came back.

Jean tried not to look shocked as the dirty young man spoke up. His dark hair was caked with specks of mud, his eyes somehow bright and alive still.

"I speak," he repeated more insistently. "Americans?"

"Yes," Jean said, gesturing Pete over unnecessarily. "We're Americans. I'm Jean Carson, Associated Press."

"Reporter!" the Bulgarian said, excited to recall the word.

"Yes." His joy over a single word gave Jean some concerns over his conversational abilities. Can we interview you?"

"Interview, yes. Okay." He bobbed his head.

With the blessing of the POWs handlers, they set into the interview, cutting through the layers. The soldier introduced himself as "Dimitar" and supplied no rank.

"Our leaders not tell us anything," the Bulgarian said bitterly. "Say this training exercise."

"But you must have known something was different," Jean said. "This war wasn't a surprise."

"No," he agreed. "Not surprise. But mistake."

"This war is a mistake?"

"Yes," he said emphatically. "Greek and *Bulgarski* can be brothers."

"If that's true then why are you here?" Jean asked. "You're fighting and killing Greeks."

"The damn Russian bastards," he spat. "Our leaders. What choice I have? I go and fight and get killed or I say no and killed. No choice." He shook his head. "No choice."

"They'll kill you if you refuse?"

He nodded again. "Kill me or I vanish. Gone. Never see me again. Family never know."

"How long have you been a soldier, Dimitar?"

"Am not a soldier," he returned. "Am engineering student."

"Were you drafted?" Jean pressed and after some explanation of the concept he agreed.

"Yes. Drafted. No school without army," he said bitterly, again adding, "No choice."

"How do you think this war will end, Dimitar?"

The young man's expression hardened. "I think we all will die. The damn Russian bastards drag us all down with them. Blood on the walls and blood in the streets."

Jean wasn't sure if he meant Bulgarians or the world at large and decided to leave the sentiment as it was. Pessimistic though it was, it would make a great soundbite.

"If you think Greeks are your brothers, do you want them to win the war?"

Dimitar had to think of the words before he could answer. "No victory between brothers. We both lose, I think. War should end. I think Greek should be free. Bulgaria should be free."

He was the enemy, at least in a geopolitical sense, and Jean wasn't sure she bought that he truly had no alternative. If he was willing to risk his life in combat against the Greeks, why not risk it for a cause he actually believed in? Still, Jean couldn't help but feel sorry for him and the others here. This was less their war than it was the Greeks' war. They seemed to have no more stake in the outcome than a piece of equipment—a truck or a tank— would have. Jean pressed on.

"If Bulgaria were free, what would you do next?"

Dimitar smiled to himself. "Finish school. Get married. Travel."

"Travel? Where would you go, Dimitar?"

"America!" The answer came without hesitation.

Jean found herself momentarily caught off guard. "America?"

"Yes. Hear rock music."

"You like rock music?"

He nodded. "Punk rock music! The Ramones, Dead Kennedys, Sex Pistols! I come to America and hear punk music."

Jean didn't have the heart to tell him that he was at least a decade too late for that. Maybe he'd find a taste for grunge if he ever got stateside. "Dimitar, thank you."

As Pete capped the camera, Dimitar's expression faded back to dejection. He knew Jean would go on to do other things and he would stay here. His own future was a Greek prisoner camp, beyond that his fate was uncertain.

"Great stuff," Pete said as they left the Bulgarians behind and continued on toward the head of the column. "And in English. Big break."

"How many POW interviews do you think they're playing on

CNN?" Jean asked, beaming. "That's going to air for sure. Now let's go see what these 'other' reporters are up to."

It didn't take long to find them. Civilians stuck out like sore thumbs amongst soldiers.

Jean was not a "car person," but she knew enough to recognize the iconic Land Rover Defender immediately. It was a mainstay across the war-torn world, which now included Greece. It was painted white and marked "PRESS," reminding Jean of the rental truck they'd used in Yugoslavia during the war there.

The sun dipped lower in the sky, just tipping toward afternoon when Jean, Hristos, and Pete reached the news crew. They were busily loading their gear into the back of the Land Rover, careful to stay out of the way of hustling Greek soldiers around them as they worked, a familiar scene to Jean.

A woman with a determined stride circled the truck, hefting a duffel back into the back of the truck, her functional ponytail swinging with each step. Jean recognized her immediately— Leanne Collins, BBC. She'd last seen her in Somalia but was hardly surprised to run into her here.

"Leanne," Jean said, approaching and extending a hand.

Leanne's expression betrayed her surprise only a moment before she grinned, shaking the offered hand. "Jean! Good to see you again. It's been too long," Leanne said, her gaze sharp and focused. Her crew continued to work, rushing around her like water around a stone as they loaded the truck with well-practiced precision.

"Likewise," Jean replied, gesturing to Pete, "You remember Pete?"

"Pete Owens," Leanne said. "Of course."

Pete, never a conversationalist, only nodded back mutely.

"Funny running into you here," Jean said.

"We've been embedded with the Greeks for a couple weeks now," Leanne replied. "Since just after the Bulgarians crossed the border when it looked like Thessaloniki might fall." She smiled, her subtly applied makeup giving her a polished, yet war-weary appearance. "I imagine you've been traveling rogue out here."

Jean nodded proudly. "Wouldn't have it any other way."

"I'm sure," Leanne said. "That sounds like you."

"Where are you guys running off to?" Jean asked, leaning on the Land Rover and trying to sound casual.

It didn't work. Leanne laughed. "Wanting to have your cake and eat it too? Looking for hot tips from the 'less fortunate' embedded?" She smirked.

Jean couldn't hold her poker face and cracked, smiling back. "You know me too well. What do you say? Help a friend out?"

Leanne shrugged. "I don't see why not. Just try not to step on our toes, okay?"

"Cross my heart," Jean said. "What do you got?"

Leanne leaned in closer as if she was afraid of the Greeks overhearing. "The Greek army only gives us scraps of information. Operational security, you know, so we're piecing this together from various sources, things we've heard, but it's not concrete."

"Sure," Jean said. "I know the deal."

"The Soviets aren't holding back. They're deploying a motor rifle corps to bolster the line here. Rumor is the railway exchange at Budapest is all gummed up with soldiers, but the lead elements should be arriving within days."

Jean furrowed her brow. "Are the Turks and Greeks cooperating on this?" She could have guessed the answer.

Leanne chuckled. "You know how the Greeks and Turks are. Not exactly a love story, is it? More like an arranged marriage." She shook her head. "I can't say there's much cooperation. At least so far as I can tell, there's a gap between their armies. The Bulgarians and Romanians see that as their ticket to advance, and they're exploiting it with everything they've got."

"And the Greeks are responding? That's where these guys are going?" Jean nodded toward the nearby tanks.

Leanne shrugged. "East. That's what I've heard. Out to Thrace, at least Kavala. Maybe Alexandroupoli."

If the Greeks *were* racing out to stop a Soviet breakthrough there, then it was a race against time. If the enemy cracked the line, they'd run all the way to the coast, cutting European Turkey from Greece with one short thrust.

Jean looked back at Pete, an unspoken question and answer relayed between them. "Leanne, mind if Pete, Hristos, and I tag along?"

"Just as long—"

"—as we don't step on your toes," Jean finished with a smile. "Right. No problem at all. You won't even know we're here."

Leanne laughed. "That's fine with me then. Just get your own ride. The Land Rover is chock-a-block as it is."

Jean offered her hand with a grin. "Deal." And so now she had the benefits of being embedded without all the hassle, an arrangement which suited Jean just fine.

***

15

Minister Gradenko hardly noticed the chill autumn wind sweeping past him, rushing along Moscow's wide boulevards. He stood beside his idling Lada, staring unblinkingly at the side door of the Soviet Union's most infamous political prison, Lubyanka. This otherwise unassuming Imperial-style building served as a nest to the vipers of the KGB. It was in that den—that hellhole—that his only son had been thrown.

Gradenko had been careless. Really it was his fault that Vladimir had been placed in danger at all. He'd included his son—because of his loyalty and diplomatic connections—in a scheme to attempt to negotiate a ceasefire with NATO. When Karamazov had sniffed out this plan, he'd visited the sins of the father on the son.

Lubyanka had become Vladimir's prison and would likely have remained that way if it wasn't for the timely intervention of Dragomirov. Now it seemed to Gradenko he'd traded subservience to one spymaster to another, for surely Dragomirov would call to collect on this favor at some point. Gradenko grimaced as if he'd bitten into something bitter. The average Soviet citizen likely considered themselves apolitical, a benefit of a system that allowed them next to no power. The consequence of an apolitical populace was that all the politicking happened behind closed doors. Every meaningful change, movement, and manipulation were left solely to the men at the top, men like Gradenko, Karamazov, and Dragomirov.

Gradenko pulled his coat tighter about himself and shifted uneasily from foot to foot. This was the appointed time and place. Dragomirov had told him Vladimir was to be released today. As he waited, Gradenko found himself wondering if perhaps his trust in the KGB man was misplaced. The thought had only just crossed his mind when the side door opened, spilling warm light from inside as a ragged figure stumbled free, blinking blearily out into the dark.

"Vladimir." Gradenko spoke his son's name automatically. He went to him. How could he not? His flesh and blood had returned from damnation.

When Vladimir saw him coming, he tried to smile. "Papa—" Whatever Vladimir had intended to say was lost in a sudden exhalation, pulled into a tight vice-like hug which Vladimir instantly returned.

Gradenko forgot the world as he held his child like he hadn't held him since was little—if ever. Vladimir had lost weight, Gradenko could feel that instantly. His son's back and ribs were more pronounced, his shoulders like guillotine blades. Dragomirov had said his son was treated well. He shuddered to imagine what qualified as poor treatment in Lubyanka.

"Vladimir," Gradenko repeated as he cradled the boy's head. "My son." The rush of joy he felt at seeing him alive and free could only compare to the joy he'd felt at his birth. It was as if he'd been given a second chance. Hot tears pricked at the corners of his eyes, threatening to roll down his cheeks. Gradenko was afraid that if he were to say more it would break whatever spell had freed his child. He was certain, however, that he would never let this happen again. If it cost him his life, if it cost him everything, he would not allow his family to be used as pawns against him.

Finally, Gradenko turned and guided Vladimir away from that horrid prison. "Home," he said the word. "Let us go home."

They made it to the car and Gradenko reached for the door, though Vladimir turned and looked back at the building with a smoldering hate in his eyes. "I don't want to go back," he said.

Gradenko shook his head. "You won't. I will make sure you never do. It—"

"No," Vladimir said, turning to meet his father's gaze. "To my job. I don't want to go back to the diplomatic office."

Gradenko blinked, dumbfounded.

"How can I?" Vladimir asked.

"We say you took a leave of absence," Gradenko replied, the lie planned in advance. "For your health."

Vladimir was unyielding. "I do not want to work for *them*." His words were directed at Lubyanka, but more than that. They were directed at the government at large. "What good is a government that arrests its citizens for seeking peace?" he asked. "I might as well go be a farmer with my sister."

Gradenko grabbed the lapels of Vladimir's coat before he realized what he was doing and shoved the young man back against the Lada hard enough to rock the car on its suspension.

Vladimir's eyes went wide with shock, his defiant anger forgotten in an instant as he stared back into his father's fiery, furious gaze.

"Don't say that," Gradenko hissed, his voice barely above a whisper. "Don't *ever* say that. Don't even think it!"

Vladimir was at a loss for words. For once in his life he didn't have a smart retort for his father's raw anger.

Gradenko had never been a harsh man. His life was one of relative convenience and ease, the same luxuries he had passed along to his children. While he was certain he'd raised his voice to them, he could never recall ever having laid a hand on them. Now, with Vladimir pressed to the car, his son could only listen mutely.

"You must go back to your old life," Gradenko explained, keeping his voice low. "And you *will* do it. They will be watching you. Understand? They will be watching and listening for just this sort of nonsense. One wrong word and you will disappear back so far down that hole that even I cannot reach you. Do you understand me?"

Vladimir could only nod.

Gradenko forced himself to release Vladimir's lapels and brush his coat off. "You will return to work tomorrow. You will tell your colleagues that you were ill and have now recovered.

You will be your old self and if you cannot do that then you will fake it."

"For how long?" Vladimir at last found his voice and his bitter disapproval.

Gradenko forced a smile onto his face. "Until you no longer have to."

Vladimir's eyes, so hard with defiance, seemed to soften, his head bowed.

Gradenko embraced him once again, kissing his son on the cheek and feeling the rough brush of beard stubble. "Come," he said, at last pulling the car door open. "We will go home and tell your mother the good news." As Vladimir climbed into the car, Gradenko felt that the coup couldn't come soon enough.

***

16

Sergeant Heathcliff leaned heavily against the ship railing, breathing in deep through his nose and then out through his mouth. In. Out. He tasted the salt spray of the ocean rushing by, foaming against the steel flank of the transport carrying the Canadians across the Mediterranean.

In. Out.

His stomach roiled like the foam below and he dry heaved. There was nothing left to expel, however, so he only convulsed impotently before groaning unhappily. He and the others had been flown in during Reforger; he'd mercifully avoided crossing the Atlantic by boat.

"This shit is for the dogs," he said.

It may have been the only way to get them to their new destination, but it didn't mean he had to enjoy it.

Just beneath his feet the name of the ship was emblazoned on the flank of the vessel. *Atlantic Queen*. The muffled thump of her engine seemed to vibrate through the whole ship. Whatever it had been before the war, it had since been pressed into service transporting troops, probably beginning with Reforger. The Canadians saw evidence throughout its interior of prior occupants. Heathcliff's bunk had the names "Alex Whence + Judy Passchendaele" carved into the painted metal frame and someone else had found a bottle of schnapps hidden in an electrical junction box.

Thinking of schnapps turned Heathcliff's stomach sickeningly and so he peered out over the dim, moonlit waters of the sea, trying to focus on the horizon to still his rebellious gut. They'd only left that morning and it felt like they still had a lifetime to go.

Turkey, their destination, seemed as alien as the Moon. Heathcliff knew less about Turkey than he did Germany, but he was assured they would take to the terrain there quickly. Arid, rocky, open. In Marseilles, they'd been haphazardly issued camouflage more appropriate camouflage for the task, courtesy of their American allies. The desert pattern camouflage reminded Heathcliff more of chocolate chip cookie dough than any desert he'd ever seen, but he had to trust it would prove effective. From what Heathcliff had heard, the uniforms were leftovers from the American Operation Crescent Storm. The tans and browns mixed strangely with their normal woodland patterns, but he had to trust it would work well in-country.

Turkey or Germany didn't really make a difference to Heathcliff. He'd fight wherever he was sent to fight, hot or cold, wet or dry. No sooner had the thought crossed his mind than he was again overcome with nausea. "Not again you bastard," Heathcliff said, gritting his teeth and resolutely staring into the dark, eyes fixed on the silvery horizon to try to retain his equilibrium.

As the nausea faded, he produced a tape player and cassette from his jacket pocket and seated the headphones on his ears before hitting play.

In an instant, he was back home. Closing his eyes he focused all his attention on the game.

"—powerplay is over... Sudbury looking to get the puck out so they can get organized."

It was a good game; one he'd listened to a considerable number of times in the year since he'd recorded it. Back then it had just been his habit, something to listen to on long deployments. Now it was a slice of heaven. Bliss on cassette. A taste of the carefree pre-war. It had been a different time then. Lydecker, and so many others, had been alive back then. Captain Werthers still had his right leg back then. None of them knew just how good they had it. Thinking of Lydecker made Heathcliff sick in a different way. He ached down to his bones, felt a sickness in his soul. A wasted life. His mistake.

"Rivers plays it ahead for O'Donnel and it's off the skate of Craigwell who takes a hit— loses the puck!"

As Heathcliff listened to the announcer, he could see the movements playing out over the ice in his mind. Players moving with the grace of dancers only to then collide, checking one another with the force of a freight train.

"Heathcliff?"

Heathcliff opened his eyes to find Lieutenant Driscoll hovering just over his shoulder. Heathcliff kept the disappointment from his face. "Lieutenant," he said, stopping the tape and pulling off his headphones. "Sorry, sir. I didn't hear you come up."

"Totally alright," Driscoll said, leaning on the railing beside him, apparently unable to read Heathcliff's mind to realize he wanted to be left alone. "Sergeant Dupont had mentioned to me that you were pretty seasick so I thought I'd come check on you."

Heathcliff refused to allow the mental image of upchucking to violate his mind and become a reality. "Fine now, sir," he lied.

Driscoll smiled wanly at Heathcliff. "Glad to hear it." He nodded at the tape player. "Music?"

"Hockey, sir."

"Oh yeah? What game?"

"Sudbury vs Oshawa. March '91." To his surprise, Driscoll's eyes lit up.

"Wolves 8-2 over the Generals," the lieutenant said without hesitation.

Heathcliff found himself smiling back. "That's right. Great game."

"Incredible," Driscoll agreed, "if you like watching the Generals lose. I didn't realize you were a Wolves fan."

"Sudbury born and raised, sir."

"You have a lot of tapes of the games?" Driscoll asked.

"This one and a few others," Heathcliff said before adding, "if you'd like I can loan you the Celestials/Wolves game."

"I'd like that," Driscoll agreed. "I wish I could return the favor, but I recorded the games on TV. The tapes are back home. No VCR." He grinned sheepishly.

"Too bad, sir."

Driscoll nodded to himself. "Plenty of time to kill and nothing to do besides damage control drills. It's going to be a long trip."

"Yes, sir."

"I'll be glad to get there."

"Yes, sir."

Driscoll fell silent for a short while as the two of them listened to the waves and wind.

"Can I ask you a personal question, Heathcliff?"

"Go ahead, sir."

"You don't really care for me, do you?" Driscoll asked, looking almost ashamed to be asking the question. Its earnestness caught Heathcliff off guard and he couldn't answer for a moment.

"I...I don't dislike you, sir."

"But that's not what I asked."

"With respect, sir, I'm here for my boys, not to make friends," Heathcliff said.

"If it's all the same to you, I think we'd operate better if we were on the same frequency, don't you?"

Heathcliff held his tongue.

"Speak your mind," Driscoll invited.

"With respect, you're green, sir." Once Heathcliff had spoken, it was like the floodgates had opened. "You weren't with us at the start. You didn't go through what we did. You didn't see what we saw. And frankly sir, I don't trust you."

The shock on Driscoll's face almost made Heathcliff feel sorry for him.

"I'm sure you're on our side, sir," Heathcliff continued. "But respectfully, trust isn't given. It's earned."

Driscoll swallowed dryly and nodded; his eyes focused on the dim horizon now too. At first Heathcliff thought Driscoll would dress him down, but finally the lieutenant spoke, voice soft. "I guess I can't argue with that. And you're right, I wasn't there at the start. I don't know what you guys went through before I got here." He was silent in thought for a bit. "But I know you were with them, and that's why I'm relying on you. The guys trust you. So why don't you work with me, eh?" He met Heathcliff's eye. "I'm not asking you to trust me, I'm asking you to help me. Help me lead these guys."

Heathcliff didn't answer right away. He thought it over a moment before offering the lieutenant his hand. It was tiring business fighting a one-man war.

Surprised, Driscoll shook it.

"I can do that, sir," Heathcliff said.

"We'll be landing in Turkey this time tomorrow," Driscoll said. "It'll mean interfacing with the Turkish army probably." He looked anxious about the prospect.

Heathcliff smiled faintly. "You're on your own there, sir."

"Dereliction of duty," Driscoll replied dryly. "Noted."

Heathcliff allowed himself a smile. "Call me when the shooting starts," Heathcliff said, pulling his headphones back on. "Until then, it's your game."

***

17

Another gray dawn broke over the endless rolling hills of Turkey, and over another day of Soviet-Arab advance.

Nabiyev rubbed eyes caked with grit and sleep and sipped tepid coffee from an aluminum cup. Packed into the belly of a BTR, he was little more comfortable than the men under his command now racing westward, driving for the Aegean Sea. Every mile they crossed put the outmaneuvered Turkish defenders a mile behind their lines, sealing their victory. So far as Nabiyev and his commanders knew, the last obstacle between them and Izmir was a scattered and demoralized flock of retreating Turkish soldiers. With the entry of Syria and Iraq into the war, where before the Turks could funnel the Soviets in through a narrow killing ground on bad terrain, now they were in serious risk of being cut off. The Turks' only hope was to retreat west and re-establish a defensive line before the Iraqis could turn in. It was Nabiyev's job to keep them running.

It would be easier, Nabiyev thought, if the Turks weren't so hell bent on fighting him every chance they got.

"Second company advancing to contact," a voice reported over Nabiyev's headphones, breathless from equal parts excitement and fear.

Somewhere in the hills ahead tank guns boomed and missiles screeched as the Soviets made contact, spreading to engage the Turkish defenders.

An apple orchard flanked both sides of the highway, trees flashing by as Nabiyev's BTR roared along. Further ahead, at the edge of the flat ground they crossed, scout helicopters and reconnaissance APCs probed forward, feeling out the Turkish lines before the rest of the battalion deployed into battle array, fanning out to envelop and pin the enemy.

"First company advance," Baranov said, sounding remarkably sober to Nabiyev, though maybe he was just very focused on this task. "Cut their line of retreat and fix them." They had to keep the Turks from slipping away again. After all, an enemy that runs away lives to fight another day. Better to kill them where they stood.

"Acknowledged."

A moment later, Baranov's soldiers were calling in artillery fire. Virtually anyone with a radio in the Soviet military was authorized to do so, which in theory offered a great deal of flexibility in the application of fire support. In practice, it was chaos.

A dozen competing voices demanded artillery rounds be dropped on *their* target as the artillery controllers argued, agreed, refused, and prioritized engagement. Only Nabiyev's self-propelled guns were able to keep pace with their rapid advance across the desert, and it was they who spoke in their booming voice as distant, unhappy thunder to their rear.

Nabiyev opened the commander's hatch of the BTR and listened to the mournful wail of shells passing overhead to drop onto the enemy before them.

"*Good hits.*"

"*I see fire. Smoke.*"

"*Boom!*"

"*Die, bastards.*"

The voices on the radio celebrated the wanton destruction as the Soviet army's main offensive weapon worked over the Turks. Soon he could see thin trails of black smoke rising over the horizon, visible over the tops of the apple trees.

At the crescendo of this attack, a quartet of helicopter gunships chopped overhead. They flew so low that their rotor wash momentarily dispelled the dust hanging around Nabiyev's column before scouring his face with a rush of windborne grit that made him flinch away.

Nabiyev pulled his dust goggles down over his eyes and made sure they were seated in place just in time to see the gunships level off their flight and fire a pair of anti-tank missiles at some unseen target. A heartbeat later a third helicopter fired, plinking off a Turkish tank or armored vehicle in the open.

Nabiyev couldn't help but be reminded of the massive "Vostok 90" exercise he'd participated in two years prior. Though they'd called it an exercise, it was really a demonstration, a carefully orchestrated display of Soviet military power with choreographed movements for massive units. It was war in ideal circumstances.

"And now here it is again," Nabiyev said to himself.

"The enemy is surrendering," someone on Baranov's frequency said.

"Take them if you can. If not, finish them off and continue the advance."

"Acknowledged."

Nabiyev waited long enough to confirm that the Turks ahead were neutralized before relaying that to General Novikov's headquarters.

"Acknowledged. The 806th Regiment will take the Turkish positions and then hold and allow the Iraqis to catch up. Once they have resumed the offensive, you will follow behind them," Novikov said.

Sit and wait?" Nabiyev was incredulous. They had the Turks on the run. "Comrade General, I have nothing in front of my regiment now. I have a clear shot to the coast."

"The 806th Regiment will hold to refuel and rearm. The Iraqis are to take point on this operation. My orders are clear. We are in danger of outrunning them. It is imperative that the advance remains cohesive."

Nabiyev didn't like it, despite it making some sense. It would earn them nothing to run off and leave the Iraqis behind only to then get caught and bloodied in a Turkish counterattack. He waited a part of heartbeats before responding. "Acknowledged." He relayed these instructions to his battalion commanders, ending with: "Baranov will move his battalion to establish blocking positions on the highway against possible enemy counterattack."

"Counterattack with what?" Baranov replied dismissively. "They are beaten, Comrade. All that remains is to finish running them down."

That was a glory that seemed destined for the Iraqis. Beside the operational concerns Novikov had mentioned, Nabiyev was sure there were political considerations at play. Was it an attempt to buy the Iraqis' loyalty by making this *their* operation? Was it an attempt to minimize Soviet losses, which were already severe? Whatever the case, it was a directive that Nabiyev had no power over and so was destined to obey.

"The Iraqis will assume our positions and continue the advance," Nabiyev continued as if Baranov hadn't spoken. "We'll resume our place as the breakthrough reserve."

"Madness," Baranov said. "We already *have* a breakthrough. If we let them go today, then we will just have to do this again tomorrow."

"If you disagree," Nabiyev said, putting an edge in his voice, "then you can explain so to General Novikov himself. These are his orders."

Baranov had nothing to say to that.

"Then we will follow behind," Abramov agreed blandly, along with agreement from the rest of his battalion officers.

Nabiyev busied himself with organizing his regiment, arraying combat units to the front and sending his surviving recon elements forward to probe for the enemy. His command BTR rumbled into the shade of an orchard, toppling an apple tree inadvertently as it ripped the earth with its tractor tires before coming to a halt. From his position he could faintly see the edges of the Turks' old position, crude dugouts and trenches scraped up at the edge of the hills beyond. Beige sand was stained black with ash in neat circles around burning vehicles. Once pristine farmland was cut with trenches and churned with craters. Scatterings of bodies and equipment lay everywhere, sooty from oily smoke.

Nabiyev took the time to light a cigarette and climb out of the BTR to stretch his legs, pacing around the command vehicle as nearby anti-air batteries took position guarding against a possible aerial attack.

Painful hours passed this way, with Nabiyev smoking and studying laminated maps he held to the hull of the BTR while he listened to rising rifle fire echoing from nearby towns. The first vehicles of the Iraqi column passed by as afternoon edged toward evening. Nabiyev watched them drive by with casual interest. It was strange to see recognizable Soviet vehicles in foreign paint schemes, BTRs and T-72s in tan and brown desert camouflage. A command vehicle flying a red, white, and black Iraqi flag roared by at speed, followed closely by a battalion of APCs. Unlike the Soviets who preferred to sit on the roof, the Iraqis rode inside the carriers. Nabiyev supposed they would learn to distrust the APCs' armor in time. Or they would die.

The infantry column was tailed by an olive drab UAZ which pulled from the main road and picked its way through the orchard toward Nabiyev's command post. He watched the 4x4 until it coasted to a halt and let out its passengers. He was surprised to see a Soviet officer, a colonel, and two junior officers.

"Hello comrade!" the colonel called, beaming excitedly. "Greetings from the 1st Hammurabi Division!"

Nabiyev glanced at his staff who all pretended to be too busy to look up. "Hello," he said. "You are the military advisor to this division?" he gestured to the passing Iraqi column.

The colonel nodded. "Davydov," he said by way of introduction. "And that—" he pointed to the Iraqis, "is the Iraqi Republican Guard."

Nabiyev raised an eyebrow. This was the vaunted Iraqi elite? They seemed somewhat ordinary to him and he didn't take that as a positive sign.

"You, my friend, are the first Russians we have met in... too long! The Iraqis—Muslims, you see? No alcohol." He smiled bashfully. "Maybe you have something to drink. We'd gladly trade for it."

Nabiyev shook his head. "I'm sorry, I have nothing for you here. I don't allow alcohol in my headquarters." He imagined Colonel Davydov would have rather found Baranov's headquarters.

Davydov frowned, his eyes narrowing slightly. It was a look Nabiyev recognized, one that was sizing up his loyalties. With Nabiyev's swarthy complexion and apparent rejection of alcohol Davydov was wondering if he was a Muslim.

The colonel waved it off. "No matter. This is a Russian unit, isn't it? I'm sure we can find some." He laughed.

Nabiyev did not, but Davydov didn't seem to notice. The colonel walked to the edge of the orchard, watching the Iraqis drive by. "A strange bunch. Devout Muslims to the death. Mostly." He chuckled. "Though don't let them fool you, they aren't as holy as they claim. I would hate to live in any city that these men pass through."

"What do you mean by that?"

Davydov glanced back at him. "You don't know? No, I see you don't. Savages. They were bad under Saddam and worse when they took over. I've seen things that would curl your hair, my friend." He stopped and glanced at Nabiyev, perhaps realizing his hair was already curly.

"And this is meant to be their best?" Nabiyev asked, disgusted. He wrinkled his nose at the thought of trailing an army of barbarians.

"Best? In a sense. Best equipped. Perhaps best motivated. Little different than the Nazi SS I think, political goons with a surplus of weapons and a deficit of humanity." He laughed again. "As bad as they are, the main Iraqi army is worse. Terrified peasants. Conscripts with nearly no training. The difference between an Iraqi conscript and a coat rack with a Kalashnikov is that a coat rack won't run away." He laughed at his own humor.

Nabiyev only felt uneasy. Now he could only wonder about the purpose of the rifle fire he'd heard in the nearby villages and hoped it was directed at enemy combatants and not civilians.

***

18

"Again!" The eternal mantra of Soviet military training. So, the inductees did it again. Climbing laboriously back inside the BTRs and waiting for the captain to blow his whistle. Their movements were sluggish, tired, worn down from fatigue, but they did it all the same.

The captain stared, eagle-eyed across the drill field until the APCs were filled with men and then blew the whistle again, setting General Strelnikov's left ear ringing.

The conscripts piled out of the APCs in a flood of uniformed bodies.

Strelnikov felt sympathetic pains in his elbows and knees as he watched the inductees bang them on hatches, rifles, and each other. Men's legs became tangled as they debarked, stumbling and falling. He could hear their swearing even from his distant vantage point.

"Sloppy," Colonel Sidorov said bitterly from beside Strelnikov. "Too slow. Half of them are already dead."

Strelnikov didn't disagree. He watched as the conscripts fanned out and threw themselves to the ground, arrayed for battle around their APCs. A BTR was little more than a "battle taxi," a means of conveyance to get soldiers into the fight. Once arrived, soldiers would need to fight dismounted. Of course, they weren't designed that way. It was intended that soldiers be able to fight from *inside* the BTR using the rifle ports along the APC's flanks. Utter madness. Strelnikov had seen countless BTRs burned up and blown out, their human contents obliterated or roasted to charcoal-black mummies. No, to survive and to fight they would have to get out quickly—often under fire—and so they practiced disembarking over and over.

The captain waited until the maneuver was finished and looked to Strelnikov for approval. Though his expression was impassive, Strelnikov saw pity in his eyes, pity for the men worn out from the same maneuver. Strelnikov answered with the mantra. "Again."

"Again!" the captain called.

This was the Soviet way of training, repetition. They were taught what to do, when to do it, and how, and then that operation was repeated until it was perfect, flawlessly executed. In this manner anyone could learn anything. The Red Army was dependent on vast masses of conscripts, many of them uneducated. Sometimes they spoke no Russian at all. To that end, trying to teach a soldier *why* something should be done became far less important than teaching him *how*. It was like teaching a monkey to ride a bike. They did not need to understand why it should be done, only that it must.

"Again!"

"You see what we are dealing with," Colonel Sidorov said, turning to Strelnikov. "These men couldn't find their asses if I gave them a map. Hopeless. They've sent inductees from all the SSRs. I have at least five languages being spoken in my regiment now."

Strelnikov remained impassive, watching the drill carried out again.

"They aren't ready to be called Guards," Sidorov finished.

"The men who earned that title are all dead outside of Zagreb," Strelnikov reminded him. It was a bitter truth, one which Sidorov visibly winced at. The 121st Motor Rifles—the so-called "Zagreb Guards"—was like the Ship of Theseus. They'd been decimated once in Yugoslavia and then again outside of Metz. How many times could they rebuild the same unit and call it "elite"?

"Captain…," Strelnikov said, eliciting a name.

"Pushkaryov, Comrade General," the captain supplied.

"Captain Pushkaryov, were you with us at Zagreb?" Strelnikov asked.

The captain puffed his chest proudly. "Yes, Comrade General! I was wounded and awarded the Order of Lenin."

Strelnikov fixed a smile on his face. "Then it's you who deserves the credit for our victory there."

The captain beamed proudly. "I serve the Soviet Union, General."

"As we all do," Strelnikov replied, looking back at Sidorov. "These men will suffice. They will have to. After all, we were little more experienced than they are now when we took Zagreb. Isn't that right?"

"Yes, Comrade General," Sidorov reluctantly allowed.

"Ordinary men are capable of extraordinary things. Remember it."

"Yes, Comrade General."

Strelnikov awarded Sidorov a fraternal pat on the back. "Carry on." The general turned his back on the endless training exercise as Captain Pushkaryov cried, "Again!" On his way across the base, he passed by the vehicle depot, noting with some satisfaction that his technicians and crews were hard at work on the new vehicles, the latest model tanks and infantry fighting vehicles. Ostensibly all these weapons were set dressing for the October Revolution parade. Strelnikov wished he believed that.

"Ah, Comrade General!" Mishkin intercepted Strelnikov with the surety of an anti-air missile, falling into lockstep with him. "I was just coming to ensure you—"

"We're on the way to deliver the welcome address to the new inductees," Strelnikov finished. "Yes. I am."

His dour attitude didn't rub off on Mishkin who pressed on undamped. "Also, there is the matter of—"

"One piece of bad news at a time please," Strelnikov cut in. "Let me fluff my feathers and then we can talk about whatever is next. It can wait?"

"I believe so, General."

"Good. These are Lukin's men, yes?"

"That's correct. They're to be moved out of the training cadre and placed with combat units this afternoon."

Strelnikov grunted understanding. He had no desire to strut around like a martial peacock today or any other day. Still, it was a part of the job and the reason why his chest was now clad with a phalanx of medals and ribbons. He felt like a buffoon, but knew that such pageantry had meaning, especially for the young and easily impressed. On the far end of the vehicle depot, he saw a gathering company of soldiers milling about before a wooden stage. "Here?"

"Yes, Comrade General. I prepared a few notes for you." Mishkin offered a sheaf of paper with neatly typed rows of text. "I was reasonably sure you hadn't prepared anything."

"Astute as always, Mishkin," Strelnikov said. "Not too long, I hope." His eyes scanned the page and he felt his stomach drop at the length of the address.

"Long enough," Mishkin said.

Strelnikov passed the time idly studying the speech as Lukin addressed his new men, calling them to attention and extolling their virtues as soldiers and the importance of duty and sacrifice, sentiments echoed in Mishkin's words. While Strelnikov's eyes scanned the page, his thoughts quickly went elsewhere. They lingered on Defense Minister Tarasov and the October Revolution parade. Strelnikov had not risen to his current post by being a fool. Whatever was going on here was deeper than surface appearances, and it cast a shadow across everything that happened.

When it was his turn to speak, Mishkin gestured him up to the stage. Strelnikov mounted the steps and came to stand behind a podium, looking out over several hundred blank, tired faces staring back at him. Among them he saw a mixture of skin tones and ethnicities, the makeup of the Soviet Union on full display here, united by uniform. They all looked impossibly young to him—like children. He had to remind himself that these *were* children, teenagers who were undergoing their first stint in the military. Maybe their last.

Without preamble, Strelnikov began the speech. "Soldiers of

the 121st Motor Rifles."

There was silence. He stopped reading and stared at the rest of the words on the page. Words that weren't his. When he looked back at the crowd, he saw the first flickers of confusion replacing slack acceptance.

With careful, deliberate motions, Strelnikov picked up the paper and folded it into squares before tucking it into his tunic pocket. Instead, he spoke to the men. "You know me," he said. "Perhaps that is arrogant to say, but I believe it is true. You know me, you know who I am. You know my reputation." A pause. "I fight," Strelnikov said. "I win when I can. But I will always fight. If you were hoping for a quiet deployment, then I am sorry to disappoint you but this will not be it. If instead you were hoping for a chance of glory...then the tides of history have placed you exactly where you were meant to be." Strelnikov gestured back over his shoulder, to the west. "An enemy slavers for our blood. They crave the destruction of the Soviet Union and communist progress. They desire nothing more than total subjugation of us all. They would see you all dead, your women and children slaves, everything we have worked to build ground to dust beneath their heels." Strelnikov tapped his chest. "We stand between them and that goal. Through flesh, blood, and iron, we will turn them back and throw the fascists into the ocean. Europe will be free. The world will be free. *We* will be free." Strelnikov rested his hands on the podium and looked the men over. "If you can commit to that dream, if you can swear your life to it, then you and I can be brothers." Strelnikov looked each man in the eyes. They would have to suffice, what other choice was there? "There is nothing more to say."

There was no cheering. Why would they after all they had seen their country put through? With the world teetering on the cusp of annihilation, there was nothing to cheer for. Still, Strelnikov saw the resolve in their eyes, felt it in their hearts. He saluted the men before surrendering the stage to Lukin without a backward glance.

Once he was away with Mishkin, his aide gave him a wry look.

"Improvisation always was your strong suit."

"I prefer to surprise my enemy," Strelnikov answered. "And what was this other business you mentioned? More functions? Are we to be fitted for new uniforms for the parade?"

"A request from the office of the defense minister," Mishkin said. "Sealed." He extended the envelope to Strelnikov who took it like it was poisonous.

The general slit the envelope with a swipe of his finger and pulled out the typed letter. It was brief, only a few sentences.

"An invitation," Strelnikov said for Mishkin's benefit. "For a meeting with Minister Tarasov at St. Basils."

"The museum?" Mishkin asked, bewildered.

Strelnikov nodded, feeling that shadow over him only growing darker. "The meeting is for tonight. Find me a truck—not a car, something unremarkable, and a driver. Someone you trust."

**

Strelnikov thought of nothing else until it came time for his journey to the city. His subordinate had secured for him an unmarked UAZ and a driver—a sergeant, one of the old guards of the 121st.

The sergeant did not speak for the long ride from the depot to Red Square and Strelnikov was thankful for that. When the countryside at last gave way to the city, Strelnikov found himself reminiscing of his distant days in Frunze military academy. Ah, to be a cadet again, carefree and young. To live in a world where his only concern had been his studies. Besides his brief stint in the academy, Strelnikov had never been much for cities or urban life. He'd grown up on a collective farm and that was where he felt most at home. The bustle and life of Moscow only made him uneasy, the sight of KGB security troops on every street corner doubled that concern. It was a far cry from the days when Moscow had been turned into a fortress in anticipation of the arrival of the Nazi war machine, but it still felt like a blemish on an otherwise pretty face.

Yes, as uncomfortable as it made him, Strelnikov also found the city beautiful. It was another world, different from his own, but stunning to look at. This feeling only intensified when, after showing the proper credentials, Strelnikov and his driver were admitted into Red Square.

It was strange, Strelnikov thought, to find such beauty in a structure so anathema to what he believed. St. Basils had been constructed by an autocratic monarch to please a tin god and a cabal of corrupt priests. Yet when he looked up at its onion-topped minarets and brick-clad tower, shining with gilded detail, he found it moved something within him.

The sergeant stopped the truck and made to get out before the general caught the man's sleeve, halting him. It wasn't customary for generals to open their own doors, but there was no sense drawing more attention to himself than necessary. The defense minister didn't call for meetings in cathedrals if he wanted them to be official.

"Wait for me here, Sergeant," Strelnikov instructed before getting out on his own and tugging his peaked cap on.

The square was cavernously large and dotted here and there with pedestrians. No one paid him any mind—military and governmental officials were a common sight in Red Square—so he made his way inside, marching briskly through the autumn breeze.

The building had ceased to be used as a place of worship decades ago. If it was at one point the house of God, then He had been evicted. In His place a cultural museum now stood, filled with artifacts celebrating Soviet culture and exposing Tsarist greed and barbarism for all to see. Above all else, it marked the ceaseless forward march of the Russian people toward ultimate victory.

It was also, Strelnikov observed, nearly deserted. The only other people he came across were soldiers, standing at each doorway as silent sentinels, watching him go by passively as he made his way through the museum, past crypts and chapels turned exhibits. While it had been stripped of its original purpose, the ornate paintings, carvings, icons and reliefs remained, giving it an air of holiness that Strelnikov couldn't shake.

Ducking through a narrow brick archway and moving past a series of velvet ropes he finally reached the tenth chapel, the church's namesake, the chapel of St. Basil. Seated on a wooden bench facing the saint's icons was General Tarasov looking like a hunched foothill in drab green. The chapel was hushed and cool, inviting despite the apprehension Strelnikov felt.

Strelnikov went to him, his footfalls echoing loudly in this silent place until at last he stopped beside the minister, unsure of how to proceed to address him. When Tarasov looked up, Strelnikov saluted him.

A slow grin spread across Tarasov's broad face. "So, you are the famous Strelnikov," Tarasov rumbled. "Please. Sit." He gestured to Strelnikov's stiff stance. "There is no need for formality here."

Strelnikov sat as instructed, laying his hat reverently beside him in the pew. He knew Tarasov only by reputation, but what a reputation it was. A man who had seen combat against the Nazis, a man who had forged the modern Soviet army. He was a living legend. "Forgive me, Comrade," Strelnikov said, "but I did not take you as a superstitious man."

Tarasov laughed like a rockslide before descending into a coughing fit. "No. I am a good communist," he said at last. "I sedate myself with alcohol rather than religion."

Strelnikov said nothing, still feeling distinctly uncomfortable and off guard. What he wouldn't give now to be advancing under NATO's guns instead of sitting in this place.

Tarasov, oblivious or unmoved by Strelnikov's discomfort, swept an arm, taking in the cluttered beauty of the baroque chapel. "Amazing, isn't it?"

Strelnikov wasn't quite as impressed but kept that to himself.

"When the people work together they are capable of miracles," Tarasov explained. "Even in those dark days, the Russian spirit was indomitable. This chapel is for Saint Basil. Do you know him?"

"I have not had the opportunity to make his acquaintance," Strelnikov replied stiffly.

Tarasov chuckled. "A mendicant of sorts. He stole from the rich to provide for the poor, went naked, weighed by chains, and chastised the tsar for impiety. Do you not see the reflection of socialist values even in that misguided man?"

"Why has my division been brought to Moscow?" Strelnikov asked with no patience for these games.

Tarasov gave him a sidelong glance, "I apologize, Comrade. I should have assumed you would be in no mood for a history lesson."

"Presently I am more concerned with making it than learning it," Strelnikov replied.

"Then firstly," Tarasov said, "allow me to congratulate you on your promotion to Colonel General."

Strelnikov felt his heart sink.

"Promotion?"

Tarasov nodded, the humor draining from his expression. "Beyond overdue," he said. "Your service to the Motherland is long and commendable. Warsaw, Zagreb, Metz, even Worms." He gave Strelnikov a sidelong glance. "It is only fitting for a man's rank to match the burden of his responsibility."

Now Strelnikov felt truly afraid. "What responsibility is that?"

Tarasov kept his eyes fixed on St. Basil's icons which cluttered the wall opposite him. "Your division will soon facilitate a change of power," Tarasov said plainly. "Your men will act as my hands in this matter and restore sanity to the government and military."

Though Strelnikov felt his heart hammering in his chest, he kept his fear from his expression, keeping his voice level. "A coup." He said the dirty word without fear. If this were not a safe place to speak, Tarasov would not be here. He had suspected as much, but never would have in his worst nightmares assumed that he would be right.

"A restoration," Tarasov corrected, not missing a beat. "To

unthrone the butcher Karamazov," Tarasov replied. "To set this government and our people back on the proper course."

"I have no interest in politics," Strelnikov said. "The machinations of the politburo do not concern me."

"You may have no interest, but you cannot escape it all the same," Tarasov said. "The chains which bind you are heavier than those St. Basil carried. It is a matter of duty."

"Duty? You expect me to march on Moscow then?" Strelnikov demanded. "Because you order it?"

Tarasov nodded. "Yes. Because I order it." There was no room for doubt in his voice. "Do I need to remind you of your oath of service? To unquestioningly obey all orders of commanders and superiors?"

Strelnikov's mind swam with thoughts flashing by too fast to parse. He felt himself begin to sweat. He wasn't accustomed to feeling fear, but he felt it now. Something in Tarasov's quiet tone and still posture suggested the demeanor of a killer, though the irony of a coup-plotter speaking of unquestioning obedience to superiors wasn't lost on him. "And what if I refuse to go along with this?"

Tarasov smiled coldly. "I will not insult you with petty threats. I will allow you to return to the war with no further trouble. You may not believe in politics, but I know you believe in the war."

Strelnikov studied Tarasov's face silently, looking for any indication of deceit. Strangely, Strelnikov found he had little fear of death, at least that it paled in comparison with his fear of becoming a traitor to the people he had sworn to serve. He would rather die than be responsible for the downfall of his nation.

"Even were I inclined to do what you say," Strelnikov said, "we have no ammunition. We are only equipped to march in the October Revolution parade."

"The parade is a pretext," Tarasov replied. "And I have seen to your ammo problem. A unit of national guard troops will occupy a nearby depot and deposit ammo before leaving. Your men will arm themselves from there when the time comes."

Strelnikov's mind raced and yet he saw the inevitable closing in on him. There was no shirking his duty, however much he wanted to. If Tarasov ordered him to do this thing, of course he would obey. Worse than that, however, Strelnikov found himself agreeing on some level with Tarasov. His former commanding officer, General Gurov, had been ordered to his death because of command incompetence. General Turgenev's pigheaded stubbornness had likely cost them victory at least once, and who could say what other chances for victory had been squandered by feeble-minded politicians and inept generals. What other explanation could there be for the complacency and incompetence that riddled the Soviet military besides rot at the highest levels? What other mechanism was there for political change in the Soviet Union than violence?

"To put who on the throne then?" Strelnikov asked. "You?"

Tarasov laughed and shook his head. "I have no interest in political games either, Comrade. I leave them to wiser—or perhaps more foolish men."

"Who then?" Strelnikov pressed. "If I am asked to commit treason, then I need a name."

Tarasov at last hesitated, clearly mentally weighing how much he trusted Strelnikov. At last, he relented. "Gradenko, the foreign minister."

Strelnikov wrinkled his nose. He could hardly put a face to the name, but he could imagine an old man in an ill-fitting suit. "A diplomat," Strelnikov said dismissively. "A politician. The Soviet Union needs a leader. A firm hand, a keen mind. Someone with vision."

"If you are hoping I will step forward, then you will be disappointed," Tarasov said. "It is not my place to rule. I am a fighter. Like you. Gradenko is a skilled leader. A man who understands politics. He will lead us well."

Strelnikov doubted that very much. If Gradenko were such a leader, then why was he hiding in the shadows while Tarasov did his dirty work for him?

"This is for the good of the nation," Tarasov said. "Truthfully, our prospects of winning this war grow slimmer every day with

Karamazov at our head. Change is needed."

"Change down the barrel of a gun."

"The only sort of change that matters," Tarasov agreed. "This is the only way."

Strelnikov had told the truth when he said he had no interest in politics, but what Tarasov said was true. He didn't know everything, but he knew enough to know that they were no closer to winning this war than they were when it began. Thousands dead, lives wasted, and for what? Sacrifice for the Motherland was noble, but only when that sacrifice meant something. For any other man Strelnikov would have refused on the spot, but for a warrior like Tarasov....

"What will you have me do?" Strelnikov asked.

***

19

It was early, but—

"He who wakes up early is rewarded by God," Yessov said with a wry smile.

"The enemy are sleeping at their posts to let us get this close," Voloshin agreed.

They'd been tracking this convoy across the last leg of their journey, all the way into the Aegean sea and to the coasts of Turkey. A juicy target, one Yessov wasn't content to let go. They were just off the coast of Turkey, by the city of Izmir. The enemy had let their guard down. After all, who would be arrogant enough to attack them in harbor like this?

As he'd done with *Gettysburg*, he simply placed himself exactly where they wouldn't expect them.

The ships were motionless now, at anchor within sight of the city. They believed they were safe here, so close to land. They were wrong.

"Have we confirmed sonar patterns?" Yessov asked.

"Yes, Comrade Captain," Sonar replied. "It's primarily civilian transports alongside a handful of escort ships, mostly Italian and French."

Yessov looked over at the waterfall display showing the overlapping sonar signals and furrowed his brow. One of the transports had an unhealthy rhythmic thump to its engines. He tapped the signal on the monitor. "Have we encountered this ship before?"

"Yes, Comrade," Sonar said, "In the Atlantic. He escaped us then."

Yessov gave the sonar operator a bloodthirsty grin. "Lucky us.

The bastard won't escape us now."

Turning back to the video replay of their periscope feed, Yessov stared at a gaggle of transport freighters, likely loaded with men and weapons intended to bolster the Turks and Greeks, one of them the obnoxiously loud freighter he'd lost before. Some of those wouldn't be arriving as expected once he was finished with them. Yessov smirked. "Flood tubes one through four."

***

It was early. Too early to be awake really, Heathcliff thought as he sat in the nearly deserted mess hall of the freighter. Only a few self-serve meal options were available, mostly cereal and lukewarm coffee, but he ate ravenously all the same. Now that they were finally anchored, his seasickness had subsided to be replaced by a deep hunger and so he ate.

Heathcliff took another bite of cereal and chewed, crunching loudly enough that he had to turn up the volume of his cassette player. It was the conclusion of the game and, in his opinion, the best part. His heart was racing, and it was only partly because they were finally here. Right now he was wholly focused on living vicariously through the electric thrill in the announcer's voice as he detailed the Wolves working the puck closer and closer until—

"Sudbury scores!"

Heathcliff held up his hands triumphantly as if that victory weren't over a year old. As he did, he heard the ship's PA system squelch to life.

"All hands to battle stations. All hands—" was all the hapless merchant marine got off before the torpedo struck.

The mess hall seemed to convulse. Heathcliff's cereal and milk sloshed across his chest and he was dumped unceremoniously to the floor, landing hard enough to knock the wind out of his chest. Dishes crashed and glass shattered as the entire vessel rocked like a wounded animal, lifting from the water before dropping back down catastrophically, breaking the ship's back.

Heathcliff felt all this happening as he desperately tried to fill his lungs with air. At last he managed a shuddering, gasping breath. As he pulled himself to his feet, he realized the ship was listing badly, something getting worse even as he acknowledged it. Metal groaned and creaked. Alarms warbled and voices shouted, echoing hauntingly in the metal bowels of the ship. What cups and dishes that hadn't been thrown to the floor now slid from the sharply canted tables to crash on the floor.

Heathcliff's blood ran cold. He found himself disoriented, at a total loss. He looked around at the others in the mess hall looking equally bewildered. His mind was frozen. Consciously he knew they were sinking, but part of him couldn't—wouldn't—accept it. It was impossible.

His lockup broke a moment later when a gray-haired merchant marine in civilian clothes stuck his head into the mess hall. "You assholes get topside now! We're sinking, goddammit!" And then he was gone.

It was all the encouragement Heathcliff and the others needed. They piled out of the mess hall and into the cramped passageway a moment before the power flickered and failed, plunging them all into darkness.

It was only a few seconds, but it was hell, jostling with unseen strangers in utter blackness. Heathcliff tripped on someone's feet and smashed his elbow against a bulkhead with a loud cry. Battery-powered emergency lights came on, casting harsh white light and black shadows across the passageway, choked with bodies, illuminating a scene from Dante's Inferno. To add to this feeling of unreality, the passageway was now canted at a 45-degree angle, forcing men to clamber on hands and feet to move through it. The ladderway was now more like its namesake than ever.

"Up, guys! Up!" Someone called.

People were shouting back and forth, questions and commands, any semblance of organization fell apart once it became a scramble to escape being sucked into the ocean.

There wasn't room for conscious thought. Heathcliff didn't even have time to be afraid, he was driven only by a desire to survive. He climbed his way down the passage and up the ladderway, trying not to tread on others or shove them aside. It took a supreme force of will not to fight for escape, to see everybody as an obstacle or competition. Still, Heathcliff and the others persisted, working their way up.

He didn't stop this relentless ascent until, finally, he emerged onto the open deck where soldiers were congregating, bewildered. No one seemed to be in charge, and there was nothing to take charge of. This ship was doomed, its lifespan likely measured in minutes. Now it was just a matter of saving as many lives as possible.

On the deck, Heathcliff could now see that they'd been struck on their port side amidships. Whatever hole was surely there was invisible below the waterline, greedily sucking in seawater and listing the freighter more and more. Fractures ran across the middle of the vessel where the torpedo which struck them had detonated. The ship's bones were broken, metal twisting and warping, the ship shifting perceptibly beneath their feet as it died.

As Heathcliff kept looking around for someone in charge, he realized that many men were looking at him. He was the man in charge. He swallowed and forced his mind into action, struggling to sort out his confused thoughts and find the steps for this situation.

"Let's get to the lifeboats!" Heathcliff called, faintly recalling his very brief damage control training.

The men moved to the left side of the ship where a crowd was already formed. Teams of soldiers worked to deploy the molded plastic, cover-topped orange boats with inexperienced hands.

A pair of harried merchant marines tried to conduct the panicked soldiers in the process, but time was short and patience thin. Some men simply threw themselves overboard, taking their chances in the sea rather than risk waiting for the rafts. The water rose up rapidly as the freighter dipped lower and lower, her hull groaning as it came apart around them.

The ship shuddered, threatening to roll over and Heathcliff swore. Someone grabbed his sleeve. Lieutenant Driscoll. "Let's try the other side!" the lieutenant said.

Heathcliff followed Driscoll uphill, struggling against the listing deck, boots slipping, until they reached the other side, now the apex of the freighter. Behind them, the angled deck into the water, ahead of them, the sloping hull of the ship, now exposed to air.

"Where are the fucking life rafts!?" someone called.

"We need vests," another said.

Heathcliff spun in a circle, trying to spot any of the more experienced merchant marines but saw only other confused, panicked soldiers. His boots slipped on the slick, angled deck.

"Over the side, guys! Let's go!" another soldier called.

Men began clambering over the railing and sliding down the hull of the ship toward the water.

"Shit!"

The ship shuddered again, throwing everyone to the deck with a screech of metal. The freighter was breaking in half, threatening to cave in in the middle. They were out of time. The only chance of survival was to get off and away.

"Take off your boots!" Heathcliff called out, in case anyone was listening, before kneeling and frantically unlacing his own.

He felt the ship shifting again. The sea foamed beneath them as it consumed the vessel.

"Sir!" a private called to Heathcliff in panic. "I can't get them unlaced!"

Heathcliff swore. The first thing to go in a tense situation was the ability to think clearly. He crawled quickly to the private, Harper, before swiftly undoing the knots and yanking his boots free. "Go!" As he said it, he realized they were virtually alone. "Come on!"

He climbed back to the railing which once looked over the edge of the ship and hauled himself over it alongside Harper.

"Where's the lieutenant!?" Harper asked.

Heathcliff spared a quick look around; it was all he had time for. No one was standing still, those still on the ship were diving overboard. "Already in the water, let's go!"

The two of them scooted to the edge of the hull and let gravity take over. They slid down the ship's flank toward the sea. A clutch of barnacles clawed Heathcliff's hip but he didn't slow down, leaping into the water as soon as he was close enough.

Harper landed beside him with a splash and they both paddled frantically, joining the panicked exodus, trying to put distance between themselves and the dying freighter. The water foamed around them, its surface coated with a spreading oil slick which slopped over Heathcliff's head with each wave. He coughed, choked, and sputtered as he kicked and swam blindly, struggling away from the dying *Atlantic Queen*.

The ship gurgled and moaned before finally upending with a spray of saltwater and tipping into oblivion, churning with foam, sucking down whoever was unlucky enough to still be onboard.

After she plunged into her watery grave, what wouldn't sink bobbed to the surface. Life vests, tennis shoes, furniture, even a few lucky, gasping soldiers.

Someone fired a flare overhead illuminating everything a flickering red.

Harper and Heathcliff paddled through the flotsam and finally found an empty orange vest bobbing in the oil-slick water. Both of them clung desperately to it, kicking their feet to stay afloat. After the ship was gone, an eerie silence settled over them. The only sound was the slosh of waves and the occasional call and response of survivors nearby.

"Holy shit," Harper said, his hair and face slick with brown-black oil. His wide eyes appeared even whiter in contrast to the grease covering him.

Heathcliff looked at the private and for a moment marveled that they had just survived that. He heard a helicopter approaching and the men in the water started waving up at it. They were within sight of the coastline, the lights of a city looking like a beacon of hope. It was a hell of a welcome, but they'd arrived. Turkey.

***

20

Bayern had once heard someone describe election night as "the political Super Bowl," which struck him as a fantastically stupid way to describe it. Also, at the moment, it felt completely apt. The voting was over, Bayern and his wife had both cast their ballots—for Dewitt of course—to some media fanfare. Now all that was left was to count them.

Bayern, staff, wife, and children, as well as a handful of reporters, had gathered in the Oval Office for the occasion. Jack and his sister Emily sat together playing with toys, being reasonably quiet and mercifully getting along. Bayern's wife, Pauline, sat behind the desk Bayern usually held, her eyes fixed on a large TV that had been wheeled in for the occasion, playing twenty-four hour news coverage of the election and providing a running tally of electoral votes.

"At this time," the news anchor said, "the Associated Press is calling the state of Florida for Dewitt. This is the first after a string of wins for Harry Nelson who has been declared in Iowa, Illinois, and his home state of New York. California is still too close to call, but Nelson seems to have taken a lead there and, with only a few counties left to count, it seems like that lead will only grow throughout the night. If Nelson wins California that will put his party up to 245 votes, still shy of the 270 needed to win. Dewitt is sitting at 256 now after Florida, with Virginia and Ohio still tallying votes. While Ohio had been polling decisively in Nelson's favor, we're seeing quite a different voter turnout here on the ground. Let's go to Aaron Papadopoulos and hear what exit polls are saying. Aaron?"

This was all background noise for Bayern. He sat away from

the others, on a plush couch, eyes glued on another TV tuned to BBC—the American networks were all focused on the election right now. This one small portable device played TV footage of the Canadian transport that had been torpedoed. Bayern watched the small dots of people throwing themselves into the black sea around them, desperate for escape. It was hard to imagine Soviet submarines still operating in the Mediterranean. Whoever that skipper was, he was good. Bayern only wished he had a chance to get him in his sights from behind the helm of an *Oliver Hazard Perry*-class.

The next news segment was little more encouraging. "More setbacks on the Greek front as Warsaw Pact armored forces have inflicted what appears to be a serious blow against the Turkish Army outside of Erdine. For more on the situation in Thrace, we go live to our journalist in the field Leanne Collins currently embedded with the Greek Army. Hello Leanne. What can you tell us?"

"Hello Robert, I'm here just south of—"

"Jerry," his wife called insistently, drawing Bayern's attention from the war and to the TV. He saw Dewitt's face flash on the screen and he smiled. "I think he did it! He won!"

"Coming back to the studio, we are officially calling Ohio for Dewitt. Virginia remains neck and neck and a recount will likely be needed, but that puts Dewitt at 273, just over the 270-vote threshold required to win. At this point, we are calling Bill Dewitt the victor."

The reporters in the room clicked on their tape recorders and zoomed in their cameras as Bayern circled around to the back of his desk where his wife sat and picked up the telephone cradled there. If Nelson had won, he would be connected with him. As it was, he was connected to Dewitt's campaign headquarters. After a few rings—

"Jerry, hot damn! We did it."

Bayern smiled broader. "Hoss, let me be the first to say, 'Congratulations Mr. President Elect.'"

"This is your win, Jerry," Dewitt said more seriously. "It should be you."

Bayern knew that the cameras couldn't pick up what Dewitt said, so he kept a plastic smile fixed on his face and shook his head. "You earned it, Hoss. A hard-fought win. This is going to be a bigger win for the American people."

"Thank you, Jerry," Dewitt said. "We'll talk soon."

"Talk soon," Bayern agreed as he ended the call. That was it. His days as president were essentially over. It occurred to Bayern that this was likely the second shortest presidential term in American history, really just the tail end of Simpson's cabinet under a different name.

Bayern felt his wife and kids hugging him and he hugged them back, the same smile frozen on his face. Since he'd gone into politics, it had always been his dream to be president. It felt strange to throw that dream away, to pass it on to someone else. In a way he had expected to feel relieved, like a weight had been lifted from him. He was surprised to find that he felt...nothing. Bayern hugged his family tighter and thought of the Canadian soldiers he'd seen thrown into the ocean, cold, wet, terrified, and very far from home.

"You alright?" Pauline whispered in his ear as they hugged.

Was he alright? Bayern didn't know, but he did the thing any husband would do. He nodded.

When they broke the hug, he found the press already queueing up to leave. They'd got what they were looking for. In their place stood Walt Harrison.

"The admiral's here for you," he said. "In the study."

Bayern looked at his wife questioningly. He saw the hurt in her eyes, but he also saw understanding. "Go," she said. "We'll be waiting when you come back. And you promised dinner."

"Dinner is still an option," Bayern said with a smirk.

Pauline rolled her eyes but couldn't help smiling.

Harrison led Bayern across the oval office and opened the door to his private study where Admiral Gideon sat looking distinctly uncomfortable, his back ramrod straight.

"Dewitt just won," Bayern said, closing the door behind

himself and shutting out the sounds of talking.

"I heard the cheering," Gideon said. "Tough race."

"It was," Bayern agreed. He moved past Gideon to take a seat on the other side of the desk. This office wasn't ornamental, unlike the ostentatious Oval Office. The desk was cluttered with books, papers, and binders. Office supplies were stacked haphazardly around the room and a desktop computer sat unused on one end of the desk, the beige plastic monitor was cold and dark.

"I thought you would be busy celebrating it," Gideon said. "Isn't there an election party?"

"I've already got a speech written up to congratulate him," Bayern said. "And another one in case Nelson won. But I didn't bring you here to talk politics." Bayern smiled patiently. "I think you know what this is about."

"I do," Gideon said, adjusting himself in his seat as if to physically brace himself for this conversation. "And I said to ask after the fourth."

"Election is over," Bayern said. "This is as 'after' as it gets. That's old business. It's time for new business."

"You want to serve again," Gideon said, a statement, not a question.

"I do. I've talked it over with my wife and it's what I want to do. Christ, it's the least I can do after pushing through the draft act."

"Respectfully, sir, that's not your call to make."

"I'm Commander In Chief," Bayern said, "At least for now. I call the shots, don't I?"

"Yes, and that's where the goddamn trouble comes from. You're not going to settle for a desk job, you want combat placement."

"I do."

"And so I'm going to have to bump someone else—someone more qualified—to put you back in the saddle," Gideon said bitterly. "We'll get accused of playing favorites, and hell, that's *exactly* what we're doing. But—same token—if I put you behind a desk, we'll get accused of the same thing. God, and if you're killed? Imagine the propaganda hit."

Bayern smiled weakly. "Based on my poll numbers, I think a good number of people will be pretty pleased actually."

Gideon let out a single dry bark of laughter. "Very funny," he said. "Mr. President...sir, there's not even any precedent for a former president to return to combat."

"Theodore Roosevelt, Junior," Bayern suggested.

"Emphasis on *junior*. He was not his old man," Gideon returned.

"Breckenridge." Bayern had done his homework. "Former vice president, led troops in battle."

Gideon snorted. "He was a Confederate for God's sake. Face it. There's no precedent for it. We're writing the book."

"Then let's write it," Bayern said. "I can't send boys out there anymore."

"So you think you'll feel better cruising around the Atlantic banging away with a sonar?"

"I think I will," Bayern said honestly, "and I think it will make this draft thing an easier pill to swallow. I won't be in the Fulda Gap, but it's something."

"Politics," Gideon said.

"Politics," Bayern agreed.

The Admiral remained impassive for a moment before sighing. "You're a real asshole for putting me in this position, but...I'll see what we can do. But you're going to have to do something for me."

Bayern wasn't used to agreeing to favors in his position. "What's that?"

"One, you're going to have to be patient. This is going to take time to get through. And don't give me that 'the war might be over by then' crap. That would be a good problem to have."

"No argument from me. Is that it?"

"Two," Gideon continued, "you need to play ball with us. You're the goddamn president, so once we stick you back in your dress blues and on the bridge of a ship, you're going to become a media darling, you know that."

Bayern did, though he didn't like it. Still, publicity was nothing new. "Deal."

"Third and last," Gideon said, "once you're back in the service you're back. I don't want one foot in one foot out. No politics. You put the uniform back on and you're government property again."

"I wouldn't have it any differently."

Gideon nodded. The pact was sealed and Bayern couldn't help but feel like he'd just sold his soul. "I'm taking you on your word," Gideon said. "Get your affairs in order, cause once we put you in, you're *in*."

Bayern nodded understanding. He only hoped he didn't wind up regretting his wish. For better or worse, his days as president were behind him.

***

21

"This is Jean Carson, live from the frontlines on the Greco-Turkish border." Jean kept her gaze locked on the cold, glass lens, ignoring the red record light, ignoring Pete squinting into the viewfinder, and above all ignoring the animal howl of artillery fire nearby. She'd been shot at enough times to recognize incoming and outgoing fire and she knew this was outgoing. Friendly.

"I can't provide all the details of what's going on here because of operational security, but I've received permission to say this much: the Greek army is coming to the aid of the Turks." As if to underscore her point, diesels roared from nearby and a pack of APCs pulled onto the main freeway going north. "At this stage it seems the Romanian-Bulgarian attack has made significant headway against NATO forces here. We're getting reports that Edirne has fallen, surrendered to the enemy and that leaves the Turkish forces left in East Thrace in grave danger of being trapped against the Bosphorus. Only two avenues for supply—or escape—remain open to the Turks: across the Straits, through Istanbul, or over the Maritsa River on the Greek border. The Romanian-Bulgarian forces could threaten either or both of those supply lanes. Now a coordinated operation is underway to clear a corridor from Greece to the Turkish corps. The Greek soldiers I've spoken to have often expressed animosity toward their counterparts in the Turkish army. It could be said that the Turks are the Greeks' enemy just after the Warsaw Pact." She pursed her lips. "But despite all of that animosity, they've come together, not as friends, but as allies. Two nations of free people working against the forces of aggression and tyranny." She paused, mentally counting to three before saying, "Cut. Okay. That's good. Was that good?"

"It's good," Pete said, lowering the camera. "Better if it actually pans out." He had no illusions about the Greeks and Turks cooperating on this.

"Pete," Jean snapped her fingers. " Come on, one step at a time. Let's try to have a positive mental attitude, kay?" Jean said, looking around at the Greek army in motion.

"Yeah," Pete agreed. "We'd better get back. I think our allies are keen to get moving."

The whole battalion was mobilizing in a hurry, forming into a growing column on the highway and racing away. The situation in Thrace was rapidly deteriorating. Time was short and no one had time to worry about two reporters and their interpreter.

Jean tucked her microphone into the messenger bag hanging at her side, then unbuckled her dark blue tactical "PRESS" helmet and tucked it under her arm. Right now she wore it for the camera because it looked good, it helped "sell" the war. Later she expected she'd be glad to have it.

Not far away, she saw the bright lights of Leanne's camera crew as she delivered her own report. The situation here was even more tenuous than they'd let on in the broadcast. Hristos told her that the word "withdrawal" was getting thrown around. If the Turks were in danger of being trapped and destroyed, they might instead withdraw to Greece. Not an ideal situation for anyone, but better than the alternatives.

The image of their Croatian interpreter, Dario, with his arm blown off flashed unbidden in her mind. Jean squeezed her eyes shut and leaned on a nearby fir tree for balance as icy cold gripped her guts. She'd been there. She could have warned him not to touch that mine. Neither she nor Dario had the slightest clue what it was, but every nerve in her body had been screaming at her to leave it be. Her conscious mind had been too rattled by the bombardment to think, but her subconscious somehow knew. The Soviets weren't in the business of delivering gifts by artillery. Nausea welled up within her.

She saw Dario bending to pick up the mine and saw it burst with painful clarity. Every visceral detail was clear in her mind's eye. His arm was obliterated in an instant, the blast working from his hand up to the elbow. She saw the pieces of him flying off with deadly velocity leaving only a red mist as the blast blew him onto his back.

She couldn't even think to stop the bleeding or treat him for shock. The shock had killed him quickly. So quickly. Faster than she had thought possible.

His last words had been spoken only to her. A waste. She didn't understand Croatian. Whatever final message he'd given had died with him.

Jean jumped when Pete touched her arm. "You okay?"

She nodded before the words had a chance to register. "Peachy," she said. "Let's get rolling." The memories couldn't catch her if she stayed moving. She stuck a cigarette in her mouth and lit it as she walked on.

She and Pete sheltered in a small stand of fir trees on the edge of the highway which was otherwise surrounded by open country. Stepping into the warm sun, Jean momentarily squinted before making her way toward a nearby grouping of APCs idling on the roadside on the banks of the Maritsa River.

"Jean, wait," Pete said, hurrying to catch up.

She sighed. "I don't have time to wait, Pete. *We* don't have time."

"We have time if you're not okay."

"That's a lie," Jean said. "Even if I weren't okay, we don't have time. Time waits for no man and it doesn't wait for me either." She stumbled down the bank of a narrow irrigation ditch and back up the other side, trailing Pete behind who struggled with the heavy camera and sound gear.

"Jesus, Jean! Stop a second!"

Jean stopped, hands on her hips, and fixed Pete with an impatient stare, cigarette hanging from her lip.

"Are you okay? I mean are you really okay? I can tell something's bothering you, right?" Pete said. "And don't give me any bullshit. I've known you too long for that."

"No, everything isn't '*okay*,' Pete," Jean said with exaggerated patience. "Is it okay with you?"

Pete didn't say anything.

"Dario got his goddamn arm blown off right in front of me. He fucking *died* right in front of me. I can close my eyes and watch him die." She blew out smoke. "No. It's not okay. But what the fuck am I supposed to do about that?"

Pete started to speak and then stopped.

"Going back home isn't an option," Jean said. She gestured back to the Greek soldiers rushing north. "The war isn't going to take a break and someone's got to document it."

"It doesn't have to be you," Pete replied weakly. "It doesn't have to be us."

"No," Jean agreed. "It doesn't. But if I'm going to have goddam nightmares, I'm going to have them here instead of back home. At least here I'm doing something. If you want to go back, I won't hold it against you, Pete. Honest. I won't. But I've got a job to do and I don't have time to fuck around."

Pete was silent for a moment and at first Jean thought he was going to continue to argue. Finally, he just nodded. "Alright," he said at last. "Just...promise you'll talk to me if you need to. Right?"

Jean puffed on her cigarette and finally nodded. She didn't trust herself to speak.

Pete nodded in return. Before he could say more, they both saw Hristos hurrying across the field toward them from the waiting APCs, waving his arm. "We go now!" he called. "We go now or they leave us behind!"

Within minutes they were riding on the roof of a boxy M113 APC, driving east, the countryside flashing by. They crossed over a pontoon bridge set up over the Maritsa into Turkey. Once on the other side the convoy turned north, driving toward the distant rumble of combat, flanked on both sides by rolling farmland dotted with clumps of trees and the occasional hill.

Jean smoked and thought about Pete's offer. She didn't have

to bear the weight of what had happened alone. But what good would it do to talk about it either? She didn't even want to think about it. What fresh nightmares would surface if she voiced her fears?

A burning M113, a carbon copy of their own, was recorded on videotape as B-roll footage as they passed slowly. Jean saw that the ramp was down and there were no bodies. She could only hope the passengers and crew had made it clear when the APC was struck.

The sounds of combat grew more intense the further they traveled. The boom of artillery joined the chatter of machine guns and whine of missiles. Cresting a low ridge, they saw more burning vehicles dotting the open plains, but these were enemies. Old BTRs and older T-55s, victim to the counterattacking Greeks.

A pair of F4 Phantoms bearing the roundels of the Hellenic Air Force shrieked by at low altitude, stabbing toward the Bulgarian lines before banking suddenly skyward, going vertical and coming around in a broad loop. At the apex of this maneuver, they each released a quartet of bombs which flew through the air, carried by inertia in broad parabolic arcs toward unseen targets which moments later thundered with high explosives.

Pete's camera captured all of this, or as much as he could keep in frame on the move.

"Enemy ahead!" Hristos told her, shouting over the rush of wind and roar of the engine. He conferred with the APCs commander through the open hatch in Greek before adding, "the lead element of the attack I think."

Jean nodded resolutely and readied herself for the approaching battle.

**

22

As the sun set over the port at Izmir, virtually the entire brigade had put to shore, following in the footsteps of the Canadians who had arrived here earlier this morning. Izmir's port was alive with the unloading of troops and gear. Harsh, yellow sodium lamps burned away the darkness at the loading docks. Cranes hefted tanks and trucks from the decks of cargo ships and men debarked on scaffolds and gangways, stepping onto dry land for the first time since embarking in France. The port seemed to be ringed on every side by light-covered hills, the city of Izmir wrapping around the bay.

Work went round the clock with empty ships ushered out to make room for fresh arrivals. Turkish police oversaw the movement of troops and vehicles, maintaining a constant flow of traffic.

Between the warships in the Aegean Sea and the anti-air batteries ringing the city, the skies of Izmir were covered should the enemy dare to venture out and attack, a prospect Gates considered quite unlikely given their mounting deficit of aircraft.

With the USS *San Jaun Hill* lurking in the eastern Mediterranean, and some fighter wings freshly based at Turkish airfields NATO held a solid edge in airpower over their opponents. Soviet numbers had been frittered away in Germany and Scandinavia, their suicidal push burning through their fleet of airframes until they could no longer justify throwing aircraft away.

Brigadier Gates took all this in at a glance, blinking tired eyes against the harsh flood lamps lighting the port with only the aid of the half-moon hanging in a featureless black sky. He stood just outside the headquarters tent of the battle group gathered here. An approaching officer startled Gates from his musing.

"Excuse me, do you have a lighter? I think I lost mine somehow in the landing." Gates would have assumed the man was American except for the red maple leaf flag patch on his uniform. His shoulder boards indicated he was a brigadier-general, equivalent to Gates's rank.

"I'm sorry, I don't smoke," Gates replied, glancing at Colonel Benson nearby. "Colonel?"

"Here, sir." Benson offered, lighting the Canadian's cigarette.

"Thank you," the general said to Benson before offering his hand to Gates. "Tremblay. You must be Gates."

Gates nodded. "Good to meet you."

"I wish the circumstances were better," Tremblay offered a cold smile. "Had a chance to meet with the French yet?"

The corps assembled here was a mix of whatever the NATO allies had available at the time. A British armored division backed by two Canadian mechanized brigades and a brigade of the French Foreign Legion—what was left of it after the bloody struggle in Bosnia, followed by the sharp counterattack around Metz. The Legion had been fighting this conflict since the very first day, and their numbers reflected that. Gates wasn't sure how they would remain combat effective after even more hard fighting here.

"No, I can't say I have."

"What a mess," Tremblay shook his head, taking a drag on his cigarette and joining Gates in watching the rest of his brigade offloading. "The Turks are getting pushed everywhere. I just heard they've shifted troops away from Istanbul to try to screen Ankara and stop the Russians there. It's got their whole line out of shape."

Gates didn't disagree, in fact he was appalled with the whole operation. "We're flying by the seat of our pants on a logistical shoestring," Gates said aloud. "We only hope the Soviets don't reach either of those cities. They won't survive a Soviet attack.

The Russians have burned damn near all of Germany."

"Half of Sweden too," Tremblay agreed, nodding. He took another drag and exhaled a cloud of smoke toward the dark port. "The Soviets will lay it to waste if they can get their hands on it."

"They're bloody lucky we arrived when we did," Gates replied shortly. "We've got good odds of stopping them short of Konya I think, if the Canadians can move fast."

The French were taking the highway south, skirting the coast toward the Syrian border, south of the main enemy effort. The plan was for the Brits and Canadians to consolidate at the city of Konya before launching a spoiling attack against the enemy south of Ankara. From there it was anyone's guess how things would develop.

"Time will tell," Tremblay agreed, continuing to smoke. "It was your boys outside Paderborn, wasn't it?" Tremblay asked.

Gates remembered the sight of the hills around the city dotted with fires and smoke, each one of them a pyre for a vehicle and its crew. He remembered the news that Colonel Dunworth had been killed. He remembered the price they paid to finally stop the Soviets. "It was."

"Hard fighting." Not a question.

"Very."

Tremblay nodded and took another drag on his cigarette, seemingly almost eerily calm. "Hard fighting," he repeated." Almost a relief, don't you think?"

The question caught Gates totally off guard and he found himself staring dumbfounded at the Canadian.

Tremblay noted his shock. "Don't get me wrong, it's a terrible tragedy," Tremblay said. "It's just that...it feels more...pure this way."

"Pure?" Gates asked, bewildered.

"Doesn't it relieve you—just a bit—to look across a field and say with certainty 'that is the enemy. That is who we must fight and kill?'" Tremblay asked. "Like pulling a bandage off. No more lies, no more pretense. No more 'peace is our profession' bullshit." He held his hands apart from one another illustrating his point. "Us and them. It's primal, a throwback to the days of hunting and gathering."

"Primal," Gates repeated, recalling an old song. "Two Tribes."

"Exactly," Tremblay said, apparently unfamiliar with the Frankie Goes to Hollywood single. "It's more sincere. We're finally doing what we were meant to do."

"I'd just as soon rather we didn't have to," Gates replied coolly.

Tremblay shrugged. "Warfare is just politics. It's just more honest."

Gates wasn't sure how to respond to that. "Honest or not, it's cost me a lot of good men."

"Me too," Tremblay said. "And that bill's not fully paid yet. We'll be watering the sand with blood soon and we've got a hell of a lot more to spill to end this thing."

The briefing they'd just come from had made the scale of their task clear: blunt the Soviet-Iraqi attack and start turning it back. Ankara must be held. Gates knew Tremblay was right, there was a butcher's bill waiting to be paid here. "We can't win soon enough," Gates said at last.

***

23

Yessov's daring attack on the anchored transports at Izmir had come just before an equally harrowing escape from NATO's search net. That close to the coast his only saving grace was the innumerable islands and channels to slip through, evading NATO patrols. As usual, he survived by doing what the enemy would not expect. Rather than fleeing west, back to the deeper waters of the Aegean, he moved north, passing between the Greek island of Lesvos and the Turkish coast separated by scarcely six miles of water at the narrowest point. It was virtually unpatrolled. Only a mad man would take this route and now Yessov was putting it behind him.

"Ahead three quarters."

"Yes, Comrade Captain, three quarters."

The *Akula*'s screws revved as the submarine's onboard nuclear reactor fed more power to the main drive. The cost of more noise was traded for the safety of depth. The continental shelf fell away here and they filled their ballast tanks, plunging deeper into the safety of the Aegean Sea.

Yessov took a sip of tea, swishing the tepid liquid around in his mouth before swallowing with a wince at its bitterness. Circling the helm, he came to peer down at the navigational plot, currently overlaid with a map of the seafloor here.

"Helm, set bearing to 320 and maintain depth. Keep us beneath the Layer."

"Yes, Comrade Captain."

"Toward Limnos?" Lieutenant Voloshin, standing opposite him, asked.

Yessov looked across the map to his XO and frowned. He

hated to explain his reasoning to anyone, even his second in command. "We won't get close to the island," Yessov explained. "This course takes us across the mouth of the Dardanelles. More traffic."

"More chances of being detected," Voloshin countered.

Yessov set down his teacup and leaned forward on the map plot, staring into Voloshin's eyes unhappily. "Yes? Perhaps you would feel safer if we let you stay back in Syria, Comrade." He saw a muscle in Voloshin's cheek twitch, but the officer was otherwise silent. "Our business is not about safety but danger. Hunting and killing."

"Hunting and killing go both ways," Voloshin said, his voice tight, restrained. "I would prefer to end this war alive."

Yessov grinned. "How many men do you think go to their deaths trying to be careful?"

"Fewer than who go being impudent."

Voloshin's retort was so unexpected that Yessov at first thought he'd imagined it. When reality settled on him, his face flushed red, jaw clenched tight, restraining an unseemly outburst of emotion. With a mental count to three, he fought down anger and maintained cool. The rest of the crew on the cramped bridge pretended to be otherwise preoccupied with their work. "What then," Yessov said finally, "would you have us do, Comrade Lieutenant?"

Voloshin struggled to answer for a moment. "I believe we must choose our targets with utmost care, Captain. This vessel is more valuable to the Party if it survives to fight. If we burn out, then NATO can simply reposition military assets from here to other theaters. There cannot be many Soviet warships left in the Mediterranean."

Yessov's tight grin slipped into a scowl again. He hated more than anything that Voloshin's answer made sense.

"We will pass across the shipping lanes," Yessov said. "Strike what we can and then—"

"Comrade Captain, contacts on sonar."

Yessov and Voloshin turned as one, watching as the tactical

plot was updated with the fresh signatures. He did not have time
to ask for details before they were given to him.

"Two surface signatures, I believe they are MEKO 200-type,
and—" the sonar operator screwed his face in concentration.
"Possibly a third contact underwater. There is too much noise."

MEKO 200, a German export frigate. It meant they could be
Turkish or Greek patrol vessels.

"Helm, ahead slow," Yessov said.

"Range? Heading?" Voloshin asked.

Sonar shook his head. "I cannot be sure. I think we are getting
echo off the seafloor." He looked up at Yessov apologetically. "I
am sorry, Comrade."

"Don't be sorry," Yessov shot back, "get me the information I
need!"

"What are they doing, you think?" Voloshin asked, standing
beside Yessov as they watched the tactical plot updated as more
information gradually came in. Both warships were advancing
line abreast, pulsing active sonar ahead of them and traveling
slowly.

"Hunting," Yessov said, rubbing his chin. The question was
"what?"

"Surface splashes ten kilometers out," Sonar said. "Maybe
torpedoes. Yes!" He pressed his headphones tighter. "Active
pinging ten kilometers out."

Yessov's stomach tightened as he imagined that whatever
they were hunting, it was one of theirs.

"New contact, screws going to flank."

"What is it?"

Sonar didn't need to consult his waterfall display; he knew
this one well enough. "Kilo-Class. One of ours, Captain."

They hardly had time to process that information when a
muffled thump echoed through the hull of their submarine.

"Undersea explosion...transients...," Sonar said, looking back
at Yessov who did not meet his gaze. "He is finished, Comrade
Captain."

"Less chance of striking a comrade then," Yessov said.

"Weapons, flood tubes one and three. Helm, rudder port."

"Yes, Captain, rudder port."

"Tubes flooded."

"Set target on those frigates—"

"Captain," Voloshin stepped between Yessov and Weapons, his expression urgent. "Perhaps we had better wait for a better target."

Yessov brushed him aside. "Target frigates and fire both tubes!"

The weapons officer glanced uncomfortably between Yessov and Voloshin who looked away. "Yes, Comrade Captain."

No sooner had they fired than both frigates accelerated and changed direction, zig zagging away.

"Evading us," Voloshin said.

Yessov shook his head. "Impossible! They are too far out to have heard our launch." The torpedoes hadn't even begun to actively ping. "Unless—"

Unless an ASW helicopter was hovering silently overhead, listening to them with a dipping sonar and calling a fresh target back to the parent vessels.

"Emergency dive!" Yessov said. "Deploy noisemaker and take us to flank speed."

Helm looked back at him incredulously. "Flank—?"

"*Dive*, you fool!" Yessov barked.

The submarine pitched down, sinking as its screw revved up to top speed a minute before Sonar called. "Surface splash overhead! Torpedo is pinging!"

"The bastards have us!" Yessov snarled, gripping a pipe for stability as the deck shifted beneath his feet.

The hull groaned in protest as pressure rapidly mounted.

"Distance to torpedo two hundred meters!"

The *Akula* shuddered as the torpedo found the turbulent water around the noisemaker and detonated.

"Hard to port," Yessov said. "Keep diving."

The *Akula* raced for the seafloor as another surface splash above them heralded another torpedo. They could outdive it.

The *Akula*'s crush depth was greater than that of the NATO Mark 46 torpedo, but only just barely. They could outdive it if they could outrun it. They had a head start but the torpedo was faster.

Yessov heard the weapon's sonar pinging through the hull of his submarine, growing steadily louder like the heartbeat of an electronic predator.

"Torpedo closing."

"Deploy noisemaker," Yessov said, biting his lip anxiously and staring only at the depth gauge. He knew it wouldn't matter; the torpedo had a firm fix on them now.

"Descending past four hundred meters," Helm said, his voice quavering with fear.

"Torpedo at two hundred and closing."

"Four hundred and fifty meters...."

Almost. They had to make it past seven hundred meters. The *Akula*'s screws chopped the water, straining to force the submarine deeper and deeper. Six hundred meters was the *Akula*'s test depth but in theory it could go all the way down to eight hundred.

In theory.

Yessov was counting on that being a conservative estimate.

"Torpedo at three hundred meters."

"Clearing five hundred fifty meters."

"We won't make it," Voloshin blurted.

"Quiet!" Yessov snapped, sweat beading on his forehead.

"Six hundred meters!" Helm shouted, nerves getting the better of him. The hull groaned like a wounded beast.

The entire crew now heard the whine of the torpedo closing on them as it passed the five-hundred-meter mark.

"Six hundred fifty...."

Yessov closed his eyes. There was nothing more he could do.

The torpedo exploded, the shockwave battering K-461, slewing the submarine and throwing the bridge crew into their consoles, or in Yessov's case, off his feet. He landed hard on the deck and rolled over with a groan. He was back on his feet in an instant. "Damage report!?"

"My God, we're alive!" Helm said.

Yessov got back to his feet and noted with satisfaction that water wasn't spraying catastrophically into the bridge. They'd survived. "All stop. Set depth to seven hundred and fifty meters." That, he hoped, was beyond reach of any of NATO's weapons. He shuddered to imagine the tremendous distance now between them and the surface.

"All compartments intact," Voloshin said. "There may have been damage to the screws but we can't be sure of that until we try to take him to flank again."

Yessov nodded and looked around at his crew, who met his gaze with expressions of mixed shock, elation, and fear. They'd survived. Somehow. No, not somehow. Because of him. He smiled proudly back at his crew. "Very good."

When he met Voloshin's gaze he saw a silent reprimand in his eyes. His XO had warned him about being rash.

Yessov thought about what Voloshin said, about staying alive. Perhaps it *was* better to fight on another day. "Hold depth. I want a full maintenance check on the sub before we leave this place." He looked back at his Voloshin. "There is no sense rushing back into danger without being sure that everything is in working order."

Voloshin masked his frustration well, but not perfectly. Yessov saw it clearly enough. They'd been lucky here, that was why they were alive. The lieutenant saluted. "Right away, Captain."

Yessov relaxed his shoulders slightly, willing his heart to beat slower. He wasn't a master of the sea here, he was as much prey as predator. He'd have to remember that if he was going to continue his mission.

***

24

The Canadians advanced northeast, racing along the D300 highway as the flat, dry landscape rolled by them. Perched atop the M113 armored personnel carriers, Heathcliff and the rest of his platoon had a good view out over the countryside. The Canadians' motley mix of woodland and desert camouflage seemed particularly out of place against the green plain. The sky bled in the dying light of the late afternoon, painting the grasslands and sandy soil in fiery reds. The sandiness gave Heathcliff hope that he would be glad for the desert tans he wore later.

"Kinda reminds me of Saskatchewan," Private Abernathy said to no one in particular. He had to speak up over the rush of wind and rattle of treads.

Heathcliff couldn't disagree. It was flat, flatter than a pancake. The only landmarks of note were the telephone poles and power lines which lined the roads with military precision, the occasional shed or farmhouse, and a conical, snow-capped mountain peak rising ghost-like from the horizon to the south, its base lost in a distant haze.

They'd seen a variety of terrain since arriving at Izmir from the rolling Mediterranean scrub of the coast to the rocky hills dotted with spruce and fir trees surrounding their assembly point at Konya, which put Heathcliff in mind of the American west. He wondered if any old cowboy movies were ever filmed out this way. Now they were into the flat interior. Perfect tank country, he mused, not wonderful ground for infantry.

Scenic or not, Heathcliff couldn't enjoy the view, he was keeping his neck craned, searching for the enemy. He and

Driscoll, along with the other officers in their company, had been briefed on what they were up against before setting out.

The Canadian brigade was the vanguard of the spoiling attack they were launching straight into the jaws of the Soviet-Arab attack. The idea was that a sharp counterattack would throw the enemy off balance and may even give them a chance of securing the highway interchange at Aksaray, thus securing the southern approaches to Ankara.

They had fairly accurate intelligence on the positioning of the enemy forces approaching, forwarded on to them courtesy of the aircraft patrols from the American carrier *San Juan Hill*. They knew the enemy was ahead of them, but their rate of advance did not suggest haste. Although, as Driscoll and the other officers were quick to point out, that could change quickly. The Soviets favored lightning speed, their movements in Europe illustrated that perfectly. Why they should be so slow here wasn't clear.

It had been days since they'd been plunged into the Mediterranean Sea courtesy of a Soviet torpedo. In the aftermath of that disaster, they'd lost a good number of their vehicles, not to mention the human cost. Heathcliff's company had been lucky; so far as he knew they didn't lose anyone. Another company they'd shared the transport with had been decimated. There was no time to mourn, and no time to delay. War didn't wait.

Now out of the confines of the coastal hills and onto the open plains, the scale of the NATO forces here became clearer. Looking left and right, Heathcliff saw tanks and APCs advancing, throwing huge clouds of dust behind them. Ahead of them, advanced recon units raced on toward their objective ahead.

The M113s rode along the main highway, avoiding the low, sandy fields that lined the road.

"Contact ahead," the M113 commander who sat unbuttoned in the commander's cupola told Heathcliff, listening intently to his radio headset pressed tight over his ears. "A town. Yapılcan."

A foreign name for a foreign place, soon to be a battleground.

Heathcliff nodded and checked that his magazine was full and locked in place.

Minutes later machine gun fire ripped out ahead, breaking the uneasy monotony.

The Canadians perked up as one, ready to spring into action. The gunfire had been relatively close, but it wasn't directed at them. Soon it was joined by more.

The M113 commander ducked lower in his hatch, eyes fixed on the town ahead. He spoke into his headset microphone and, at his word, the APC veered off the road with a squeal and clatter of tracks. It joined the others in the platoon as they fanned out, trading the highway for the soft farmland around them, chewing parallel ruts toward Yapılcan.

Heathcliff yanked back the bolt on his rifle, feeding a round into the chamber. "Looks like they're going to make us work for it today, guys," he said.

Heathcliff clung to the metal hide of the M113, feeling his heart beating slow and steady as the town of Yapılcan grew larger. Boxy beige buildings with dull red roofs poked from amongst sporadic scrub. It was the only cover to speak of for miles around, so if the enemy managed to contest their advance things could get bloody quickly. Finally, the APC shuddered to a halt at the edge of a construction yard scattered with old work trucks and cement drainage pipes.

"Let's go!" Heathcliff called, leaping off and landing on the soft ground, knees absorbing the impact. He sprung back to his feet and dashed a few dozen meters to one of the man-sized cement pipes and threw himself down behind it, sighting his rifle toward the town ahead as the others joined him, each man a few meters apart. Heathcliff looked back in time to see Lieutenant Driscoll crouch walk into cover beside him.

The lieutenant adjusted his helmet, catching his breath as he stood up to peer out over the pipe. Heathcliff watched a platoon of Leopard 1 main battle tanks roaring forward, past his platoon, still traveling along the highway which bypassed the town. The sounds of gunfire only grew more intense around Yapılcan and was soon joined by the whistle of mortar fire.

"Sounds like the enemy got here first," Driscoll said. "Let's move up. Keep low, wide dispersion. Heathcliff, can you take Dupont's men on our right?"

"Sir," Heathcliff said.

"That road there," Driscoll pointed ahead. "The one perpendicular to the highway."

"I see it," Heathcliff returned.

"We'll move up to the roadbed. We can lay cover fire for the advance on the town."

It was scant cover, but the best the area offered. It would have to do.

"Say when," Heathcliff said.

"When." Driscoll slapped his back. "Hop to it!"

"Dupont? Let's move," Heathcliff said, rising to his feet.

"*Oui.* Okay, *allons y*! Go!" Dupont said.

The Canadians rose up and moved forward as fast as they could, while staying in a low crouch to avoid sticking out as they crossed the open field toward the road. Men moved in leapfrogging dashes, pausing at parked trucks and other scattered construction equipment to cover one another's advances as they drew steadily closer to their destination. Each step was painful. Heathcliff was terrifyingly aware of how vulnerable they were here.

He led the way and reached the road embankment first, throwing himself down in the dust. Dupont crawled up beside him, the others fanned out across the road edge.

Finally, the platoon reached the roadbed, crawling to the edge of the road and sighting their weapons across it. Heathcliff caught his breath and looked around, ensuring that his men were in position.

The nearby Leopard tank platoon halted in a line and fired a volley of shells into the town with thunderous booms. Masonry crumbled and wood frames burned while the tanks adjusted fire, demolishing any structures which seemed to harbor the enemy.

Heathcliff craned his neck, looking down the line to see

Driscoll. They were in a bad spot here and couldn't remain long.

"Do we move?" Dupont asked, half-rising to his feet.

Stuttering gunfire sent them all ducking back, automatic fire sweeping across the highway as an unseen Iraqi machine gun position bracketed them.

Heathcliff slid further back behind the road embankment, feeling more exposed than ever. If the enemy adjusted some mortar fire this way, they were finished.

He didn't need to worry.

The Leopards spoke again and the apartment building firing on them erupted with staggered explosions before sagging and collapsing in a shower of cement blocks and brick.

Off to his left, Driscoll rose to his knees, waving to catch Heathcliff's attention.

"Dupont, Heathcliff, take your men forward!" Driscoll called.

Heathcliff flashed a thumbs up and turned to Dupont. "Sergeant, cover fire."

"Where?"

"Everywhere, just hit them!"

"Cover fire!" Dupont shouted and began firing bursts indiscriminately into town.

"Mandeville, Harper, on me!" Heathcliff called, rising to his feet and clambering over the lip of the embankment and dashing across the highway, his boots throwing loose pebbles of asphalt as he ran.

The two privates followed hot on his heels before he reached the other side and slid down into the relative cover of the weeds. Moving forward again, they found a low cinderblock wall framing out a backyard and sheltered there.

"Dupont, move up!" Heathcliff shouted back, voice cracking to be heard over the ringing in his ears. When he turned back around, he saw a flash of movement in a window of the apartment building overlooking them. He didn't hesitate. He shouldered his rifle and unloaded half a magazine into the open window.

A panicked burst of return fire cut back, snapping overhead

before the shooter was hit and flopped lifelessly back into the building.

"Shooters!" Heathcliff shouted. "They're in this apartment, watch it!"

Dupont's section maneuvered to cover the approaches to the building, watching the windows carefully.

Heathcliff's pulse raced as he likewise circled in, inching along the cinderblock wall, creeping closer to an alleyway and a visible side door. He hardly noticed the roar of the Leopard's engines as they advanced or the bursts of gunfire elsewhere in town. All his focus was laser honed on that doorway and his finger hooked around the trigger.

The door flew open and a man in a foreign uniform burst out, boots skidding on the pavement.

Heathcliff cut him down with a burst of rifle fire.

A second man, carried by momentum, fell out of the doorway, trying frantically to turn on the threat.

Another burst ended him. The soldier—an Iraqi in khaki and tan—flopped dead, his helmet striking the pavement with an almost-comical metallic "bonk."

"Surrender!" A voice called from the doorway, speaker unseen. "Do not shoot! Surrender!"

Heathcliff kept his sights on the doorway, heart pounding in his chest. "Come out!" He called. "Hands up! Throw out your weapon!"

Somehow the enemy soldier made sense of Heathcliff's commands. A Kalashnikov clattered out of the doorway followed by a helmet.

"Come out!" Heathcliff roared again, sweat beading on his forehead.

A young man in Iraqi khakis stepped out, hands held nervously aloft, eyes wide with terror. "Surrender!" He repeated. "Surrender!"

"On your knees!" Heathcliff gestured with his rifle and the Iraqi complied, looking equally exhausted and relieved.

"Mandeville, check him."

The private bounded forward and shoved the Iraqi onto his face with an excess of force as he quickly patted him down. Once he was confirmed unarmed and his hands securely zip-tied behind his back, Heathcliff allowed himself to relax. He crouched beside the Arab. "How many more?" He asked, pointing toward the apartment.

The Iraqi sputtered something unintelligible.

"Soldiers?" Heathcliff tried. "Friends? Surrender?"

The Iraqi shook his head.

"Well?" Dupont asked, arriving on scene.

"Either he doesn't know or the answer is 'no.' Either way, I'm not taking chances. Smoke the place."

"*Oui*. Parker!" Dupont called another soldier and the two of them set to work throwing live grenades in through the building's open windows, each blast shredding a room. Working methodically, they left the building uninhabitable in short order.

The sounds of battle were fading north. The Iraqis were already in retreat. Heathcliff intended to keep it that way. "Alright, check mags and let's move out! We'll link back up with the rest of the platoon. Let's go."

"*Allons y!*"

***

25

Moscow—like any sufficiently large city—never truly slept. Even a strictly enforced military curfew could only limit the nightlife of the city so much. The staff of the Soviet Foreign Ministry knew that better than most. While many others were sitting down to dinner in their flats, a select few labored on in the Stalinist high-rise, working past the death of daylight.

Gradenko paused his own typing to look up at the small black and white television perched beside the desk he sat at. A monotone TV anchor reported the news as it was given to him, reading the script dryly. The American election was over and Dewitt—Bayern's hand-picked successor—had won. There went hopes for Gradenko's easy diplomatic win, though he doubted that Nelson would have been as pliable as he had hoped. Even America's left-wing seemed to support the continuation of the war, at least for now.

The planned naval victory in the Norwegian Sea had become a disaster. What had been intended to shake American resolve for victory only strengthened it. The better part of twenty years of Soviet naval buildup was wrecked or sent to the bottom of the ocean in mere days.

"The introduction of a new conscription act from Bayern's regime in Washington is a further sign of crumbling American military infrastructure. With the American public deeply dissatisfied with the war and moral plummeting, the American government has implemented mandatory military service which was last in effect during their failed occupation of Vietnam," the news anchor continued dispassionately, accompanied by footage of Bayern solemnly signing the act into law, inducting a fresh wave of soldiers into their army.

It was insult to injury and Gradenko shuddered to imagine the long term ramifications of this. What clearer sign was there that America intended to see this war to its conclusion?

"They've been fighting this war with one hand tied behind their backs...," Gradenko said to himself.

The Soviet Union was inducting more and more of its young men to throw into the meat grinder, fresh waves of conscripts to bolster flagging lines in Germany, Scandinavia, and now Turkey and the Balkans. They were stretched very near to the breaking point already and America had only just begun its own draft.

"Comrade Minister," the deputy minister's voice drew Gradenko's attention from the TV playing in the background and back to the work at hand. "Were these for the Hungarians or the Bulgarians?" He held a stack of hand-typed booklets.

"Bulgarian," Gradenko said, squinting at the foreign text. "I think. Check with Sergei. He reads it, I don't."

"Yes, Comrade." The deputy minister—the same one who had so valiantly tried to protest the declaration of war on Sweden— was subdued but focused, like all of the small group of trusted staff here hard at work.

The operation Gradenko oversaw in the Foreign Ministry's bullpen was absolutely unsanctioned and—strictly speaking— deeply treasonous. It was for this reason he had only included the bare minimum of personnel—men and women he could trust.

Gradenko looked about himself at the handful of clerks and deputies transcribing hand-written sheets of paper using a battery of typewriters. The sheets were Gradenko's own original writings being rapidly translated by a quartet of harried interpreters converting his thoughts into German, Czech, Slovakian, Hungarian, Polish, Romanian, and Bulgarian.

They were *Samizdat*. Illegally produced subversive written material. Gradenko wrote each one mirroring the style he remembered from his youth, the booklets and amateur magazines passed around by dissidents. They ranged in topic from overt criticism of the Soviet Union to simply being amateur translations of unsanctioned works. It was through *Samizdat* that Gradenko had first read *the Lord of the Rings* as a young man. Now he used the same medium for a different purpose.

The *Samizdat* he wrote told stories of hardship and suffering, misery and pain. He wrote of brave young men of the Eastern Bloc herded to their deaths by uncaring Russian overlords, Soviet masterminds callously sucking the life from their so-called "fraternal allies." These brutal accounts were intermixed with stories of hardships back in their home countries, conscription, shortages, mercilessly suppressed riots. Some were real, others were fanciful, the products of Gradenko's mind. Each was engineered to elicit the response he sought. Fury. Anger. Blind, seething rage. The kind of anger that drives men to the streets. The kind of anger that swept through Berlin in 1953, Budapest in 1956, and Warsaw in 1989, regime-ending anger.

"Here," Gradenko said, pulling a sheet from his typewriter. "Irina, can you make this Polish?"

The translator leaned from her desk beside Gradenko and took the sheet, scanning it over before adjusting her glasses. "Without difficulty, Comrade." It was a lie. She was exhausted, her eyes red and shadowed with fatigue. They had all been at this for hours. But once started they had to see it to completion, the longer this took place the more risk there was of being discovered.

This whole operation was carried out right under Karamazov's nose. After all, who would suspect treason on this scale from within the Foreign Ministry's halls?

The fact that Dragomirov was on their side was little comfort. Certainly his control over the KGB wasn't absolute. Karamazov had allies everywhere. They simply could not allow themselves to be discovered. Gradenko had told no one of this operation. Not Tarasov, not Dragomirov, not even his son. Total secrecy would be required. Only the promise that this activity would ultimately lead to peace motivated his trusted circle.

The door opened and everyone looked up, tense, only to relax at the familiar sight of Rurik, his motorcycle helmet under his arm, goggles on his forehead. "Done," he said tiredly.

"Another batch," Gradenko's deputy minister told him, gesturing to a twine-bound stack of *Samizdat*. "For the Bulgarians. You know the drop off location?"

Rurik, a bold young man with more bravery than a file clerk ought to possess, sighed but nodded. Rurik, in addition to youthful bravery, possessed a Riga Delta moped and so worked the job of delivering the contraband materials by hand. He shuttled from workers' barracks to collective farm to flat block and back to the office for more. If he were to be caught, it would likely be the end of his life, but he toiled on. "Hand them to me, Comrade," Rurik said, pulling his goggles back down, "and I will be back in a flash."

Gradenko was particularly proud of his Hungarian writing. It centered around the establishment of a Hungarian military draft. After their failed uprising in '56, the Hungarians had had their military burden eased. Now, with the rumor that it would be imposed upon them again, he hoped to stir their hearts to the same violence they had exercised in their uprising.

Rurik took the stack and was off again on his odyssey.

Almost the instant the doors closed behind him, one of the phones rang, that of Gradenko's secretary.

The work stopped and all eyes went to the phone anxiously. Gradenko's secretary wasn't working, she wasn't among his trusted employees, so he crossed the room and answered himself. "Gradenko."

"Comrade, let's meet for drinks." It was Tarasov.

"It isn't a good time," Gradenko replied calmly. "I am up to my eyeballs in paperwork."

"It never is a good time," Tarasov replied. "And yet there is always something to celebrate. I have good news and I have need of your special skills. I can have my driver meet you."

Gradenko glanced at his own driver, currently at work bundling stacks of *Samizdat*. "No need," Gradenko said. "I have mine. I will come to you."

"My office," Tarasov said. "In Moscow."

Gradenko was grateful not to have to descend into the ghoulish subterranean city. "I will be there shortly." He hung up the phone and stared at it for a moment, lost in thought, before returning to the open office floor where his co-conspirators were still hard at work on their treason.

"Comrades," Gradenko said, holding up his hands for attention.

They looked up from their work, typewriters falling silent, the shuffle of paper ceasing. There was a painful hope in their eyes, one which Gradenko was afraid of failing. None of them were fools, each understood the risks here and each understood the benefits. They were more than his co-workers, more than friends. They had shared in his suffering. Gradenko wasn't the only one among them to have a family fallen afoul of the KGB, disappeared into Lubyanka or Siberia. They'd lost their own loved ones to the state security. People who desired nothing more than peace, prosperity, and freedom, consigned to confinement.

Others had family and friends called up by the draft, sent to the killing fields of Germany, the frigid gravelands of Sweden and Norway, or lost in the desolate Turkish hills. For what?

"Comrades," he said again, this time with the truest meaning behind the word. "It is time for us to go home and place our faith in our work. I cannot thank each of you half as much as you deserve. I can only promise that when all of this horrible nightmare is behind us, you will be properly recognized for what you've done here. This is the first step in a fight which will return us to normalcy. Each of you deserves more than I can give you at this moment, so I will only offer you this: return home to your families and be safe. The plan will be set in motion soon. I cannot say when, but soon." He fell silent, ensuring they understood the gravity of his words. "You must speak to no one else about this. Trust no one. Any word, any single word could be enough to destroy everything. Look among yourselves, comrades, remember these faces. Remember whose trust you hold and who stands to suffer if you betray that trust."

His fellow revolutionaries looked among themselves, perhaps wondering if this would be their last time meeting.

"Go home," Gradenko repeated. "And leave the rest to me."

***

Arbatskaya Square and the General Staff building where the defense ministry headquarters was only a few minutes away from the foreign ministry. The trip was made shorter by the lack of traffic due to the curfew. Gradenko's credentials got him access to the headquarters and, as usual, Gradenko was struck by how hideous the building was. Far from the elegance of Tsarist architecture, the General Staff building was a cubic, soulless thing. The squared building was dotted with square windows and otherwise nearly featureless.

Lack of aesthetic care was the least of his concerns. He passed the security checks with little hassle and was at last admitted to Tarasov's office. Gradenko couldn't recall ever visiting it before and was somewhat surprised to discover that the wood-paneled room was well-furnished and decorated. A broad window framed by velvet curtains looked out on the empty streets, on the other wall a heavy wooden desk penned Tarasov in. Above and behind the desk was a large oil painting of Georgy Zhukov, hero of the Great Patriotic War and former defense minister himself.

"Please, Comrade, come and sit," Tarasov said, indicating a plush chair facing his desk.

As Gradenko crossed the room, he couldn't help but note a display of memorabilia on a credenza set against the wall. A pair of (presumably deactivated) Soviet-made stick grenades sat beside a well-lacquered PPSH submachine gun propped up by its iconic drum magazine.

Also on the credenza were a number of framed photographs, the most interesting of which showed Tarasov as he had been during the Great Patriotic War. It was a photo of a group of soldiers carrying submachine guns and belts of grenades posing beside a burned-out German halftrack on the edge of some Belarussian village.

Hanging above the credenza was a threadbare crimson Soviet banner stitched with a slogan. "Forward to Berlin!"

Gradenko passed by all of this without comment and took a seat opposite Tarasov.

"You may speak freely," Tarasov said, producing a bottle of vodka and two glasses from beneath his desk. "My people have swept this room thoroughly." He sat the glasses down and poured two heaping shots. "Karamazov in all his arrogance considers me beaten. Filed away."

Gradenko had to take Tarasov at his word. He took a glass in his hand. "Health," he said.

Tarasov echoed the toast and they both downed the vodka in one gulp. No sooner had Gradenko set his empty glass down than Tarasov was pouring a second set of shots.

"I have secured the cooperation of General Strelnikov," Tarasov said.

"Strelnikov?" Gradenko repeated, surprised he recognized the name. "The one who took Zagreb and broke through at Metz?"

"The same," Tarasov said, swallowing his second shot, eyes watering. "A good man. A soldier. Loyal. He commands the forces that will march in the October Revolution Parade and is quite popular within the army and the population at large as I understand it. A hero of the Soviet Union. His men will be the ones who ensure Karamazov is removed."

"And he can be trusted?" Gradenko asked.

"Loyal," Tarasov repeated. "He can be trusted unto death."

"That is the good news then?"

Tarasov nodded and studied his empty glass, seeming to consider a third shot. "When can we expect the uprising to begin? It will be impossible to move forward before that point."

Gradenko could only shrug. "Men are not machines. I have given no timetables. All I can say is 'hopefully soon.' Perhaps sometime after the October Revolution parade. We can scale up rhetoric and calls for action then."

Tarasov took all this in with impassive nods. "There is also more ordinary business to consider." He leaned back in his chair which squeaked dangerously.

"The Navy, eager to avenge their humiliation in the Norwegian Sea, has proposed a solution to the stalemate in Turkey, but there is a political angle."

"There always is," Gradenko replied. "What this time?"

"Two regiments of naval infantry and proper fire support stand ready to land and attack Istanbul," Tarasov said. "They will be supporting a renewed Bulgaro-Romanian offensive, backed with a fresh tank division sent in from the Far East."

"Two regiments?" Gradenko wasn't a soldier but— "Will that be enough to take the city?"

Tarasov shrugged. "It is hard to say. With the intervention of our Arabic comrades, the Turks have had to transfer forces East. They're stretched thin, but if the Turks make a fight for it, a city like Istanbul can soak up a whole army if we let it."

"What then?" Gradenko asks. "Where does my department fit in this?"

"The Turks must abandon Istanbul," Tarasov said plainly. "They must be made to see what will happen if they don't. The operation will proceed in twenty-four hours, whether they agree to cooperate or not."

"And you want them to surrender the city without a shot?" Gradenko asked.

Tarasov nodded, his jowls jiggling. "Like Paris to the Nazis. Make them understand what will happen if they make us fight for it."

That wouldn't be an issue. There were plenty of ruined cities in Germany that would illustrate that point well. Istanbul was a vital strategic point. The question then would be if the Turks were willing to burn the jewel of their crown to spite their enemy.

Gradenko didn't believe they were. "I will call a meeting with the Turkish ambassador straight away," Gradenko said. "I have back-channel access through Austria." He hated to play the part of a bully, but if threats spared the city from destruction and advanced the Soviet cause, then a bully he would be.

"Good," Tarasov said. "Then that is all." He poured himself a third drink and laughed. "Istanbul. Constantinople. Tsargrad." His laughter came again, loosened by the alcohol. "At last."

***

Held in reserve just for this moment, the Soviet Black Sea naval infantry brigade unleashed its wrath upon the tranquil shoreline north of Istanbul, their target: a village named Ağaçlı.

The rolling yellow sands, once a haven for fishermen and lovers alike now oversaw an armada of war. Steep, scrubby hills dotted with concealed Turkish defense positions stood silently ready in the dim early-morning light.

The first notes of this new invasion were the booms of explosions followed by the echoing howl and whines of trans-sonic cruise missiles as they obliterated Turkish fighting positions. Mere minutes later, the calm waters of the Black Sea were dotted with hovercraft and landing ships as they closed in, deploying the brigade to the nearly undefended shore.

Missile trails streaked across the sky overhead before arcing down further south, detonating across Istanbul Airport with reckless disregard for civilian casualties.

Off the coast of Ağaçlı, the lead landing hovercraft cut the waves before hauling themselves ashore with a roar of turbofans, disgorging infantry and armor. Amphibious APCs and light tanks followed in their wakes, wading ashore to drive inland. Where they met resistance it was swiftly crushed.

With their lines both east and west stretched thin, the Turkish army did not have enough left to defend every inch of their extensive shoreline. Now they were paying the price.

Helicopter gunships cut the air overhead, racing by, rotors roaring, as they prowled for targets. The staccato rhythm of gunfire echoed across the hills as they struck down feeble attempts by the overwhelmed Turkish defenders to mount a counterattack.

No sooner had the lead elements of the naval infantry cleared the beach than mobile SAM sites sprang into action, forming a protective shield against any possible NATO airstrike on this toehold. Offshore, the ships of the Black Sea Fleet held steadfast, their guns and missiles trained on the horizon, overlooking the landing.

Within hours the beach was the rear area, and the first battalions of the naval brigade were driving inland across rolling countryside toward the suburbs of Istanbul—a blade poised to sever the sinews that bound European Turkey to Anatolia. If the Turks chose to defend the city, it would be to that ancient place's detriment. A city which had survived crusades would be rendered to dust and ash by modern firepower. The choice was simple, one which had been offered to Turks by ancient conquerors in the past: submit or burn.

**

26

The dawn sun shone golden and bright behind the Soviet column coming down out of the hills. Far to his left, alone, a snow-capped mountain rose at the edge of the plains. Lieutenant Colonel Nabiyev watched the rolling hills fall away as they came within sight of Aksaray. The city sprawled before them, wholly visible as his regiment crested a hill and carried on down the highway. It seemed to stretch all the way to the far horizon, an impressive vista. Smoke curled up across the city, combat between the Iraqis and scattered Turkish forces. Despite this, Aksaray had been given up without a fight, much like Istanbul, Nabiyev thought, if the news was to be believed.

Nabiyev kept his dust goggles down, protecting his eyes from the cold air whipping by as the BTR rumbled at top speed toward the city, joining with the rest of Novikov's division. For all the elation he felt at seeing another enemy city conquered, he also felt frustration.

The Iraqis had stopped again and Nabiyev could do nothing but clench his fists in impotent rage. That they could stop their advance at all, let alone *again*, blinded him with fury.

The highway was lined with idling vehicles, a confused mix of Soviet and Iraqi trucks and armored vehicles, the lead elements of Soviet forces tangled with strung out Republican Guard logistics.

Nabiyev listened closely to the divisional radio band, hungrily seizing on any scraps of information he could get about the broader tactical picture. The Iraqis were supposed to be wheeling and driving on Ankara, the Turkish capital only 200 kilometers northwest. Centrally located, it was a prize beyond compare, not just for the obvious political ramifications but for operational ones as well. With Ankara in their control, they could choose their next thrust at their leisure. North to the Black Sea coast to trap yet more outflanked Turkish defenders? West toward the Aegean Sea? South to the port of Antalya? Turkey was coming apart at the seams. All that was necessary was speed, something the Iraqis seemed to lack.

Nabiyev's radio crackled, carrying Abramov's voice. "And what is the reason they have stopped this time? They can't possibly be lost."

Sighing, Nabiyev toggled his own radio on. "Your guess is as good as mine. I have yet heard nothing from the Iraqis or from General Novikov." He could have relayed this question through Colonel Davydov, but he doubted he'd get a clear answer and had no real desire to speak with the man.

Nabiyev passed a platoon of Iraqi tanks parked on the side of the highway outside Aksaray, eyeing them warily. For all that he'd heard of the "battle hardened" Iraqis, they seemed nearly useless to him, incapable of maintaining a simple advance against minor opposition. With the Turkish army forces here outnumbered, any set piece battle inevitably resulted in the defenders being outflanked or overwhelmed. So instead, they'd settled on a strategy of hit and run attacks, striking at long distance and then quickly falling back before the Iraqis could drive them off. When the Republican Guard had started ferreting out these raids with attack helicopters, the Turks had started posting SAMs and man-portable anti-air weapons in ambush positions. The result was that the initial race southwest had become a crawl.

"If they advance much slower, the enemy will have completely rebuilt their army by the time they reach Ankara," Abramov said.

Now Baranov chimed in. "They conduct next to no reconnaissance. I have had my flank struck twice by Turkish forces. Such complacency is criminal!"

Nabiyev didn't disagree with his subordinates' assessments, but he could not allow such defeatism to take hold. Like it or not, the Iraqis were their allies. "We will have to ensure we are doing everything in our power to assist and motivate our allies," he said.

"Perhaps a 155-millimeter shell up their backsides will motivate them to advance," Baranov retorted, the radio fuzzing.

"I will speak with General Novikov to try to ascertain the cause of this delay and ensure the column gets moving again," Nabiyev said. "Until that point, maintain vigilance. We're lucky that NATO hasn't yet deployed air assets here." A strung-out armored column in the open doubtlessly made a juicy target for NATO's ground-attack wings. Nabiyev had no desire to see his men become statistics.

"Remind the general that *we* achieved the breakthrough and were ready to exploit it when our *allies* were given precedence over us," Baranov said. Nabiyev thought he detected a slurring to his speech, but it was impossible to tell with the poor quality of the transmission.

Nabiyev didn't deign that with a response, instead he switched to the division frequency. "Nabiyev of the 806th to HQ." Nabiyev counted seconds until he got a reply.

"Headquarters, go ahead."

"The Republican Guard have halted their advance. Repeat, *halted* their advance. What is the cause of this delay?"

Seconds ticked by and Nabiyev was about to repeat the question when General Novikov came over the line. "The report is a Western NATO brigade on their flank. The Iraqis have readjusted their forces to clear the enemy back before advancing on Ankara." His tone was brusque, clearly just as annoyed as Nabiyev and his subordinates were.

A *Western* NATO brigade? The thought chilled Nabiyev's blood. The Turks were stout defenders but stymied by a lack of the most modern NATO gear. The Western NATO powers didn't have such shortcomings. He shuddered to imagine what firepower they may have up their sleeves.

"Affirmative, 806 acknowledge."

"The Republican Guard will drive back the enemy and then the

Iraqi Army will ensure the flank is secure before we continue on to Ankara."

The Iraqi army, Nabiyev noted sourly, made the Republican Guard appear professional and he doubted they were any faster. More delays.

He lifted his goggles to rub his eyes, feeling the sting of the cold air on his cheeks. He longed to reach their rendezvous point beyond this city and dig in for the night in the hills opposite Aksaray. He was desperate to stretch his legs again and free himself from the metal confines of this command vehicle.

He was tired. Everyone was tired.

But they were so close to victory.

Novikov continued, oblivious to Nabiyev's exhaustion. "Take the 806 regiment forward, deploy en echelon west of the city. Once you have reached the former Republican Guard positions, have your men dig in. I won't have us caught in the open."

Nabiyev didn't like the caution he sensed in Novikov's tone. Was there more on their flank than a lone NATO brigade?

"806th acknowledged." Before Novikov could end the transmission Nabiyev blurted a question. "Are we expecting a full enemy counterattack?"

Novikov hesitated before answering. "It may well be."

"And if it is?"

Another pause. "Then we will fight them."

***

27

Peering from the ground floor window of an apartment block on the edge of town, Heathcliff had a clear view of the loose ring of burning Iraqi tanks that surrounded the town of Yapılcan. Haphazard and piecemeal attacks had finally tailed off; it seemed like they were learning they couldn't shift this position without intent. It wasn't a lesson Heathcliff wanted them to learn.

Sliding back from the window, he sat on the bed in this room, glancing around at the interior, casually wondering what sort of person had lived here before they'd—presumably—been sent fleeing west. And, assuming this apartment's owner was still alive somewhere, they were one of the lucky ones.

In the first hours after the Canadians took this place back from the Iraqis, a stream of civilians had fled in whatever vehicles they had on hand. Those who couldn't flee were hunkered down in basements and homes, hoping to ride out what came next.

Sergeant Dupont was preceded by the smell of cigarettes. "Any change, *mon ami*?" He stubbed his cigarette out on the wall and peered outside.

Heathcliff shook his head. "After the last tank push, nothing."

They were both anxious. They'd learned how the Soviets operated and learned what to expect. But the Iraqis were a new element in war. While they were supposed to follow Soviet doctrine, practice often differed from theory.

Heathcliff was only a warrant officer, but he knew enough of the battlefield to know that his platoon and battalion were dangling on a hook right now. The rest of the brigade was further back, leaving him and his man with their necks on a chopping block. He didn't know *why* that was, but he knew enough to know he didn't like it.

"Seen the lieutenant?"

Dupont jerked his head. "Next door."

Heathcliff slung his rifle, patted Dupont on the shoulder, and worked his way out of the apartment. The main living room was strewn with ration wrappers and trash, all the furniture pushed to the walls to provide as much protection as possible. His men had bedded down in buildings like this across town. It was sheer luxury when compared to roughing it in the field like they had in Germany. It was a luxury Heathcliff was trying not to get used to.

Nodding at men as he passed, he left the building and jogged across the street to the opposite apartment block.

It wasn't long before he located Driscoll in an upper-floor hallway, looking out of a window half-blocked by furniture. He lowered his binoculars long enough to recognize Heathcliff.

There wasn't time for a greeting before they heard the howl of incoming artillery.

Soldiers shouted warnings and threw themselves down, under furniture and into cover where they could find it. Moments later the first shellfire walked over the town.

Each detonation sent a bass thump through Heathcliff's guts and shook the building. The tempo increased, shells falling faster and faster until the sound was nearly continuous. Windows shattered and glass sprayed across Heathcliff's back. Only minutes later, the shelling let up enough for Heathcliff to crawl over to Driscoll, close enough that they could hear one another by shouting.

"Enemy counterattack!" Driscoll shouted. "Get me the radio!"

The radio operator crawled to join Heathcliff and Driscoll on the floor by the shattered window.

As Driscoll coordinated with company HQ, Heathcliff risked a look out the window. Rising dust across the horizon made his stomach churn. Driscoll was right, it was a counterattack. A big one.

Rifles and machine guns began to bark and chatter as the Canadians engaged at long range, plinking at the advancing Iraqi vehicles with little apparent effect.

Driscoll grabbed Heathcliff's sleeve to get his attention. "Battalion is drawing back! We're holding the door."

Heathcliff's stomach knotted itself but he nodded, what else could he do?

Nearby Canadian Leopard tanks engaged the Iraqi armor and soon shells were flying back and forth across the open ground to the east. A T-72 exploded, hurling its turret into the sky as all its ammo cooked off at once. Return fire knocked out a Leopard, its crew bailing out to flee on foot into town.

Fresh shellfire came in from the unseen Iraqi artillery, demolishing more buildings and dropping a thick smokescreen over the town, blotting out Heathcliff's view of the enemy.

"Get the platoon back," Driscoll said. "Not safe here anymore."

"Let's go!"

Together they ushered the platoon out of the high rises and onto the streets, falling back through the dense artificial fog toward secondary positions. The midday sun cut strange, twisting patterns in the smoke billowing through the town's streets. The smokescreen swirled into eddies as soldiers dashed through it.

Heathcliff came to rest behind a low cinderblock wall and caught his breath, tasting the metallic smoke in the air. Peering over the top he could faintly see the tops of the few tall structures in town. The apartments they'd abandoned were struck with shellfire, probably from tanks or BMPs and caved in with eruptions of dust and smoke. Shrapnel and splinters perforated a water tower which leaked like a sieve before a support leg buckled and it toppled. Beyond it the skinny minaret of a mosque exploded from a direct hit, raining masonry and dust down on the town. The entire east side of Yapılcan was being systematically demolished by fire.

Movement ahead in the smoke caught Heathcliff's eye.

"Contact!"

A mottled tan and brown BMP-1 emerged at high speed, racing down a narrow street toward them.

A Canadian Carl Gustaf recoilless rifle barked, the shell exploding on the BMP's sloped frontal armor. The round penetrated the BMP's thin armor and blew out the driver's hatch. The BMP slewed off the road and smashed into a storefront, the building collapsing on top of the stricken APC.

A second BMP followed, veering around the first before braking hard. The tracked vehicle rocked forward before lurching to a halt. Iraqi infantry debarked through the rear doors, nearly invisible in the smoke and dust.

"Infantry!" Heathcliff called, shouldering his rifle and firing long bursts into the enemy. He was gratified to see them dropping left and right, caught in the open.

The BMP reversed unexpectedly, its treads flattening the dead and living alike as the Iraqis tried to scramble out of the way. The wails of half-crushed Iraqis echoed in the street.

The Carl G spoke again and de-tracked the enemy APC which juddered to a halt a half-second before it exploded, flames spewing from hatches and igniting a nearby house.

The Iraqi attack was uncoordinated, but it was fierce, and it was substantial. Gunfire echoed out all around them as infantry swarmed the town.

Heathcliff ran down the line, ducking through cover until he found Driscoll shouting into the radio. "Can't stay, sir!" Heathcliff said, shouting over the din.

Driscoll ignored him, focusing on the radio. "-heavily engaged!" He said. "We'll hold as long as we can. Out."

Heathcliff grabbed his arm to get his attention. "Sir! We can't stay!"

Driscoll pulled free, eyes wide with fear and anger. "We hold, Heathcliff! Orders are to hold until the battalion is clear."

Suicide.

Heathcliff bit his lip and looked around at his men firing like wild into the dust and smoke. "No chance." He shook his head.

"No way! They're killing us, sir!"

"You think I don't know that?" Driscoll returned.

The howl of artillery fire sent them diving flat again. Shells burst and Heathcliff heard the beehive buzz and hiss of shrapnel whirling through the air around them. A soldier beside him jerked and curled up tighter.

When it stopped Heathcliff turned the soldier over and saw him clutching his gut, teeth clenched. "Fucking got me," he said.

Heathcliff gestured to another soldier. "Get him back!" He turned to Driscoll, but the lieutenant spoke before he could.

"We've got a job to do, Warrant Officer! We do it or we die trying! That's the game!"

Heathcliff wanted to argue, but found he had nothing to say.

"Contact right! Contact right!"

Machine gun fire chopped through an Iraqi platoon that fell back quickly, filling the air with rifle fire. An RPG corkscrewed overhead and blew a hole in a house's roof behind their line. There was no running, not yet. All they could do was fight, so they fought. It was only minutes, but it felt like hours.

Heathcliff fired off magazine after magazine until finally the order came.

"Fall back!" Driscoll called. "Heathcliff, make sure we don't leave anyone behind!"

"Sir!"

The surviving Canadians leapfrogged back, dashing from cover to cover, withdrawing toward their waiting APCs, Heathcliff among the last to fall back. Bullets whizzed by, but none found them. The Iraqis seemed hesitant to close to range with them again and finally they were clear, running in the open back to the APCs parked at the west end of town.

"Go! Go!" Heathcliff called, sprinting with all he had.

More shells came in, a parting gift from the enemy. One burst thirty yards to their right and a soldier went down with a grunt.

Heathcliff stopped, frozen between the APCs and the ruined town. The wounded Canadian, Private Bevin, tried to get back to his feet, but his right leg was limp and he fell on his face again.

Swearing at himself, Heathcliff went to him.

"I got you, Bevin! Give me your hand, drop the rifle!" He said. With some effort he crouched and pulled the man up onto his back, grunting with the strain, feeling his legs shake.

"Don't drop me!" Bevin groaned.

"Not gonna drop you," Heathcliff said.

Another shell exploded in a nearby house, obliterating it in a hail of shingles and shattered cinder blocks.

Flinching away, Heathcliff ran for the APCs, counting the remaining yards. His breath roared in his ears, his heart thundering. Each step made his legs quake, threatening to buckle. When he reached the M113 and staggered up the ramp, he tripped, falling forward into the waiting arms of his comrades who pulled him and Bevin in. The APC roared into gear, ramp raising as it fled, firing smoke grenades to conceal its retreat.

Heathcliff caught a glimpse of Leopard tanks reversing and firing before the ramp closed and they were away.

***

28

"They've taken the bait." Brigadier Gates studied the map spread on the folding table beside his headquarters APC, now updated with fresh enemy positions. Further to the south, the French had blunted a half-hearted Syrian advance and were rolling them up in conjunction with air and missile strikes from the battlegroup off the coast. *San Juan Hill* was working overtime.

Further north, a NATO defensive line was drawn across the open plains east of Konya with Tremblay's Canadians holding the northern stretch and Gates's British holding the southern stretch. If Gates were to drive only a mile or so east, he would reach the trenches and fighting positions they'd finished carving out. Relentless combat in Germany had taught many lessons to his men, but one of the most important was the need to dig in quickly and efficiently whenever time allowed. Within two hours his brigade occupied reasonably secure defenses. Another two and they had the extensive trenches they now occupied. The Canadian gambit at Yapılcan had served the dual purpose of getting the Iraqis' attention and buying time for his men to dig in. Now it was time for the next step in the operation.

Gates looked from the map to his assembled subordinate officers, standing in a semi-circle around the map table. Their expressions ranged from stoic concern to open enthusiasm. The enemy was going over to the attack, coming straight at their prepared lines, exactly as they hoped.

"The enemy is dancing to our tune," Gates said. "And we aim to let them play straight into our hands."

"Advanced recon teams and cavalry scouts report that we're

facing an Iraqi Republican Guard armored division—the cream of the Iraqi crop as it were. They're newly equipped—T-72s from the Soviet Union I'm told. But you lads have had no trouble destroying those before."

A few chuckles, tense, but a necessary off-letting of anxiety. Whatever air of danger the T-72 might have held before, the war had long since been shattered. Half-blind and poorly armored, they were more often targets than killers. Still, they were capable of being deadly in the right hands and right circumstances. He'd lost enough men to them to know that.

"They will come down the D300," Gates said, tracing the highway with a finger. "And run straight into Tremblay's men. We expect the Canadians will hold brilliantly. While they do, we will sweep up and over the open ground here—" he moved a hand south to north, "strike their rear and shatter them." Gates said, expressing the crux of the NATO plan in simple terms. "It doesn't seem that they know we're here. They've made no allowance for flank security from what we've seen."

The Republican Guard seemed to be blindly stumbling forward, groping in the dark for the Canadians even as they were stung incessantly by withdrawing NATO forces. Overconfident aggression married to staggering incompetence was a recipe for failure, one Gates hoped to exploit.

"Once they're crushed we can roll the whole Iraqi line up and drive on their supply lines and liberate Aksaray." Gates looked over the map, hands clasped behind his back and nodded, satisfied. "Questions?"

"What about the Russians?" Colonel Benson asked. "Where are they?"

"Mostly to the north," Gates said. "Pushing for Ankara and being thoroughly stymied by our friends the Turks." Gates grinned humorlessly. "As for our operating area, there is a motor rifle division at Aksaray. Seems to be in reserve, but it's not their best. Reservists and conscripts. More of the same we've faced before." He only hoped that turned out to be true. "Anyone else?"

No questions came. These men were experienced

professionals. They knew their work.

Gates nodded. "Return to your units, gentlemen. When we go, we go all in. A backhand blow to send them reeling. Once Aksaray is liberated, then Ankara's flank is secure and the Turks can redouble their efforts on stopping the Soviets on the Black Sea coast."

A simple plan, but like all plans one he was sure wouldn't survive the opening shots of the engagement.

***

29

Pete swore under his breath as he and Jean ducked deeper into the shallow dugout they occupied with Hristos and a handful of Greek soldiers peering watchfully into the dark ahead with bulky night vision goggles. Jean thought they looked insectoid this way, almost biomechanical. From the side she could only just see their eyes lit by the green glow of the displays inside the goggles. Their lips were skinned back into tense, predatory grins as they observed the fight ahead, mostly invisible to the naked eye.

Pete also saw the battle through the lens of his camera which was likewise night vision capable. They all saw more than Jean, who only could make out the flash of explosion, flicker of flames, and ragged lines of tracers cutting the early dawn. She hadn't slept that night and had instead spent it busily gathering interviews from the Greeks, recording voiceovers, and filming a segment about the state of the war in the Mediterranean. She felt a little like a ghost, almost like she wasn't real. On a conscious level she knew that was fatigue—exhaustion, sapping away her ability to feel present. But on another level, she welcomed it. How else could she watch impassively as young men destroyed one another? She thought of Captain Kalatzis and Dimitar. She thought of Dario.

A fireball blossomed in the dark scarcely two kilometers ahead, throwing stark shadows across the open ground before them. Momentarily it illuminated the vast graveyard of the Bulgarian army strewn across the plains here. Tanks, APCs, trucks, and bodies—hundreds of bodies—lay still on the earth. The rolling farmland they fought on reminded her of the Midwest—of home, if home were a gray, twilight hell. Pillars of smoke stabbed skyward across the horizon-to-horizon battlefield, the remnants of a Bulgarian battalion run down by the Greeks, a product of the Warsaw Pact's desperate need to close the escape route for the Turks. But now a fresh enemy had taken the field and were launching a pre-dawn attack. The Soviets were here. And it was to their detriment.

To Jean's left an anti-tank missile streaked from a launch tube, crossed the open ground in a few heartbeats, and struck another half-visible Soviet tank, causing it to blow its top. The ammunition inside cooked off, vaporizing the crew and shooting the turret into the air like a cork from a champagne bottle.

It was a bloodbath. Jean didn't have to be a soldier to recognize that. She only had to count each destroyed Russian tank and note, with some satisfaction, that she hadn't seen nearly as many Greek losses.

Despite all their bloody-mindedness, the Soviets could learn. The armored attack drew back to be replaced with a helicopter assault. A pair of gunships crested the distant horizon, silhouetted against the purple sky before they threw a salvo of rockets in a parabolic arc toward the Greeks and ducked away.

The rockets fell on the Greek positions to Jean's left, out of sight. She heard a staccato rumble as the rockets burst in sequence, leaving her no clear idea how badly that attack had hurt.

She and Pete watched in mute awe as the Soviets battered themselves bloody in a sequence of futile assaults on the Greek position, attacking up and down the line and interspersing these raids with a rain of artillery shells and flares before at last they let up. As the sun crested the horizon, it painted a scene of carnage, a veritable parking lot of ruined vehicles jammed up on roads and scattered through fallow fields.

The Soviets attacking here were not the battle-hardened troops of the German front; these were fresh reservists, inexperienced and making the same mistakes they had made in the opening days of their invasion of Germany and the Greeks were making them pay for it in blood.

Hristos crossed himself in the Orthodox fashion.

Jean only stared dumbly at the vast graveyard the Soviets and Bulgarians had left behind, fraternal socialist allies together even in death.

Pete hefted the camera off his shoulder. "Jean, tape."

It was a well-practiced exercise by this point. Jean pulled a fresh tape from the bag and passed it to Pete who reloaded the camera with professional smoothness. He shouldered it again just in time to catch a quartet of Greek Leopard tanks snort plumes of diesel smoke and haul themselves out of fighting positions off to their right.

Just a mile to the south, hidden behind the rolling terrain, a column of Turkish army equipment streamed west, escaping the pocket the Soviets had formed with their capture of Istanbul. The escaping Turks carried on, crossing the Maritsa River under shellfire from the Russo-Bulgarian attack and passing into Greece proper.

Two of the lead Leopards fired, one after another. Jean felt the concussive boom of their guns in her chest and saw something erupt in flames further away, maybe a fleeing Soviet tank caught in the open.

She felt the tempo of battle shifting subtly. The Soviet attack was rapidly losing steam in the face of staggering losses. Soon they were deploying billowing smokescreens in the early morning twilight and dropping back behind the horizon to escape the ferocious Greek defensive fire.

One of the Greek soldiers beside Jean spoke and Hristos translated. "We're counterattacking."

The Greek forces gave their enemy no breathing room, no time to collect. They smelled weakness and they intended to exploit it. Pete caught it all. Jean waited until the tanks passed out of sight and Pete stopped filming before she spoke to Hristos. "Can we follow them? Can we get closer?" It had been a constant question during her time with the Greek army and the answer had almost invariably been the same.

"They will not get any closer until they are called," Hristos explained. "But they say we may go and examine the closest enemy tanks." He gestured to some of the burnt-out vehicles a few hundred yards away.

Jean looked at Pete and raised an eyebrow.

Her cameraman shrugged. "You're the boss, Jean. I go where you go."

"Then let's go. Hristos, you can stay here." Jean didn't fail to note the relief on Hristos's face. She thought, and briefly, of Dario, his bloody, shattered stump.

With a boost from Pete, she pulled herself from the trench and into the open, feeling momentarily exposed, even as the sounds of fighting moved further and further away. She offered a hand to Pete and helped him from the trench. Out of the cold, damp dugout they felt the warmth of the sun on their skin, chasing away the nip of winter. They crossed together, walking over the churned grassland toward the nearest tank. A T-55. It was remarkably intact aside from a mangled left tread which was tangled like a shoelace, twisted to the side of the vehicle where it had thrown the track. Some of its road wheels were blown away by the same force which had thrown the track. The hatches were open and there were no bodies. The crew had escaped and fled, or at least died somewhere else.

Jean and Pete came to stand by the tank and Jean reached out, brushing her hand over its cold metal hide. Some of the green paint flecked away beneath her fingers revealing a thick coat of white.

"Winter camo," Pete said, brushing off his own paint chips. "Maybe a Far East unit."

Jean let the green paint chip fall away and looked around at the battlefield again. It was a sobering sight and reminded her a little of the Marines in Yugoslavia. They'd been driven to exhaustion by relentless Soviet attacks there, worn down almost to nothing. The Marines had ultimately managed to escape. Jean wondered if these Soviets would be so lucky. "Let's do a segment here," she said.

"Here?" Pete looked surprised, but Jean paid no attention.

Her mind was already set. She nodded and brushed her hair down, accepting the microphone when Pete handed it to her. She positioned herself in front of the destroyed tank, lit by the rising sun, and stared into the lens as Pete counted her down. She didn't know exactly what she intended to say, but she knew whatever it was was going to be good. Pete's countdown ended and he pointed to her. Recording.

"I'm standing here on the latest battlefield in what feels like an endless trail of them across Greece—across Europe—this place a graveyard for the young men who crossed it: Soviets, Bulgarians, Romanians, Greeks, and Turks. Those who seek to steal our freedom and those who fight to defend it." She walked, Pete panning to follow her, dragging the camera's gaze across the rest of the battlefield and the multitude of ruined tanks, a highway of death.

"The Soviet Union continues its brutal assault on the people of Europe, but here at least they have been turned back. Their tools of war left burning under a rust sky." She stopped walking, leaving the wastes behind her. "Each day—each and every day, we hear stories of fallen cities and towns, miles of territory lost to the enemy, casualties mounting. The Turkish army has been through the worst of this these past few days. Alone, they might have capitulated. But now they stand united with the rest of NATO, brought together by a mutual love of freedom and an unwillingness to submit to tyranny. Brothers in arms."

As she continued to pace, Pete's lens came into sight of the withdrawing Turkish columns in the far distance, dots moving over a ridgeline in a solemn funeral procession.

"The Soviet attack here has been thoroughly blunted, their supposed Bulgarian allies suffering terribly." She paused. "They've paid a horrible price for their masters today. A price I am not sure they will willingly continue to pay for much longer. What will happen to the Eastern Bloc when the fear of Soviet reprisal is overcome by a justified rage for the generation thrown away on the battlefield here? In the past hours we've seen huge amounts of destroyed and abandoned gear strung along the roads around us. The Hellenic Air Force and the rest of NATO have wreaked a deadly toll on the Warsaw Pact forces pressing south. It's too soon to say for sure, but unless something changes...." Jean shook her head. "Something's got to give."

Only days ago, it had felt like they were on the ropes. Now something had changed, some subtle shift in mood. As the weather cooled and the days grew shorter, the Soviet's thrall armies seemed to fall apart under sustained operations. A broken machine rattling itself to pieces, Jean thought.

"The Turkish army is driven back but unbowed. The Greeks defiant. I can only report on what I see and what I hear and what I'm seeing is a turning point. The people I've spoken with are optimistic. They say their nation has faced impossible odds before, unstoppable enemies, the Persians, the Ottomans, the Nazis, and now the Soviets." Jean set her jaw. "Victory, they say, is now only a matter of time." A pause. "Jean Carson, Associated Press."

Pete cut and lowered the camera. "Good stuff." He hesitated. "You really believe all that?"

Jean heard an approaching engine and looked back to see a Greek APC approaching them from the way they'd come. "I do." She handed the microphone back to Pete and met the APC and Hristos who climbed out first, beaming.

"That's it!" he said triumphantly.

"What's it?"

"They're out," he said. "The enemy are retreating." He grinned somehow broader. "By God, Ms. Carson, I will get us all a round of Ouzo once we make it back to somewhere decent."

"I'll take you up on that," Jean said, distracted as she noted a Greek officer in the cupola of the APC, speaking quickly into a microphone. "Captain," she asked. "What's next? If Greece is safe, what's next?"

Hristos relayed the question, though from the captain's expression Jean imagined he understood her meaning even without Hristos. His answer was short. Hristos repeated it with a wry expression. "We go north."

Jean followed his gaze. North, over the border, into Bulgaria. Far enough on this line and they'd reach Sofia. Further, Bucharest, then Budapest, then...where did it stop?

***

30

Heathcliff lay on the edge of the trench beside Lieutenant Driscoll. The late afternoon sun beat down on them as they peered over the ramparts of the simple earthwork toward the distant horizon across miles of open farmland toward a rising dust cloud and movement.

"Here they come," Driscoll said, observing the enemy through binoculars. He passed them to Heathcliff. "It's a hell of a lot of them."

Heathcliff took the binoculars and almost wished he hadn't. By virtue of the flat terrain ahead of them it felt as though he could see forever, and what he saw was an entire armored regiment on the attack, or at least the lead elements of one. Instead of saying any of this he said "BMPs."

"Looks like BMP-1s," Driscoll agreed.

Heathcliff scanned the line carefully, peering into the dust clouds. "Don't see any tanks yet."

"Yeah, just infantry," Driscoll said. "For now."

"Hoping to flush us out."

"Most likely."

Heathcliff felt his stomach knot with fear, but he only nodded stoically, handing the binoculars back. He felt he needed to say something to Driscoll after he'd pressed the lieutenant to abandon the town. But what was there to say? Driscoll was right. This was their job, after all. Heathcliff felt it was his duty to keep the platoon alive, but sometimes it was just as much his duty to put their lives in danger.

"Check the sections," Driscoll said, glancing at Heathcliff. "They might try to stand off and shell us or something. Make sure we've got good cover. I want to draw them in."

Heathcliff couldn't help but notice the edge in Driscoll's voice, as if he were eager to get to grips with the Iraqis.

"Yes, sir." Heathcliff would just be glad when this was over. He scooted back from the rampart and dropped back into the narrow trench, hurrying along from section to section, checking with the men. Machine guns and Carl Gustaf anti-tank weapons were sighted, stacked, and ready. Riflemen stood on the firing step or stood by, ready to take position. Some of them smoked anxiously.

"Put that out, Mandeville."

"Sorry, sir."

"Looks like trouble," Dupont said in French when Heathcliff reached him. His eyes were fixed on the horizon and the growing dust cloud there.

"Trouble for them," Heathcliff replied. "Your section ready?"

"Ready," Dupont agreed. "If we can get the bastards close enough to hurt."

"If they want to get to us they'll have to get close," Heathcliff said. "Try to flush us out."

"Unless they find a way around. Or they just bury us with bulldozers."

Heathcliff shuddered at that mental image. "I didn't see any bulldozers."

"Maybe not," Dupont said. "Then we'll be ready."

The Soviet artillery batteries were too far out to hear the rumble of guns, but they heard the freight train wail of shells clearly enough.

"It's that time!" Heathcliff called out.

"*Attache ta tuque!*" Dupont shouted in response, calling his men to arms.

The first shells landed moments later, bursting across the plain. The deep booms and ear-shattering bangs battered the trench. Deadly fragments hummed and screamed through the air overhead. Heathcliff was grateful for the protection of the trench as he made his way back toward Driscoll and the center of the line. Only a direct hit or an airburst right overhead posed any real risk to them. Heathcliff knew that consciously, but animal fear tore at the back of his mind all the same.

By the time he reached the lieutenant, the barrage was walking callously back and forth over their line, churning the earth to craters. Heathcliff noted that there seemed to be fewer dud shells among the Iraqi guns than the Soviet batteries. He imagined it was because these stocks were fresher.

He'd only just thought it when the shellfire tapered off, replaced instead by the boom and whistle of BMP 73-millimeter guns.

Heathcliff risked a peek over the parapet in time to see a shell explode a few dozen meters ahead of the trenches, falling short. A poor shot, abysmal really. Heathcliff hoped it would prove prophetic.

The rest of the BMPs joined in the fire as they crossed the last leg of their journey. The IFVs' guns boomed and barked, throwing shells across the Canadian line, mostly doing nothing but churning earth. Heathcliff reached Driscoll in time to see the Canadian response to the shelling. A pair of TOW missiles streaked out from the nearby heavy weapons section and struck two BMPs, exploding them both catastrophically. Fireballs rolled out, scattering fragments of steel across the plain and painting the sandy earth black with ash.

Heathcliff expected the Iraqis to shift fire to this new threat, to maneuver, or really to do anything besides what they actually did. Being fired back at seemed to bewilder the enemy and sent them into a panic. Half of the BMPs immediately reversed, deploying smoke screens to escape out of range of the TOWs while the other half continued to sit immobile, shelling the Canadian line.

Seconds later, Heathcliff glimpsed dark shapes rising over the horizon, a pair of aircraft closing at supersonic speed—Iraqi or Soviet, he couldn't be sure. He ducked down in the trench just before a missile trail cut the air above them, lancing from west to east to strike one of the enemy aircraft with an echoing bang.

The Canadians craned their necks to watch as the skies above them were suddenly alive with activity. Iraqi F1 Mirages and Turkish F-16s climbed, twisted, and dueled overhead. Missile streaks cut the air, often terminating in explosions, sending flaming wrecks spiraling to the earth.

A broken Mirage splashed across an open field, trailing a cascading fireball over the earth.

Some of the men cheered weekly as the Iraqi fighters were driven off, but their excitement was short lived, erased with another fusillade of fire from the BMPs.

"Infantry!" Someone shouted. "Infantry in the open!"

The BMPs unloaded their troops who were hurrying forward now, fanning out into loose battle lines and advancing directly into the jaws of the Canadians.

"Open fire!"

Machine guns and rifles ripped out, bullets scattering across the plain, kicking up plumes of dust and cutting down Iraqi troops in the open—too far out to do more than fire back blindly or throw themselves to cover.

Some of the BMPs that had previously been stationary began to advance. It was as if, Heathcliff thought, the Iraqi squads were each operating alone. Every man for himself with next to no coordination in this attack. It was a shooting gallery.

Rifle fire panged off the hull of an approaching BMP before one of Dupont's Carl Gustafs banged and punched a hole in the vehicle's flank. Black smore poured from hatches as the Iraqi passengers and crew scrambled free, only to be cut down by more gunfire.

Another BMP roared forward from the smoke now obscuring the battlefield, alarmingly close to the Canadian trenches and Heathcliff. It stopped and dropped its ramp in time to be struck with another Carl Gustaf, this one deflecting off the sloped front armor. It made no difference to the crew who similarly abandoned their vehicle in a panic.

Heathcliff squeezed his trigger and swept them with automatic fire, dropping two men and sending the others to the ground.

Beside him, Driscoll pulled the pin on a grenade. "Grenade out!" He rose and hurled it like a baseball, dropping it behind the BMP, among the debarked infantry. It exploded and threw an invisible cloud of fragments through the men sheltering there. Someone howled in pain, but the sound was lost in the roar of gunfire.

The remaining stalwart BMPs began to withdraw in a cloud of smoke, another pair taken out in short order by TOW fire.

Heathcliff fired another burst at the Iraqis fleeing on foot before he saw they were throwing down their weapons and running for their lives. He decided to save the ammo.

"We've got more coming," Driscoll said. He was kneeling now, disregarding the safety of the trench rampart in order to better see the enemy. Heathcliff had to admire that kind of disregard for the enemy, even as he knew it was his job to curb that sort of foolhardy behavior.

"Sir, better lay back down."

Driscoll ignored him. "Tanks. T-72s, I think."

T-72s would be tough work for the infantry. Even the TOWs weren't guaranteed to breach T-72 frontal armor. If the Iraqis had coordinated with their armor, they may have at least gotten close enough for their infantry to try to clear the trenches.

Driscoll was on the radio in an instant, speaking with battalion fire support.

Heathcliff watched the tanks drawing closer, linking up with some of the retreating BMPs to come back around in a half-hearted second wave. This restored bravery was rewarded with a shower of artillery. Shells burst among the Iraqi formations, taking out a handful of vehicles before they could get much closer.

The T-72s fired on the advance, their shells screaming over the Canadians or exploding ahead of the trenches without effect. One lucky round sailed past and struck a half-concealed M113. The shell ripped through the APC and set it burning, the surviving crew bailing out desperately.

Before the Iraqis could capitalize on this small success, a flight of Turkish F-4 Phantoms screamed by, pulling away after releasing cluster ordinance which exploded in the face of the Republican Guard armor assault, wrecking more tanks.

Perfectly on time, a company of British Challenger tanks roared over a distant hill to the south and into sight of the enemy. A heartbeat later they fired as one, obliterating a half dozen enemy tanks. The British cruised on, plowing across the open fields, banging away and popping off T-72s like fireworks.

Suddenly Heathcliff and his platoon felt very small compared with this titanic display of firepower. The Canadians stopped firing to watch this microcosm of the British advance in awe. Soon enough the Challengers vanished from view again, continuing to drive on the Iraqi flank and rear.

The Iraqis apparently had enough. They fell back, the tanks emitting smoke to conceal their retreat, racing back to prevent the British from cutting them off.

Dueling fighters crossed the skies just above the horizon as NATO aircraft punished the Iraqis for daring to sally out. Soon enough, the sky was all but clear of the enemy.

The Iraqis were on the run.

***

For how much they'd been built up, Gates was shocked by how fast the Iraqi attack disintegrated. These were men supposedly battle-hardened from a decade of conflict with Iran, well versed on the lessons of war, trained and equipped by the Soviet Union, and slavering for blood. The Republican Guard, Iraq's answer to SS storm troopers, had turned out to be a paper tiger. A paper tiger now totally off balance.

The Canadians had done an admirable job of halting the Republican Guard attack, bloodying their noses in the process. Now Gates and his brigade swarmed forward to finish the job. Challengers fired on the move, smiting T-72s and T-62s from well outside of their own ability to fight back. It was a shooting gallery. The perfect killing ground of Turkey's broad fields was dotted with burning vehicles. Gates followed behind the cutting edge of his advance, glad to be the attacker for a change. As he rode, he looked out over the carnage the retreating Iraqis were leaving behind and pressed his headphones to his ears, listening to Benson's report.

"The Canadians are saying they've annihilated an entire armored brigade in the open. The whole division could come apart at the seams," Benson said breathlessly. "We're moving up but the Iraqis are slowing our advance."

"We have air assets on standby," Gates said. "Use them. Plaster any strong points. Or bypass them. Let the Canadians mop up behind us."

"No, sir," Benson said. "Not resistance. Prisoners. We're overwhelmed with prisoners. Too many surrenders."

Gates almost couldn't believe his ears. "Too many prisoners?"

"Yes, sir."

Were it not so macabre he might have laughed. "By God, Benson, tell them to start walking west if they want to surrender. Let the Canadians deal with it. We haven't got the time. If they fight, kill them where they stand."

"Yes, sir."

This was their moment. With the Iraqi flank falling to pieces, they couldn't let up. Gates didn't get his Waterloo in Germany, but here it was in Turkey, staring him in the face. His single armored brigade couldn't destroy the Iraqi army alone, but with the rest of the NATO battlegroup at his back and the Turkish Army switching over to the counteroffensive, they might be able to smash an Iraqi armored division. If they set them running now, it would be that much easier to undo the rest of them later. They had to capitalize on this victory, and they had to do it quickly.

As Gates's APC crested a low scrubby ridge, he was met with the acrid smell of burning tanks. The wrecked, blackened hulks which dotted the open ground around him were visible even in the fading daylight. His APC crawled forward slowly, mindful of the columns of defeated prisoners trudging past, their hands on their heads. There were so many that Gates could hardly believe it. Hundreds, maybe thousands. The Iraqis were disintegrating.

All across the plain Gates saw the marks of war. The flat landscape bore the scars of recent conflict, with smoldering wrecks of both Iraqi and Western tanks scattered across the horizon. He noted far more of the enemy's losses than his own though. Gates kept half a mind on the radio, listening to his battalions maneuvering through and around the routed Iraqi remains, occasionally breaking up pockets of enemy resistance. With the reduced visibility the fighting was more intense than it had been before, but so far was no real challenge for his men.

"General Gates, our forward scouts have made contact with fresh enemy ahead. Looks like the Soviets." Colonel Benson's voice carried a note of urgency which Gates could hear even though the heavy distortion on the radio.

More than his subordinates' concern, Gates was surprised with such a concrete identification of the enemy. With visibility nearly down to zero and both Iraqi and Soviet forces using much the same equipment, he wasn't sure how Benson could be confident in his designation. Gates adjusted his microphone. "Soviets? How can you be so sure?" Gates asked, his mind already racing through the possibilities.

"They're standing their ground," Benson replied. "If they were Iraqis, they'd be running by now. These are disciplined troops."

Soviets. Gates furrowed his brow. The stalwart Soviets changed the dynamics of the battle. It meant a well-organized and formidable opponent—one that couldn't be underestimated. In ideal circumstances he had no doubts that his brigade, backed by the rest of the NATO forces here, could punch through a single Soviet motor rifle division, but these were far from ideal circumstances. Still, there was only one answer.

"We can't afford to let them regroup," Gates said. If the Soviet-backed Iraqi forces managed to escape to more defensible positions, it would complicate the already challenging task of dislodging them. "Benson, ready for an attack," Gates commanded, his tone resolute. "We can't allow them a moment to breathe. I'll get this up the chain to division command. I think we have a real opportunity here. We can't allow them to slip away." Even as he said it, Gates doubted that escape was the Soviet's plan. It seemed they intended to fight.

"It's getting quite late, sir," Benson said. "It will mean a night operation."

"A night operation will give us all the advantages," Gates replied. "Leave the details to me."

"Sir!" Benson replied quickly.

As Benson carried out his orders, Gates couldn't help but think of Colonel Dunworth being cut down outside Paderborn. This battle felt like a continuation of the struggles they had faced together. Dunworth's memory fueled Gates's determination to succeed.

There wasn't time to dwell on the past. Gates established a connection with divisional command and wasn't surprised to learn that other units across the front were reporting similarly dramatic success. The enemy was disintegrating. If they could press this advantage, then maybe they could do more than secure an important city. As the coordinated assault began, Gates felt a surge of adrenaline. The sun dipped lower on the horizon, casting long shadows across the plains as the British and Canadian forces advanced.

***

31

The Republican Guard was crumbling, virtually annihilated on the field and now the rest of the Iraqi army threatened to implode with fear and confusion alone. The sun dipped to the west, plunging the countryside into a red haze as the sun set on a bloodbath.

Nabiyev was only a regimental officer, it wasn't his job or responsibility to understand the greater operational situation here, but he almost couldn't help it. The radio traffic he heard on the Iraqi bands was not good. Although their words were foreign to him, their tone wasn't. Panic. The mainline Iraqi army, lukewarm soldiers at the best of times, were already faltering. It was clear that their flank was turned and they'll all be trapped by a raging NATO spearhead if something isn't done soon.

Nabiyev followed his general's instructions to the letter, maneuvering his battalions and deploying them as instructed into defensive positions in the plains west of Aksaray as the sky faded from red to purple and then was blotted to darkness by falling night. No one explained the battle plan to him, but he understood it all the same. The fighting positions his men had hastily dug for their tanks and APCs would soon be put to use.

When Novikov finally explained his intentions to his regimental commanders, it was almost superfluous.

"We are being pressed everywhere and I can get nothing from the Iraqis," Novikov said, the thick radio distortion doing nothing to mask the anger in his voice. "With night coming we will have a reprieve to stabilize our lines. Our division must stand firm. We will stop the enemy here and allow the Iraqis time to regroup." Novikov paused before adding, "Tomorrow we will let the enemy come to us and we will destroy them."

Novikov's certainty gave Nabiyev pause. "How can we be certain the enemy attack will come tomorrow?"

"The Anglos are already stopping their pursuit. A night operation against unreconnoitered lines would be foolish. It will take them some time to reposition. I expect the attack at dawn tomorrow at the earliest." His tone suggested he would tolerate no more questions. "By then maybe we can get some sense into the Iraqis."

"Yes, Comrade General."

As much as Nabiyev hated to sit and allow the enemy the initiative of attack, he understood the logic. What else could they do? In a straight fight in the open, they would be easy picking for superior Western main battle tanks, something the Iraqis had learned too late.

As daylight quickly gave way to night, the Soviets navigated in the darkness only by the invisible light of their infrared spotlights. If the retreat wasn't screened soon, it would become a total rout. The massive Iraqi military would be run down like dogs on the open road, the entire campaign undone. Nabiyev was already seeing the first disordered columns of Iraqi forces streaming through his lines, weapons abandoned, some even fleeing on foot—uselessly. There would be no escape that way.

While the Iraqis went to pieces, their Soviet allies remained resolute. There was no other choice.

Nabiyev buttoned down in his command APC and waited, each moment his regiment dug in was another moment the West drew closer. This showdown would decide the course of this campaign. Victory or defeat hung in the balance and there was nothing to do but wait.

***

Gates's brigade deployed in the dark. Using night vision, they moved as easily at night as they might in the day. They'd survived the hell of the initial weeks of the Soviet attack and so they were no strangers to sleep deprivation. They were old hands at this game now and so they moved through the dark like coyotes, slinking to established positions outside of Aksaray, ready to pounce. All the days and weeks of preparation, trading their temperate uniforms for desert camouflage, deploying across the Mediterranean, was coming to a head. Now they would measure themselves against a new enemy, one who had proved up to the challenge in the past, but Gates had faith in his men. How could he not after all they had accomplished?

The night would be their shield. Whatever safety the enemy thought it provided them would be illusory. There would be no respite in the dark.

Strangely, Gates found himself wishing for the battle to begin. At least in battle there was no time for doubt. As he waited, he found himself thinking of Tremblay's words about the purity of war. It was rubbish. The only thing pure about war was its barbarity and inhumanity. But perhaps there was something to be said for doing away with pretense. He would be glad to be at the enemy and have this over with.

Companies of Challengers formed up on the plains, guided by advanced night optics and skilled crews. Whatever stubborn, bloody-minded discipline the Soviets had would not save them. Gates was sure of that. Tank platoons formed into companies, and companies into battalions as they prepared to charge forward.

The distant rumble of tanks and the staccato bursts of machine gun fire to the north signaled the commencement of the attack. The Canadians were going in.

***

Heathcliff and his men advanced through the night, cloaked in darkness. News that they were following hot on the heels of the retreating Iraqis wasn't exactly welcome, but in a way, Heathcliff preferred attacking to sitting and waiting. The interior of the APC was dimly lit, the others packed in with him were only half-visible. They were exhausted, having fought most of the afternoon and being given no time to sleep, but war didn't wait. They'd gathered their strength just after sunset, boarding APCs and advancing in the wake of the retreating Iraqis. They passed through the Iraqi graveyard that now lay in front of their positions, the men and machines of the Iraqi Republican Guard laid to waste. As they moved beyond the battle lines, they'd seen further carnage, a terrible toll reaped on the fleeing enemy by NATO air strikes.

Anti-aircraft fire lit the night ahead, the horizon flashing with lines of tracers streaking toward the stars above. The aircraft evidently circling and swooping overhead were invisible in the dark, only apparent by the occasional bomb or missile detonating with a bright flash on the ground.

Heathcliff hoped the Soviets were so preoccupied with these relentless airstrikes that they wouldn't notice this ground assault until it was too late.

The cadence of the M113's engine changed as it slowed, the Canadians drawing near to the Soviet lines.

"Here we go," Heathcliff said, pulling down his night vision goggles. A moment later Heathcliff and the others in the M113 were jolted together as the vehicle lurched to an unexpected stop. The ramp lowered almost before anyone could give an order.

"Everyone out!" Heathcliff called, joining the others in the section as they surged out of the APC and into the darkness outside. Everything glowed a sickly green through the lenses of his NVGs. He was overcome with a stark sense of agoraphobia. The vast, flat farmland stretched before him; a dim plane married to the star-filled sky. Heathcliff's night vision gear made the stars overhead glitter as bright as flares. The forms of his comrades fanned out in the open as artillery fire crashed down on the enemy lines several hundred meters distant.

Heathcliff adjusted his NVGs to ensure they were securely in place as he lay flat, staring out toward the shellfire pounding the Soviet positions which he could only just make out as earthen ramparts ahead.

As the barrage tapered off, Driscoll called an advance. The platoon rose up and moved forward, staying low. As Heathcliff watched the last few NATO shells explode over the Soviet lines, he hoped against hope that they would find nothing left alive when they reached the trench.

The enemy's survival was confirmed a moment later as a tank shell tore by and ripped into a distant M113 obliterating the lightly armored APC in spectacular fashion. The blast lit the dark with a flare of fire and black, oily smoke. The explosion sent a shockwave through the night, scattering debris and shrapnel.

"Contact!" someone screamed pointlessly.

The Canadians threw themselves flat or staggered away from their own APC, seeking cover amidst the chaos while the APCs frantically reversed, firing their smoke grenade launchers to conceal their hasty retreat. The rumble of their engines echoed through the desert as they withdrew, soon lost in the cacophony of gunfire which drowned out the mechanical sounds of war.

Heathcliff lifted his head from the ground, peering ahead. He couldn't see the enemy, but they were ahead, snug in their trenches. They couldn't stay here. There was only one possible order and Driscoll gave it.

"Forward! Advance!"

"Dupont, cover fire!" Heathcliff snapped.

Dupont's section lashed out, firing blindly ahead, sweeping the air with machine gun fire as the others in the platoon rose to their feet and surged forward, masked by the smoke and dark.

Darkness let the Canadians close range quickly. The Soviets fired several parachute flares which illuminated the battlefield in a flickering twilight, but it wasn't enough.

Heathcliff led the section forward, the air thick with the acrid scent of burning metal and the chemical tang of the M113s fading smokescreens. When they closed to within a hundred yards of the Soviet positions, he could see the mounds of raw earth that formed the parapets of the enemy trenches.

At a word, the section leaders fired Carl Gustafs into these makeshift fortifications, blasting gouts of dirt into the air and suppressing the defenders within.

Heathcliff threw himself flat and belted off half a magazine at the trench lip, stitching the air and keeping the defenders from firing back. The deafening echoes of gunfire battered his eardrums. He fired another long burst and then waved Dupont's section up, leapfrogging them forward while the enemy was pinned down.

Somewhere nearby he heard the bark of tanks and shriek of missiles—unseen forces dueling around him—close, but not close enough to have any impact on his platoon. Another heartbeat later and Dupont and his men came forward like ghosts from the haze. The soldiers jogged up to join Heathcliff when a burst of gunfire lashed out from the Soviets and dropped Dupont and one of his men.

Heathcliff's heart skipped as the sergeant fell, clutching his thighs and groaning. His men threw themselves flat while the rest of the platoon renewed their fire, saturating the Soviet positions.

Heathcliff rose to his feet and dashed over to Dupont, heedless of the danger, before throwing himself down by the sergeant who was cursing in French. Without a word, Heathcliff tore open the med kit at his waist and produced a tourniquet. He tied the first one in place and started working on the second one, noting with alarm the dark blood seeping from Dupont's thigh and staining the sand.

"Both legs? Christ," Dupont groaned. "Bad luck."

"Bad luck would be dead," Heathcliff said, glancing over at the other fallen soldier who lay silent and motionless nearby.

"Go," Dupont said, brushing Heathcliff away to finish cinching the second tourniquet himself. "Go! I can do this."

Heathcliff slapped a friendly hand on Dupont's shoulder before turning and returning to the attack. In the moments it had taken him to tend to Dupont, Driscoll had guided the platoon to within striking range of the Soviet positions and now men were lobbing grenades into trenches and foxholes. Panicked shouts were followed by bangs and pitiful wailing as the men within were perforated by shrapnel and deafened by the blasts.

With Dupont down, Heathcliff took control of his section. "Go! Harper, come on." He led a fire team forward, the three of them dropping into the narrow trench. Heathcliff landed on a dead Russian and immediately put three rounds through a wounded man rolling on the trench floor beside him before Harper swept past him, firing blindly around a turn in the trench.

"Surrender! Surrender!" The voice was thickly accented, the words unmistakable.

"Come out!" Heathcliff shouted, weapon trained on the blind corner. "Throw down your weapons and come out!" He couldn't remember how to say it in Russian. Either they understood or they didn't, and if they didn't, he would just cut them down.

They understood. Two soldiers staggered into view, their hands out. One bled profusely from a fragmentation wound to his face. Both were dirty and bedraggled.

Harper and another private threw them both to the ground and patted them down for weapons while Heathcliff and Mandeville finished clearing this small fighting position. Only the dead manned it now.

As Heathcliff and the others dragged their prisoners from the small trench, he heard the distinctive roar of diesel engines. In the distance, through the smoke and darkness, Challenger tanks charged forward like Napoleonic cavalry. Their superior optics and thermal sights gave them a decisive advantage over their Soviet adversaries in the dark and they fired as they advanced. The British armor tore through the Soviet tanks with relentless efficiency.

Heathcliff, momentarily forgetting his own role in the carnage, marveled at the unleashed fury of the Challengers. Their shells punched through the Soviet defenses, creating a path of destruction in their wake. Lieutenant Driscoll grabbed his arm, startling him. "All clear?"

"Clear sir. Two prisoners."

Driscoll eyed them. "Two more than I wanted. Leave someone

here to watch them and the others. We're moving up. I'll be damned if we let the Brits leave us behind."

Heathcliff smiled. "Sir. Mandeville, watch Ivan and his buddy. If they try anything, shoot them."

"No argument," Mandeville said, eyeing the Russians coldly.

Driscoll lifted his night vision goggles, revealing a ring of dirt around his face. "Let's keep them rolling." They had more trenches left to clear.

"Sir!" Heathcliff checked that his rifle was still loaded. "First Section, with me!" There was no other way for him to lead but from the front. He weaved through the twisting Soviet trench network, taking off his own NVGs and pausing only long enough to let his eyes acclimate to the dark.

Reaching a bend in the trench, Heathcliff pulled a grenade from his vest and ripped the safety pin free, letting the arming handle fall away. He counted to two and lobbed it over the top of the parapet and into the neighboring trenchline.

Someone cried out in fright before they were snuffed out by a bang.

Heathcliff was right behind it, looping the corner, firing bursts from his rifle. He caught a Soviet trooper in the back and sent him sprawling as another dropped to cover.

More rifle fire from behind Heathcliff peppered the Russian and he rolled over, limp and dead.

Heathcliff exhaled uneasily and continued on.

Tracer rounds flashed and careened overhead. Flames from burning vehicles cast a faint reddish glow over the upper parapets of the trench while the trench floor itself was bathed in darkness, occasionally thrown into flickering light by Soviet parachute flares.

As the Canadians strode over dead bodies and shell casings Heathcliff wondered if this was how his ancestors felt at Vimy Ridge driving out the Germans. Reaching another bend in the trench, Heathcliff pitched a second grenade around it. The blast ruined his hearing, but he paid no mind. Leaning carefully around the edge, he put a burst through the chest of a Soviet on his knees, dropping him to his back.

Gunfire lashed back at him, sending him ducking away.

Harper blind fired around the trench wall as Heathcliff reloaded his rifle with shaking hands. "Get a grenade on those guys!" he shouted, barely hearing his own voice over his ringing ears.

Two more grenade blasts stopped the enemy gunfire and Heathcliff finally gathered the courage to peek again. The trench ahead was empty except for dead bodies, and a Soviet soldier trying to sit up though his right arm was mangled and his legs evidently limp.

Heathcliff put two short bursts through the hapless enemy soldier who flopped back, dead at last.

"Okay, let's go." They moved forward again, this time toward what seemed to be the rear of the fighting position. Only his fear of ambush kept him from dashing ahead. When at last they reached the rear of the trench network, he ducked up the small ramp leading back to ground level and faintly saw figures fleeing into the dark.

"Infantry!"

Staccato rifle bursts dropped more troopers, more intent on fleeing than fighting as they raced back for waiting APCs. "Bring up the Carl G!"

But they didn't get the chance. Following a low howl, Soviet artillery fire slammed down around them, sending Heathcliff and the others scrambling back into the safety of the trench. The barrage tore the earth around them impotently as the enemy slipped away.

Driscoll caught up to Heathcliff's section a moment later. "All clear here," Heathcliff said, shouting over the barrage. "Enemy's running!"

Driscoll nodded. "It's up to the Brits now!"

***

32

Colonel Nabiyev surveyed the unfolding chaos from the vantage point of his mobile command post. The once-mighty Soviet division, a formidable force on paper, now lay in shreds. The reality of the situation was a bitter pill to swallow as he watched the disintegration of his command.

The oncoming British tanks thundered over, around, and through the Soviet fighting positions outside of Aksaray, now devastated and abandoned. Flames licked from burning tanks and craters which dotted the fields now torn by war. Nothing moved as the British infantry debarked from APCs to storm into the trenches and clear them of any surviving enemies.

This was the scene unfolding behind Nabiyev as his headquarters company fled east, following the general rout of the rest of the division.

The West shattered his regiment like glass. Abramov's battalion withdrew in tatters and he'd lost all contact with Baranov. Nabiyev, however, was far too afraid to feel shame or anger. He was far from safe yet.

Jets thundered overhead, the screech of their engines lost in the night sky above. He had no illusions as to whose jets those were as his BTR rolled past a burning SAM launcher. NATO ruled the night and the skies, and now both were his enemy.

The low fly by was followed by a thunderous explosion and a fireball ahead as something valuable was destroyed further up the highway. The blast momentarily lit the convoy choking the narrow highway into the hills, a long string of Soviet trucks and APCs doing everything they could to get away from the pursuing British behind them.

Nabiyev toggled on his radio, checking that it was tuned to the regimental command frequency. "Alexandrovitch? Damn you. Where are you?"

Static was his answer.

Alexandrovitch's battalion was meant to be their rearguard, dug in along this road to stop—or at least slow NATO pursuit.

Nabiyev looked over his shoulder in time to see another fireball light the night followed quickly by two more. He was nearly thrown from the BTR when it braked hard, shuddering to a halt, narrowly avoiding a collision with a stalled fuel truck ahead of them.

Nabiyev saw that the truck's tires were blown and it was leaking fuel from a dozen holes through the tank. The doors were open. Whatever crew had survived this attack had abandoned it. Nabiyev's eyes widened at the sight of the fuel spreading across the highway.

"Get us off the road!" he shouted down into the BTR. "Get away from the truck, you fool!"

The driver swore back at him, wrestling with the controls and fighting the BTR off the road and over a ditch, onto the dry scrubland of the hillside by the road.

Further ahead, the highway was jammed—backed up with vehicles—destroyed, abandoned, or both. NATO aircraft were turning this road into a highway of death. As the relentless air strikes continued unopposed, the night sky to the east transformed into a canvas of fiery destruction. He was beginning to wonder if any of his men would make it out of here.

Even as he looked, he saw another flash of an explosion, this one dangerously close. The shockwave washed over him and he ducked into the BTR in time to be thrown around as it bounced through an unseen gulley.

The driver swore again and down shifted, trying to work the vehicle free. The engine roared, tires spun, and the BTR shook violently, shifting only deeper into the ravine, now hopelessly stuck.

"Bastard!" Nabiyev shouted, pounding his fist on the cold

metal hull, unsure if he was cursing the vehicle, the driver, or the gulley.

"We are stuck, Colonel!"

Nabiyev bit off his first response. After he was sure he would say something constructive, he addressed his staff again. "Burn whatever documents we have," he said. "Destroy the radios. We'll go on foot."

To their credit, the staff followed his orders, lighting a small sputtering fire with the few maps and papers onboard while another soldier smashed the radio faces with the butt of his rifle. Nabiyev climbed from the BTR and checked the action of the carbine he carried before looking around, peering into the fire-lit dark. He knew there would be no escape without a vehicle of some kind.

"Now we need transportation."

The men of the BTR made their way back to the road only to see that nothing was moving. Whatever could drive on had, either becoming ensnared in the jam ahead or getting picked off by air strikes, although perhaps some had gotten lucky and slipped out. Nabiyev wouldn't be among them.

He felt a growing pit in his stomach, matching the distant approach of tank engines from further down the hill. The enemy.

They'd bought time for the Iraqis to regroup and escape. He only hoped it was enough. Whether or not any of Novikov's division survived was beyond him to say. All he knew with certainty was that the 806th motor rifle regiment and the vaunted Iraqi Republican Guard were no more.

He looked at his men, each of them looking at him for orders, for a way out. They hadn't yet realized there wasn't one. He tossed his carbine aside and looked at the others. "Get rid of them." One by one they threw their guns aside. The approaching engines grew ever louder. Nabiyev resolved to handle even this indignity with all the professionalism he could muster. As he saw the faint outline of the first NATO vehicle crest the ridge west of them, he held his hands over his head. "Do any of you speak English?" He asked his staff. "It will make this next part easier."

***

Gates's command APC crawled up the hill slowly, following behind the leading edge of his tank battalions as they cut through the routed Soviets. It was slow going, weaving around the tangled mess of burned out and abandoned vehicles packing the road. He'd thought the carnage across the open plains was staggering, here it was almost beyond belief. Everywhere he looked the ground was full of wasted trucks, tanks, and APCs of every description. There were fewer obvious bodies, but they were there all the same. Either cooked skeletons, half-glimpsed in burned out trucks, or blackened, burned forms scattered around craters and blown-up tanks—crew who had bailed out in flames only to die in agony mere steps away.

Gates's APC slowed to indelicately ram a blackened UAZ off the road and into a ditch. As they continued on, he didn't need the night vision goggles mounted to his helmet. So many fires burned in this valley that everything was lit in flickering red. It looked like Hell.

As they drove, Gates listened to radio communication from Benson's regiment ahead.

"We've hit another Soviet blocking position about two miles up," Benson said. "They're well-positioned and backed with some kind of SAM umbrella. The Turks say they can't get at them and I'm still waiting to get an American stealth fighter tasked with clearing them back, but for now I think we've hit our limit, sir."

"We can't get boxed in here," Gates replied. "I'll see about turning their line further south. Maybe the French can push them."

"We've destroyed two divisions at least," Benson said. "I've counted about a hundred tanks. Maybe more."

It was unquestionably a victory, but it wasn't quite the end. Not yet.

Further ahead the horizon flashed with explosions—artillery fire—though Gates couldn't tell whose. Gates thought of Paderborn. Although the slaughter there paled in comparison to what was inflicted here, he wondered if this was what it would have looked like if the Soviets had broken his line there, if Dunworth's counter attack had failed.

Further on, a column of POWs marched back under the watchful guns of a handful of British soldiers. Gates ordered his APC off the road to let the prisoners pass and watched them go by. To the rear of the line, he was surprised to see a man in an officer's uniform marching with his men, hands on his head. Gates couldn't identify Soviet ranks, but noted two golden stars and two stripes on his shoulder boards. They locked eyes in passing, conqueror and conquered. Gates saw no regret in the Soviet's eyes and knew there was no pity in his own. That officer was lucky to be alive at all, and if he hadn't wanted to end up a prisoner, then he should simply have stayed home.

"Driver advance," Gates said at last, eager to get out of this killing ground and to his next command post. Ankara was safe, for now at least. The Iraqis were routed, their vaunted Republican Guard annihilated, and the Soviets bloodied. It felt like they'd stopped the invasion. Now it was time for a new chapter, he thought. Liberation.

***

33

Bitter winter wind swept through the vehicle depot like enemy fire, tugging at caps and coats as Strelnikov led his officers across the snowy lot. The snow was no obstacle, little more than a dusting. It accumulated in cracks and crevices, forming small pools around tires and treads, and was swept away where it lay in the open. General Strelnikov hardly noticed the cold, after all it was no match for the chill in his blood. The lot was dark, far from the harsh floodlights of the rest of the base, lit only by the moon which hung overhead.

Nearing the middle of the lot, he saw his goal. A command BTR with its canvas tent deployed sat waiting for them, though otherwise deserted, just as he had ordered it.

Strelnikov lifted the tent flap and wordlessly stood aside as the officers filed in, holding their coats closed, collars turned against the cold. He saw unspoken questions in their eyes. Sidorov stopped for half a moment and looked as though he might actually give voice to these concerns. What *were* they doing out here? The colonel kept the question to himself and filed in, trailed at last by Mishkin and then Strelnikov himself.

Once in the relative shelter of the tent, Mishkin busied himself with igniting the crude kerosene heater in the middle of the enclosure. It would make the space marginally more livable in the brutal cold, though Strelnikov knew in actual combat it would just provide another heat source for NATO thermal sights to detect. He banished the thought and looked over the men gathered here, colonels and majors, the commanders of his regiments and the command staff of his division. Just days ago, they'd had the dubious honor of marching through Moscow's

Red Square in celebration of the October Revolution. In another time it would be an experience Strelnikov would savor, the accomplishment of a lifetime. As it was, he could only think of it as a dress rehearsal for what was to come.

Their eyes were all on him now. They rubbed warmth back into numb ears, noses, and hands but did not speak. Even Mishkin finally finished with the heater and stood silently watching him. How to begin? How could he relay to them what Tarasov had so bluntly expressed? It was obvious to all present, without being told, that something monumental and unorthodox was happening. Strelnikov's sudden promotion to Colonel General alone had made that crystal clear. He was still unused to the new rank on his shoulders but wasn't entirely displeased. At least if he should ever encounter that bastard Turgenev again, it would be as equals.

"What is to be spoken of here is of the utmost secrecy," Strelnikov said at last.

These were the men who'd led at Zagreb, Metz, and Worms. They'd faced down death, but how could he ask him to do this thing?

"I have received orders directly from Comrade Minister Tarasov," Strelnikov continued carefully. "Orders which supersede those issued by the Stavka, Politburo, or normal army command." He saw their eyes widen. This was far beyond normal, already bordering on treasonous.

Strelnikov rubbed the bridge of his nose with a finger, eyes squeezed shut. It was a display of weakness and he cursed himself for it. These men needed to see strength and determination, not uncertainty and doubt. Finally, he opened his eyes. If he were going to involve them, he could do nothing but give them the truth. "We have been gathered to this place to act as a bargaining chip in a political scheme," he said at last. "A plot to overthrow Secretary Karamazov and install an opposition leader. One more competent."

He expected an outburst of questions, but he was met only with well-disciplined silence. Sidorov, Lukin, Mishkin, and the others waited for their general's word. "Your oaths of service require you to unquestioningly obey all orders of commanders and superiors," Strelnikov continued, unwittingly echoing the same words Tarasov had used to browbeat him into cooperation. He shook his head. "But I absolve you of this requirement. This is an order you do not have to follow." He looked each man in the eye, allowing his gaze to linger for a heartbeat. "If any of you oppose this plan, please speak now. I will honor your opinions and release you from this duty." He looked them over again.

Not one spoke. He saw uncertainty in their faces, but he also saw admiration, dedication.

Colonel Sidorov finally broke the silence. "You said yourself, Comrade, we've laid siege to the gates of Hell. We've faced the devil before," he said. "We will gladly do so again by your side."

Strelnikov couldn't help it, a smile forced its way onto his otherwise stoic expression. He nodded finality. "Very well. It is not in your nature to be pawns, I know, but know that I would not ask this of you if I did not believe it was the right thing."

"What can we expect?" Lukin asked.

"A time will come—soon—when we are called on to enter Red Square again, this time as invaders. Our job will be to secure the city, subdue the security troops, and maintain order."

Lukin nodded.

None of the others looked more than slightly perturbed by this. It was far from welcome news, but none of them had any love for the KGB or its minions.

Strelnikov tapped Mishkin with two fingers. "Colonel, I will need a special company for the main thrust on the Kremlin. Reorganize our newest battalion." He looked at his other officers. "Think of names, men who you know and can trust."

"The Old Guard?" Mishkin suggested.

"The Red Square Guards," Strelnikov corrected. "A full company of trusted veterans. Pull them from wherever they can be found. I must have a unit that will not falter."

"We must be cautious," Sidorov said. "With so many fresh inductees if we pull too many veterans—"

"I leave that to your discretion. Give me one hundred men beyond reproach. That is all I ask. I will lead them myself." There was no argument. "Keep all of this from the men. Trust no one but those gathered here," Strelnikov warned. "When the time comes...we will have to trust that each man will do what he is told."

There was much left to discuss, but there was nothing further to say. All that remained of their treason was the plan itself. "Let us set to work."

***

34

Though the news was good, it did little to ease Gradenko's tension. Sitting on his living room couch beside his wife, they watched on Programme One as Soviet soldiers, laughing and grinning, linked arms on the shores of the Sea of Marmara. On cue from their lieutenant, they held their arms overhead triumphantly, some held red Soviet banners aloft, fluttering proudly.

"This is footage from Turkey where our brave soldiers have secured a hard-fought victory over NATO forces," the news anchor explained, his voice deadpan. "With the Turkish Straits secured, the Soviet Union has at long last achieved a strategic goal which has been desired since the time of the tsars. Not only has the loss of Constantinople to the Turks been avenged, but now the Soviet Union alone controls access to the Black Sea."

The footage switched to show a soldier playfully bathing in the waters of the Marmara as his comrades laughed.

"Tens of thousands of NATO soldiers were trapped by this lightning maneuver," the anchor said, narrating footage of Turkish soldiers marching into captivity. A victory for certain, but Gradenko did not see tens of thousands. He saw dozens, maybe hundreds. "With these straits now secured, military traffic is free to flow into the Mediterranean and disrupt enemy shipping, further weakening their war effort." The anchor shuffled papers. "In domestic news, the price of bread grain has fallen again as—" the anchor stopped, glanced off camera, looking bewildered and perhaps afraid. Then the signal abruptly terminated, replaced with footage of a ballet.

Gradenko sat forward on the couch, staring at the screen as

his heart and mind started to race. He recognized the ballet, it was Swan Lake. They'd played the same thing during the media blackout after General Secretary Andropov died while deliberations had been held to determine his successor.

Katya seemed to read his thoughts. "Has someone died?"

Gradenko was just starting to hope it was Karamazov when the window glass of the large picture window in their living room vibrated with the boom of loudspeakers and the chanting of gathering crowds.

Gradenko felt his stomach tighten as he rose to his feet.

"Andrei? What is it?"

Gradenko pulled the curtains aside and his fears were confirmed. A river of humanity moved by on a distant street, barely visible beyond the small pond beside their apartment. The crowd snaked along after a praetorian guard of men wielding handmade banners with crudely stenciled slogans.

They were too far away to read, but Gradenko could imagine their demands, they were the same ones people in the Soviet Union had always clamored for, the same that the Poles had demanded in 1989. More liberties, more freedoms, less restrictions and now—most treasonously—peace.

It was finally happening. Gradenko couldn't be sure exactly what had done it, which straw had broken the camel's back, but if he had to guess he would say the news of staggering casualties among the Bulgarian and Romanian Peoples' Armies had been one straw too many. The Romanians and Bulgarians had bled for the victory the Soviets were now claiming on the news. It only added insult to injury.

He should have felt some satisfaction, or at least some relief that his plans were finally coming to fruition, but he couldn't shake the feeling that the threads of that same plan were in danger of unraveling at any moment. This was what he wanted —*exactly* what he wanted—and yet it felt so wrong. It was anathema to him to bring such strife and discord to the heart of the Soviet Union. The realization that this chaos was a result of his own hand left a pit in his stomach.

Just above the bass rumble of the protestors he heard the shrill cry of sirens. An anemic police response to a sudden surge of political activism they were doubtlessly ill-prepared to handle. With so many reservists called to the front, who was left to suppress dissent in Moscow?

The column of protestors he could see approached a weakly held police roadblock and showed no inclination to yield to authority. Gas grenade launchers barked and plumes of white tear gas filled the air, driving back the guest workers at first before they rallied and stormed forward, chasing off the police with a shower of bottles, bricks and cries of triumph.

Time was growing short. Soon the whole city would be deadlocked with chaos. If he was going to move, he had to move now.

His wife stood beside him observing the gathering storm, gripping his arm tightly.

"This is it," Gradenko said, his gaze fixed on the unfolding protest. His wife only held him tighter. He'd told her nothing of his plans or his role in this, but she was no fool. She had to suspect his complicity based on stoicism in the face of this chaos. "I must go," he said finally, forcing the words out.

Katya looked at him, eyes wide with fear and uncertainty, but she didn't argue. The lines etched on her face told the story of a life lived in the shadows of political maneuvering. She embraced him. "Please be careful," she said.

Gradenko couldn't promise that and so only silently held her.

As they parted, Gradenko couldn't shake the persistent trembling in his hands. The fate of his nation hung in the balance, and Gradenko couldn't escape the feeling that the discontent he had conjured here could spill out of control, raging like wildfire, consuming everything in its path.

***

Gradenko's driver was forced to take a roundabout route to Red Square, weaving a delicate patchwork of blocks in the hands of the swelling numbers of protestors and those still held by KGB security forces and city police.

They cruised past a rough sawhorse barricade manned by a phalanx of police in riot gear, shields interlocked, waiting to receive the advance of a chanting mob of Romanians and Poles, already hurling bottles and bricks.

Gradenko turned in his seat, looking through the rear windshield he saw the orange flash of fire, a so-called "Molotov cocktail" splashing against the riot police line. His stomach tied in knots. Only the knowledge that this sacrilege against the Soviet Union made his plans possible allowed him to continue at all.

The Kremlin had returned to its original use as a fortress. The towering red brick walls were no longer decorative but instead created easy choke points, now firmly held by KGB troops armed with rifles and machine guns. They begrudgingly allowed Gradenko entry, more concerned with the booming echoes of chants that reverberated through the city.

When Gradenko got out of the car, he spared a look to his driver. "Stay here until it is safe."

"Y-yes, Comrade!"

Gradenko arrived in the Politburo chambers just as several others did, finding a scene of unfolding chaos.

Karamazov sat like a mad tyrant, eyes wide with shock and fury as a quartet of stone-faced KGB men surrounded him. One of them, Gradenko saw, was the current KGB chairman, Dragomirov.

Karamazov's advisors, their faces etched with concern, briefed the general secretary on the rapidly deteriorating situation.

"Security troops across the city are drawing back to Red Square and the Kremin," one of the advisors said. "Once we have secured the area, we can begin dispersing the rioters." This withdrawal, Gradenko knew, would only further embolden the protestors, leaving vast swaths of the city effectively lawless.

"The protests are spreading out of control," another said, "and it's not just guest workers—local Muscovites have joined the foreigners. Their numbers are growing exponentially."

Karamazov listened intently, his brow creased with worry. These protests were no minor setback—such discontent could easily become viral. With Moscow paralyzed it was only a matter of time before the chaos spread to other cities: Leningrad, Minsk, Baku, Kiev, Novosibirsk. It was a threat not just to his authority, but the very fabric of the Soviet Union.

"What steps have been taken to limit the spread of information?" Karamazov demanded.

"Programme One has been taken off air, Comrade Secretary," another advisor replied. "Instead, we are broadcasting pre-recorded television, ballet I believe."

Karamazov met Gradenko's eyes. They both knew that the West would be watching closely, and they couldn't afford to project weakness. The longer the chaos continued, the more vulnerable his regime would appear.

Gradenko did not need to feign the concern on his face. In this case the cure may very well prove worse than the disease if they failed to curb the protests after the fact. Whatever they were going to do, they would have to do it quickly.

"We can have a helicopter here in five minutes," one of the advisors said. "Aerial evacuation to your dacha or the remote command station."

"Evacuate?" Gradenko blurted, outraged and horrified by the suggestion, not least because it would disrupt his plan. "You cannot be serious."

The security officer who spoke grimaced at this unwelcome solicitation. "The situation in the city is tenuous. Safety cannot be guaranteed."

Karamazov slammed a fistful of paper down on the table. Gradenko's eyes went to it automatically and he saw his own handiwork, poorly printed *Samizdat* in a rainbow of colors and languages. "Right under our noses," Karamazov spat. "They've fermented rebellion. The ungrateful bastards are rising up beneath our feet like rats from a sewer."

Gradenko glanced at Dragomirov, afraid for his gaze to linger too long. "Without the KGB noticing?" He had to fight to keep a grin from his face and saw Dragomirov blanch appropriately.

"Our resources have been directed toward the detection of foreign assets. Domestic surveillance—"

Karamazov waved a hand, silencing Dragomirov. "Whatever the case, it has happened."

"And our security forces can't handle them?" Gradenko asked.

Dragomirov paused, hesitating appropriately long. "We are stretched very thin. We don't have a hope of controlling crowds of this size without more application of force."

"You start shooting those people and rebellion will become a revolution," Gradenko shot back. "One you're apparently ill-prepared to contain."

"Even so, we don't have the manpower," another KGB officer, glowering at Gradenko. "And so, evacuation—"

"Will erase whatever legitimacy this body has," Gradenko said, gesturing around himself and summoning all his fury and courage. "You may run, Comrade, but I will not, and we will see who holds the reins of power when you surrender the Kremlin to a seething mob of foreigners."

This goaded Karamazov, just as Gradenko hoped it would. "There will be no evacuation. This is our capital, damn it! There must be options. We must have more security forces."

The suggestion had to come from Dragomirov, not Tarasov, not Gradenko, but someone Karamazov trusted. The chairman did not disappoint. "There is an army unit deployed nearby," he said. "On reserve."

"Who?" Karamazov blurted.

"The 121st Zagreb Guards Motor Rifle Division. They conducted the October Revolution parade recently. I am reluctant to deploy an army unit in Moscow but...."

"They were the ones who cleaned Warsaw in '89, yes?" Karamazov asked.

Dragomirov gave a slight shrug. Why should he know?

"I believe so, Comrade Secretary," Gradenko said.

The General Secretary growled impotently, holding his head in his hands. Sending in the army would turn Moscow into a battlefield. But it was a battle Karamazov expected he would win.

"Send them in. Crush the protests." He looked back at Dragomirov. "Secure order and give me back my city."

***

35

The tanks, trucks, and APC's of Strelnikov's division idled in the dark. Their heavy diesel engines churned and purred, filling the air with exhaust. The call hadn't gone out to them yet, but they were ready all the same.

The command had gone from Strelnikov down, passing from regiment to battalion to company to platoon. Be ready to advance on Moscow. If any of the soldiers questioned these orders, none did so aloud. Men donned weapons and gear, secured helmets and ballistic vests and mounted the vehicles just as they would have in Germany. Battle was battle and an enemy was an enemy, no matter if they were German, American, Croatian, Hungarian, or Pole.

Strelnikov walked the line, the distant city lights of Moscow behind him. The low clouds overhead glowed red in the reflected urban light. The asphalt was cool and hard beneath his booted feet and it vibrated with the thrum of engines. It was starting to snow, coming down in flurries, the wind whipping it through the column and accumulating in small drifts and clumps.

Soldiers called to him in passing, doffing helmets and raising rifles.

"Strelnikov! Strelnikov! Strelnikov!"

The name on every set of lips. His name. He said nothing but walked the line in silence, his conscience weighing on him. None of these men knew that they were soon to again write the name of his division to history. He only hoped it would be for the better.

Ahead he saw Mishkin waiting just off the main road. A collection of headquarters trucks marked a meeting of his command staff. Strelnikov stepped from the road and onto the cold, crushing earth. His breath plumed visibly as he came to stand before them. The same men who swore to follow him to Hell stood arrayed for his orders.

Strelnikov looked at Mishkin wordlessly, a question unspoken.

"We have received an official order from the Politburo," Mishkin said, speaking carefully. "They ask that we move into the city and quash the disturbance at once. We are to use all available means to do so."

Strelnikov had no qualms about shooting protestors, armed or otherwise. He'd seen it done in Warsaw in '89. He would see it done here. It was raising his sword to Moscow, to the Soviet Union itself, which bothered him. He looked back over his shoulder toward the lightening sky that marked the city.

"Now is the last chance," Strelnikov said, his back to his officers. "If any of you cannot do this thing, I ask now that you step away. I will not hold your loyalty against you." When at last, he turned back around, none of them had moved.

"This is a difficult thing we must do," Strelnikov continued. "Mine is the hand which holds the blade. No one else need bloody their hands. I only ask that you are with me."

"We are with you, Comrade General," they chorused.

Then the die was cast. "See to your men."

The officers left for their regiments and battalions and Strelnikov left with Mishkin toward his command company, now accompanied by the company of Old Guards Mishkin had assembled, hard-faced men who bore the marks of war. At first glance they looked disordered, a mess of men in poorly fitted kit, smoking and chatting amongst themselves. But to Strelnikov's eyes these were his men, veterans of Zagreb. He could trust them unto death itself.

Strelnikov climbed quickly atop the new BMP-3 he'd selected to command the guards from. Mishkin joined him. Standing on the vehicle's rear deck, Strelnikov looked toward the city again. Though it was too far away and too loud here, he could imagine the sounds, the chanting, the shouting, the crash of plate glass windows. The Soviet Union stood on the brink of disaster, a collapse which could see the promise of communism undone. Enemies without and enemies within threatened her. The man leading the Motherland was a self-serving snake and his advisors were stooges and sycophants. Victory could only come from strong leadership. Strelnikov only regretted that he must be the one to see things set back to order.

"We are ready, Comrade," Mishkin said from beside him, buckling on his helmet and awkwardly adjusting the folding carbine slung at his side. He offered an identical carbine to Strelnikov.

The general took the weapon and pulled on his own helmet. It was time.

***

The 121st Zagreb Guards moved through Moscow like a bayonet through flesh. The roar of engines and chatter of machine guns broke the spell of chaos that had fallen over the city. It was just like Warsaw, Strelnikov thought, looking at the heaps of bodies that filled the roads which the treads of his tanks crushed beneath them. Tanks and APCs smashed through burning barricades of city buses, tires, benches, anything the rioters could pull together. Blood-stained banners fell, emblazoned with slogans about democracy or freedom. Empty ideals that could do no more to stop a bullet than the linen sheets they were printed on. With the application of raw violence, the protestors filling the street evaporated like snow against flame.

Secondary to their mission of clearing out the rioting guest workers, the Soviet troops secured vital infrastructure across the city. Intersections, bridges, telephone exchanges, broadcast studios, and police stations. Each heartbeat carried Strelnikov and his men closer to the point of no return: the Kremlin, a roughly triangular walled fortress pressed to the banks of the Moskva river between the Bolshoy Kamenny and Bolshoy Moskvoretsky bridges. That second bridge was the target of Strelnikov's Old Guards.

Strelnikov peered from the commander's hatch of his BMP. With his helmet, weapon, and ballistic vest, he looked just like the rest of the soldiers clinging to the outside of the vehicles. Their breath fogged visibly in the chill air, mingling with exhaust smoke. After the initial carnage, the city now appeared deserted. Moscow's residents were either holed up in their homes or rioting elsewhere.

"Resistance is fading away, Comrade General," Mishkin said over the headphone Strelnikov held pressed to one ear. "The rioters are fleeing in all directions."

"Pursue them," Strelnikov said. "The more we kill now the less trouble there will be later."

"Yes, Comrade General."

Strelnikov's thoughts weren't on the riot though, they were already reaching toward the heart of the city and his mission there. "Mishkin, see to securing the city. I'm taking my company on."

Mishkin's tone was robbed of any gravity by the poor quality of the radio. "Yes, Comrade. Be careful."

What he was about to do was anything but careful. Strelnikov turned the toggle on his radio and was connected to his company command frequency. It had been many years since he'd held company command. It felt simultaneously small and huge. Compared to the bulk of his division a company was nothing, a pawn, a chit to be traded away. But here, now, he could nearly look each of his men in the face. He could count the vehicles on his fingers; there were scarcely ten altogether. A fragile thing. A glass knife now in his hands.

He didn't bother to introduce himself, they would recognize his voice. "Company advance. A left turn. On to Red Square."

The platoon leaders didn't argue and didn't question, they'd been well-selected. Continuing on, the company advanced through the harsh glow of the streetlamps. The treads of

Strelnikov's BMP rattled as they approached the Bolshoy Moskvoretsky Bridge, crushing the detritus of the riot beneath them. The bridge crossed over the cold, dark waters of the Moskva River leading directly to Red Square. He could clearly see the ancient buildings of the Kremlin, the palace and the cathedral where he'd first learned about this treason. The general wondered to himself how the old Tsars would have felt seeing the revolution which destroyed them now threatening to destroy itself. The thought brought a grimace to his face. He didn't believe in this mission, but he believed in Tarasov and he believed in victory. It would have to be enough.

Ahead, at the far end of the bridge, a pair of UAZs were parked nose to nose. Four KGB security troops with rifles waved flashlights at the approaching soldiers, bidding them to stop or turn back.

"Column halt," Strelnikov said into his headset microphone.

The drivers of the BMPs did as they were ordered, slowing to a stop facing like a lance toward the bridge and the Kremlin beyond. For a moment there was only the sound of the idling engines and the growing tension with the KGB.

Strelnikov's hand-picked men stood on one bank of the Moskva River. On the other side lay treason. Once they crossed, there would be no turning back. The weight of his decision felt crushing, overwhelming, yet somewhere in the back of his mind Strelnikov recalled history. He spoke before he knew exactly what he would say. "God-like Rome, be friendly to my quest." The words of Marcus Lucanus's *Pharsalia* came easily to him from studies of his youth. It seemed a fitting address to the Third Rome from the man who would march his legion upon it.

"The man who makes me your enemy is the one at fault. It is his acts that make me your foe. Here we abandon peace and broken laws," Strelnikov said. "Farewell to treaties. Fortune, guide me." He grit his teeth, willing victory. He concluded the martial prayer. "War is our judge, and in the Fates our trust." Strelnikov lapsed to silence, looking over his chosen company assembling in the dark with a grim stare.

With his resolve steeled, he finally addressed his men clicking on his radio. "Our orders were to rid Moscow of the traitors who would see her destroyed," Strelnikov said, speaking slowly and clearly so there would be no misunderstanding. "The orders I give you now are both new and the same." This was the moment where the loyalty of the Old Guard would be tested. "All beyond these waters are the enemies of the Motherland. They are no different than the Western fascists." He knew it wouldn't take much encouragement to turn his men on the hated internal security troops. All of them, after all, knew of the deep paranoid fear inspired by the unfeeling security apparatus of the state.

"Spare no one," Strelnikov said. "Trust no one. Free your hate and visit the pain they've inflicted on us back to them. Our mission is to restore order to Moscow and the Motherland and so we shall."

He swallowed, allowing his platoon leaders enough time to consider these orders before he gave his new command. "Company, advance."

No one moved. Not a single BMP advanced an inch. They sat and idled as they had before, facing the sparse KGB patrol on the bridge.

Strelnikov would not repeat the order and he would not look around for support. Though his palms sweated and his heart thundered, he only stared ahead expectantly. as if his men would move at any moment.

And then they did.

The first BMP roared into gear, coughing a stream of exhaust, soon followed by another and another. The second platoon followed behind the first, and the third behind them. Strelnikov's command section likewise went into gear and rumbled onto the bridge, passing over the Moskva—the Rubicon.

The army tracks drew nearer and nearer, now within a stone's throw of the KGB trucks. Soon enough it became clear that neither side wanted to fire first. Any charade of camaraderie had fallen away and now each found themselves on a collision course they were desperate to avoid.

Strelnikov could only faintly hear shouting over the sound of the engines, the rifle section of the first BMP and the KGB troops shouted back and forth as the vehicles drew nearer. Last minute entreaties to yield or clear a path.

The KGB broke the spell with gunfire first. The strobe of automatic fire lit the bridge.

It was met tenfold by the motor rifles. Autocannon fire shredded both UAZs and rifle fire scattered and dropped the KGB men one by one until all of them were dead.

The lead BMP clipped the UAZs aside, sending them skittering away on burning tires.

Like that, the spell was broken, their hate unleashed. Now all KGB forces were met with gunfire, mostly precision bursts of autocannon fire down the broad avenues of Red Square.

"Company, deploy by platoons and advance," Strelnikov said. "Secure the Kremlin gate and advance within."

It was like a sick mirror of their well-organized performance here just days before. Where the October Revolution parade had been neat, orderly, and clean, this advance was anything but. Fire, smoke, bodies, the roar of diesels. The Tomb of Lenin passed by, its angular block structure looking sinister in the light of a burning KGB armored car.

The gates of the Kremlin were just ahead. Gunfire lashed out at his men from guard posts beside the gate. Machine guns and autocannon fire reduced these to smoldering ruins in seconds.

Strelnikov checked the carbine slung over his shoulder, half-pulling the action back to see the steel-jacketed cartridge already in the chamber. He let the action snap closed as the BMPs raced for the gate.

***

36

The sounds of the distant protests were blocked out by the walls of the Kremlin. The same wasn't true for the crack and rattle of gunfire. Each set of gunshots that rang out made Gradenko jump nervously. He stood anxiously by a vaulted window looking down on the grounds outside the palace knowing he would see Strelnikov's men any moment now. It's just a matter of time.

A hand clapped onto Gradenko's shoulder, making him jump again until he saw it was Tarasov, his face grave. "It's time," He said.

Gradenko nodded shakily, knowing that by this time tomorrow he would either be General Secretary...or dead.

"Once your man arrives we can move," Gradenko replied.

A BMP in mottled camouflage paint emerged from the Kremlin gate at top speed, sprinting in faster than Gradenko thought possible. It hit a parked KGB truck so hard and so fast that the jeep simply rolled beneath the BMP which momentarily rocked back as its treads chewed and crushed the UAZ's frame.

Gun and autocannon fire lashed out, sweeping the yard around the Kremlin. KGB troops retreated in disarray or surrendered. Strelnikov's BMPs stopped and the troops riding them leapt off, fanning out and gunning down their enemy —fighting or surrendering alike. In a struggle for absolute dominance, there was no room for mercy.

"Let us go," Gradenko said.

They encountered Dragomirov waiting for them in a gilded hallway. His normally unflappable calm seemed frayed. His eyes were wide, nervous. "Your man knows to meet us here?"

Dragomirov asked Tarasov.

"He knows," the old general replied calmly as gunfire banged out in the halls of the Kremlin.

Moments later, an infantry squad rounded the corner, weapons ready, looking very out of place against the casual opulence of the palace. Mottled uniforms contrasted sharply against gold-accented white walls.

The sergeant leading the men called for a halt. "Friend or foe?" he called to Gradenko and the others.

"Friend," Tarasov said, stepping forward, hardly leaning on his cane. "Of yours and General Strelnikov. Where is he?"

"Here." Strelnikov arrived on the heels of his men. He was, Gradenko noted, almost indistinguishable from them. Unlike Tarasov, who wore dress uniform, Strelnikov wore battle fatigues. Still, Gradenko recognized him. He recalled his face from the parade. Strelnikov had ridden standing in a UAZ. Dressed in full military regalia, he'd saluted Karamazov, Gradenko, Tarasov, and the other elite of the Soviet Union as he led his division past.

It was all Gradenko could think of during the October Revolution parade, that this hatchet-faced man was his only hope. The beautiful symmetry and precision of their march through Red Square days before had become a grotesque parody of their rough and deadly performance now.

Strelnikov pulled off his helmet and passed it back to a lieutenant behind him who in turn handed him a peaked cap which he snugged on, letting his Kalashnikov hang from its sling. Once the hat was in place, he saluted Tarasov crisply, his face betraying no joy or pleasure. "We have done as you asked, Comrade General. The city is secured, the KGB subdued, the Kremlin in your control."

Tarasov looked from Strelnikov to Gradenko, allowing a faint smile to ghost his expression. "Then all that remains is Karamazov."

"We must arrest him," Gradenko said, willing his voice not to waver as he addressed Strelnikov and his men. "Alive if possible.

It would be better."

Strelnikov absorbed this instruction without a change in expression. He looked to Tarasov who nodded in turn. "Very well," Strelnikov said. With another gesture to his lieutenant, Tarasov was handed a carbine. The defense minister checked the magazine and loaded the weapon with expert smoothness.

"We strike this blow for the Union Herself," Tarasov said, speaking with an almost religious fervor that Gradenko had never seen outside of cloying Great Patriotic War films. Gradenko shared none of the Defense Minister's reverence for this act of brutal violence, but he also agreed it must be done, and it wasn't being done for his personal benefit.

The quartet set off, Strelnikov and Tarasov leading the way with bold strides. Gradenko followed anxiously behind them with Dragomirov in his wake. Strelnikov's soldiers melted off by twos and threes, dashing through the Kremlin's finely paneled halls, boots thumping over plush carpets. Gunfire rang out occasionally, sometimes preceded with shouted calls for surrender, sometimes not.

When they reached the General Secretary's office, two sergeants threw themselves against the tall, white doors, bursting them open. They filed in, rifles leveled, followed closely by the leaders of the coup.

Karamazov stood at the far end of the ostentatiously large office behind a heavy gold-inlaid desk. A pair of men in suits wielding automatic pistols stood to either side of him, weapons trained on the door and the coup-plotters they framed.

No one moved. No one breathed. Fingers tightened precipitously on triggers, nerves frayed.

"General Secretary," Gradenko spoke at last, taking a bold step forward to the front of the group, forcing his voice calm and level. "We are here to place you under arrest."

"Arrest," Karamazov spat the word. "On what pretense?"

"What pretense was there for my son?" Gradenko said, voice devoid of emotion. He hadn't planned to say it, but now that it was out, it felt right. "For any of our sons and daughters?"

Gradenko continued.

Karamazov grinned wildly, eyelids peeled back so far as to seem gone. "Petty revenge," he said. He might have intended to say more, but one of his bodyguards half-turned, angling toward one of Strelnikov's soldiers.

The motor rifle sergeant fired first and then the air became a storm of bullets and wood splinters.

Gradenko's hearing was lost in an instant, replaced with a roaring ring as he staggered back and threw himself to the opulent carpet, hands on the back of his head. He looked up to see General Strelnikov firing wildly from the hip, teeth clenched. One of the army men went down, his face covered in his own blood.

Dragomirov started howling and thrashed around on the floor beside Gradenko.

Then it was over.

Gun smoke curled in the air; steel gray shell casings lay scattered across the plush carpet. Dragomirov moaned despondently, holding a hand against his side, blood soaking through his dress shirt and suit coat. Beyond him, Tarasov's massive form lay on his side in pooling blood. Karamazov and both his men were dead.

Gradenko's heart beat hard and fast, his eyes darting around to take all this in. His gaze jolted from one horror to the next until they came to rest on Karamazov. Dead. On his back, mouth agape, arms limp at his side. Dead.

Dead.

"Get him out of here," Strelnikov said, gesturing to Dragomirov. His soldier instantly obeyed, lifting the wounded KGB chairman from beneath his shoulders and dragging him off, calling for a medic.

Gradenko rose unsteadily to his feet as Strelnikov knelt beside Tarasov, a pair of fingers pressed into the defense minister's soft, jowled neck. His expression was as slack as Tarasov's. Finally, Strelnikov brushed Tarasov's eyelids closed and stood. It was over.

"It's done," Gradenko said, looking around him. "I am sorry that it has come to this."

Strelnikov looked blankly at Gradenko, making no reply. He turned in place, surveying the carnage.

Gradenko's mind finally began to open to hope. They'd done it. He could not mourn for Tarasov now, and he wondered if he would at all. Now all that remained was to clean up the mess and move forward. "Your men have the city in hand?"

"Not a person will move without my authorization," Strelnikov said, voice cool. "Moscow is in my hands."

Gradenko nodded, stepping over the blood stains on the carpet and forcing himself closer to Karamazov's body. Seeing it firsthand still did not make it feel real. He felt like he might awaken from this dream at any moment. "We—" Gradenko stopped himself. Tarasov was dead. Dragomirov wounded, who knew how badly. He was alone now. "I will prepare a statement to issue. I believe Comrade Karamazov was tragically killed in the violence surrounding the riots."

Strelnikov did not object.

"And then we can set things right," Gradenko continued. "Undo what has gotten so far out of control." His heart rose in his chest at the thought.

"Set things right?" Strelnikov asked, startling Gradenko. When the Foreign Minister turned, he found the general standing over Tarasov's body, staring accusingly at him. "What will you do?"

The answer was so obvious that Gradenko was shocked a general of Strelnikov's caliber couldn't figure it out. "Make peace, Comrade General. End this war."

※ ※ ※

Strelnikov's ears were still ringing. Perhaps he'd misheard the thin, bookish foreign minister. "Peace?"

"With the West," Gradenko confirmed. "An end to all this senseless bloodshed."

Strelnikov was unable to respond. He saw smoking fields of his dead. Row upon row of coffins and headstones. He saw the burn wards in Germany, overflowing with his soldiers. Boys with lost limbs and mutilated faces. Lives ruined. Lives lost.

"All that bleeding," Strelnikov said, clenching his carbine in white-knuckled grip. "All that bleeding we did. What was all that for then?"

Gradenko's already pale face paled further. He gaped for a moment, stammering. "W-we all made sacrifices in this war, Comrade General, but—"

"Sacrifices?" Strelnikov repeated. "No, *Comrade*. We did not *all* make sacrifices." He stabbed an accusing finger at Gradenko. "What sacrifices have you made? Where are your children, *Comrade*?"

As Gradenko backed up, hands raised placatingly, both men came to the same realization at the same time. Each of them recalled that power flowed from the barrel of a gun and Strelnikov was the only one in the room with one.

"General," Gradenko said warningly. "This is what Comrade Tarasov was after."

"To throw away everything with a scrap of paper? A white peace stained with our blood? A peace begged for after the West struck first?" Strelnikov asked. Anger left his voice. Anger was replaced with a confidence that Gradenko seemed to find even more frightening. Strelnikov's mind raced as possibility dawned on him. The sheer vista of possibility now open before him was staggering. It would have cowed a weaker man, bent or broken those without the resolve to see what must be done. Strelnikov was not afraid. He would act.

"We would need to negotiate a settlement," Gradenko replied.

"Defeatism." The accusation from Strelnikov's lips mirrored one leveled at him when he'd lost his army command. This time though he was sure the barb had found the right target. *Here* was the defeatist standing before him. This peevish academic, so enthralled with the West that he would sell his people's honor in order to appease them. "Defeatism," Strelnikov repeated. "No.

This is a chance to fix things. To bring about victory." Now he voiced his realization. "I wield the reins of power here," Strelnikov said at last, gesturing with his carbine. "I control Moscow. I control the Kremlin. I control the heart of the Soviet Union, and I control you, Comrade Minister."

Gradenko's fear rapidly became horror. Sweat beaded down his cheeks. "Impossible."

"Reality," Strelnikov countered. "How many rifle divisions does the foreign ministry have?" He allowed himself a grin to see this sniveling politician at a loss for words. It was men like Gradenko who had dragged his country into this war in the first place, men who gave foolish political directives while stooges in army command carried them out. It would all stop now.

"You don't have the connections to keep this country together," Gradenko reiterated. "You are just a general!"

"I am willing to wager I am presently the Soviet Union's most famous general," Strelnikov returned.

"Once you declare yourself a petty tyrant then everything will fall apart!" Gradenko blurted, anger no longer in check.

"Petty tyrant," Strelnikov repeated, smirking coldly. "How is that different from what our late Comrade Karamazov had done? Or Comrade Andropov? Kruschev? Stalin?" He grinned evilly. "How is that different from what you yourself had intended, Comrade Minister?"

Gradenko sputtered, at a loss for words.

"You fear chaos? You fear the Soviet Union will collapse? Then you will have to ensure that does not happen," Strelnikov said.

Gradenko's face flushed red. "You're destroying everything, can't you see that? We can end this war!"

"And we shall," Strelnikov said. "With victory."

Gradenko stared back, wide-eyed, dumbfounded, a man who had expected to be crowned Tsar only to discover that someone else had plucked the crown from the gutter.

Strelnikov smiled triumphantly. At last, he could make all these sacrifices count. He could make them matter. "I have restructuring to see to," Strelnikov said. "I don't care to rule. I care to win. If there is nothing else, I must see to my men."

Gradenko watched him leave, boots leaving red prints across the white carpet, striding confidently from the room and into command of the Soviet Union.

AFTERWORD

Thanks so much for reading! Please be sure to leave a review and let other people know what you thought about it.

https://www.amazon.com/gp/product/B0D3WP7XB1

Also consider following me on Twitter to be kept aware of upcoming releases or feel free to drop me a line on email.

TKBlackwoodWrites@Gmail.com
https://twitter.com/TkBlackwood

ABOUT THE AUTHOR

T.k. Blackwood

T.K. Blackwood is a full time IT professional and part time writer who lives in North Carolina with his wife, child, and too many reptiles.

IRON CRUCIBLE

A conflict nearly fifty years in the making spills from boardrooms and back alleys into open battle on land, sea, and the air. The showdown of the century is here, East versus West with the fate of the world at stake.

Blue Masquerade

The year is 1992. Over twenty years have passed since Soviet General Secretary Leonid Brezhnev was assassinated by a crazed gunman. Since that time, the Soviet Union has been put on a course toward economic success—and war.

In the Balkans, Yugoslavia's collapse into ethnic violence draws NATO and the Warsaw Pact to the brink of Armageddon. Armies deploy and fleets maneuver. Political intrigue engulfs Moscow and Washington, and paranoia radiates from the Iron Curtain. In the zero-sum game of Cold War, neither side can afford to blink or back down.

A conflict nearly fifty years in the making spills from boardrooms and back alleys and explodes into open battle on land, air and sea

Red Front

The year is 1992.

The unthinkable has happened. East and West are on a crash

course for war, and the battlefield will be Germany. Peace is no longer an option and all bets are off as the Free World and the Communist Bloc descend into war. NATO forces scramble to grapple with the Soviet juggernaut, as the Reds pull out all the stops - and engineer a secret plan - to crush them in a single mighty blow. The future of humanity tilts in the balance.

Welcome to World War III.

White Horizon

The year is 1992.

The Soviet Blitzkrieg in Germany has been beaten to a bloody halt along the Rhine River. The Reds rush masses of teenage conscripts and rusty reservists to the front, while NATO scrambles to mount a killing blow against their reeling nemesis.

The flames of war spread north to Scandinavia, embroiling Sweden and threatening Norway. In this grinding war of attrition, both sides endure, and the death toll mounts. Is a breakthrough at hand or has the carnage only begun?

Black Seas

The year is 1992. Europe is in flames. Scandinavia is under siege. Only Norway holds out against the Soviet war machine. And now the pride of the Soviet Navy, the Red Banner Northern Fleet, sallies out to finish the job.

With their armies facing annihilation, and World War III at a tipping point, the combined navies of NATO stand ready to receive their enemy. Europe's greatest naval battle since Jutland, the first carrier battle since World War II, is about to begin.

Printed in Dunstable, United Kingdom

70273574R00160